'Fun... unapologetic, and shameless in the best possible way, thi... a YA heroine (and a book) that you've never seen before' Lou... O'Neill, award-winning author of *Asking for It*

...is book will make you laugh out loud, nod in agreement, ...ringe with recognition, and stand up and cheer. I adored it' ...atherine Webber, author of *Wing Jones*

'I ...ved it. Hilarious and feminist (and full of foofers)' K... is Stainton, author of *If You Could See Me Now*

'I LOV... D this book! A really smart, relevant and switched-on explo... ion of teen sexuality, gender and slut-shaming' Kath... ne Woodfine, bestselling author of *The Sinclair's Mysteries*

'P... lliant. Hilarious. Important. Pick this up and spend the ... t of your life wanting to be best friends with Izzy O'Neill' ... nantha Shannon, author of *The Bone Season*

'Funny, feminist, rightly furious – this'll be HUGE' Jim at *YAYeahYeah*

'If you are alive right now, experiencing the world as we live it today, you must read this book' Imogen, *Goodreads*

'Izzy is one of the best narrators I think I have ever read; she manages to be witty, irrever... ...bsolutely loved her a...

THE
EXACT
OPPOSITE
OF OKAY

LAURA STEVEN

First published in Great Britain in 2018
by Electric Monkey, an imprint of Egmont UK Limited
The Yellow Building, 1 Nicholas Road, London W11 4AN

Text copyright © 2018 Laura Steven

ISBN 978 1 4052 8844 6

A CIP catalogue record for this title is available from the British Library

67998/1

Typeset by Avon DataSet Ltd, Bidford on Avon, Warwickshire
Printed and bound in Great Britain by CPI Group

To Toria and Lucy, a.k.a. the Coven – because in the immortal words of Kelly Clarkson, my life would suck without you

Hello

Look, you probably bought this book because you read the blurb about how I'm an impoverished orphan and also at the heart of a national slut-shaming scandal, and you thought, *Oh great, this is just the kind of heart-wrenching tale I need to feel better about my own life*, but seriously, you have to relax. I am not some pitiful Oliver-Twist-meets-Kim-Kardashian-type figure. If you're seeking a nice cathartic cry, I'm not your girl. May I recommend binge-watching some sort of medical drama for the high caliber of second-hand devastation you're looking for.

Either that or you saw the nudes, which, y'know. Most people have. My lopsided boobs have received more press attention than your average international epidemic, which I bet the super-virus population is furious about. All that hard work attempting to destroy the human race gone unnoticed.

In all seriousness, I don't know why my publisher asked me to write this book, because apart from that one time I accidentally ate a pot brownie and broke into the old folks' home, my life really hasn't been all that interesting. But we'll get to that in due course. It's not actually relevant to the sex scandal or anything, but it is hilarious on a fairly profound level.

I know, I know, it's highly confusing that I'm referencing the fact this is a book you bought – unless you pirated it, in which case joke's on you because this PDF is set to self-destruct in forty-five seconds – but the reason is that I am incredibly meta and pretentious, and I wanted to make your brain hurt like it did when you watched *Inception* for the first time.

First, I guess I better explain how I got to this point: eighteen and internationally reviled. But instead of wasting time typing it all up for you, what I'm going to do is copy-paste entries from my blog so you can catch up, and add valuable retrospective insights in square brackets. By my calculations this should take up at least ninety-five percent of the manuscript, which is a big win for me because it means significantly less work on my part. When in doubt, always do the least amount of work possible, in order to preserve energy for important things like laughing and sex.

Don't look at me like that. This is a book about a sex scandal: did you really expect me to be a nun and/or the Virgin Mary?

Tuesday 13 September

7.01 a.m.

Honestly, I swear I'm the only person in the universe who realizes how pointless life is. People act like mere existence is some beautiful gift, completely overlooking the fact that said existence is nothing but the result of a freak accident that occurred a cool 13.7 billion years ago.

Not to rain on the parade or anything, but we're all doomed to a limited number of sun orbits before we finally kick the bucket and end up in the same infinite hell as Donald Trump and Adolf Hitler. Perhaps I'm overthinking it, but what we do between now and then barely seems worth getting out of bed for.

Maybe I'm being melodramatic. I just really hate getting out of bed.

2.47 p.m.

Just had a career counseling session with Mr Rosenqvist, who is Swedish and very flamboyant. Like *Brüno* but less subtle. Actually I think *Brüno* was Swiss or Austrian or something, but whatever.

The point is I can't look at Mr Rosenqvist without seeing Sacha Baron Cohen in a blond wig.

The dude tries really, really hard to make sure everyone FOLLOWS THEIR DREAMS [he is very shouty, hence the caps lock] and TAKES THE PATH LEAST TRAVELED and STOPS INJECTING HEROIN ON WEEKENDS. [I hilariously added that last one myself. To clarify: nobody at Edgewood High is in the habit of injecting heroin on such a regular basis that it would be of concern to our career counselor. In fact, if you are a lawyer who's reading this, please ignore every such allegation I make throughout this manuscript, because I really don't need to add a libel suit to my spectacular list of problems.]

We're sitting in Rosenqvist's minuscule, windowless office, which I'm pretty sure is just a repurposed broom closet, if the lingering scent of carpet cleaner is anything to go by. He sits behind a tiny desk that would be more suitable for a Borrower. There are filing cabinets everywhere, containing folders on every single student in the entire school. I would imagine there's probably some sort of electronic database which could replace this archaic system, but Bible Belt schools really love to do things the Old-fashioned Way™.

So he's all: "Miss O'Neill, have you given mach thought to vat you vould like to study ven you go to college next fall?"

[I'm going to stop trying to type in dialect now as I don't

4

want to appear racist. If you can even be racist to white Scandinavian men, which I'm not sure you can be.]

Breathing steadily through my mouth in a bid to prevent the bleach smell from burning away my nostril hair, I'm all: "Um, no, sir, I was thinking I might do a bit of traveling, you know, see the world and such."

And, to be fair, his subsequent line of questioning regarding my economic situation is probably quite legitimate, given that my grandma and I currently require more financial support than the US Army.

"So do you have money saved up to fund your flights at least?" he asks, completely unperturbed by the decades-old feather duster that's just taken a nosedive from the top shelf behind him. As an aspiring comedian and all-round idiot, it's very challenging for me to refrain from scoring the duster according to Olympic diving standards. 8.9 for difficulty, etc.

But back to the issue at hand: my negative bank balance. "No, sir, for I am eighteen and unemployed."

Patiently moving the feather duster to a more secure location in his desk drawer, he shoots me a sympathetic look. A waft of moldy apple stench floats out of the open drawer, and he hastily slams it shut again. This place must violate at least a dozen health codes. Is that the patter of tiny mouse feet I hear?

"I see. And have you tried to find a job?"

"Good God, that's brilliant!" I gasp, faux-astounded. "I had

5

not previously considered this course of action! Have you ever considered becoming a career counselor?"

In all seriousness, this is a sore point. For the third time this year, I just handed out my résumé to every retailer, restaurant and hotel in town. But there are too few jobs and too many people, and I'm never top of the pile.

He sighs. "I know it's stating the obvious. But, well . . . have you?"

Grinding my teeth in mild irritation, I sigh back. "Yessir, but the problem is, even the most basic entry-level jobs now require at least three years' experience, a degree in astrophysics and two Super Bowl trophies to even be considered for an interview. Unfortunately, due to my below-average IQ and complete lack of athletic prowess, I am thus fundamentally unemployable."

So ultimately we both agree that jet-setting to South Africa to volunteer in an elephant sanctuary, while very noble and selfless, is not a viable option at present.

Rifling through my shockingly empty file, Mr Rosenqvist then tries another tactic. "What subjects do you most enjoy in school?" He tries to disguise the flinch as he spots my grade point average.

I think about this for a while, tugging at a loose thread on the cushioned metal chair I'm perched on. "Not math because I'm not a sociopath."

He laughs his merry Swedish laugh.

"Or science. See above."

Another endearing chuckle.

As a feminist I feel immediately guilty because everyone is trying to encourage girls into STEM subjects now, but to be honest I'm not dedicated enough to the Vagenda to force myself to become a computer programmer. Sometimes you have to pick your battles.

The thing is, I know exactly what career I'd like to pursue, but I'm kinda scared to vocalize it. Most career counselors are interested in one thing and one thing only: getting you into college. Schools are rated higher according to the percentage of alumni who go on to get a college education, and thus career guidance is dished out with this in mind. If the Ivy Leagues don't teach it, it's not worth doing. And, believe it or not, the Ivy Leagues do not teach comedy.

Plus, the chances of success in my dream job are not high. Especially for a girl like me.

Rosenqvist continues his gentle coaxing. "What about English?"

Nodding noncommittally, I say, "I like English, especially the creative writing components. And drama." Before I can talk myself out of it, I add, "Sometimes I write and perform sketches with my friends. You know, just for fun. It's not serious or anything." Judging by the tingling heat in my cheeks, I've flushed bright red.

But despite my pathetic trailing off, he loves this development.

His little blond-gray mustache jumps around his face like a ferret stuck in a combustion engine.

"FANTASTIC! FOLLOW YOUR DREAMS, MISS O'NEILL!" [Told you.]

So now, despite the fact that it's not exactly a reliable career path, I have a backpack stuffed full of information on improvization troupes and drama school and theaters that accept script submissions. I'm actually pretty grateful to Rosenqvist for not immediately dismissing my unconventional career ambitions, as so many teachers have before.

He even told me about his friend who does reasonably priced headshots for high-school students. Granted, this sounds incredibly dodgy, but I am giving him the benefit of the doubt here because I would be quite upset to discover Mr Rosenqvist was earning commission by referring his students to a pedophilic photographer as a side hustle.

5.04 p.m.

On Mr Rosenqvist's jolly recommendation, I find myself voluntarily staying behind after school to talk to Mrs Crannon, our drama teacher, about my career. Like, I am actually spending more time on campus than is absolutely necessary. Of my own free will. This is clear, unequivocal evidence that mind control is real, and that my lovely, albeit shouty, Scandinavian career advisor is in fact some sort of telepathic Dark Lord. It's the only explanation. Well, not the *only* explanation. For those who do not believe in the supernatural, it is of course possible that Rosenqvist performed some sort of lobotomy on me during our session.

[For all my cynicism and wit, I do actually genuinely care about writing. But, as much as I would love to be, I'm not clever in the traditional bookish way – more in the "watches a lot of movies" and "is very talented at taking the piss out of everything" way. Which means academia is not exactly my preferred environment, due to the lack of emphasis on movies, and the general dissuasion of piss-taking. It's almost like teachers don't *want* to be told their subject of expertise is a cruel and unusual punishment for being born. Weird.]

Anyway, Mrs Crannon's office is up a random back staircase behind the theater. I traipse up there once the final bell has rung and all other sound-of-mind students have evacuated the premises. I'm armed with a notepad, a sample script, and a metric crap-ton of peanut butter cups, since I assume talking to teachers in your spare time is much like getting a tattoo – you have to keep your blood sugar consistently high in order to survive the pain without passing out.

Mrs Crannon is a lovely woman. She dresses in purple glasses and Birkenstocks and crazy tunics, and veers toward the eccentric side of the personality scale. And she always gives me great parts in school plays because I'm loud enough that the tech department doesn't need to supply a microphone. I'm currently playing Daisy in *The Great Gatsby*, for example, despite not being elegant or glamorous in the slightest.

I've always liked Mrs Crannon, but in a Stockholm Syndrome sort of way. I mean, do any of us *really* like our teachers? These are the important philosophical questions, people.

When I walk in, she's sitting behind a desk piled high with playbooks, coffee mugs and a massive beige computer from the nineties [good old budget cuts]. The whole room smells of dusty stage costumes and stale hairspray. My favorite smell in the world.

"Izzy! It's lovely to see you outside of rehearsals for once."

She ushers me in and I take a seat on quite literally the most uncomfortable plastic chair I've ever had the misfortune to encounter. It is the Iron Maiden of the chair world. I'm not exaggerating.

"Thanks," I say, trying to give off the pleasant expression of someone who is not in severe physical discomfort at the hands of a chair-come-torture-device. "I brought peanut butter cups to compensate for the fact I'm keeping you from getting home to Mr Crannon."

"Actually, I have a Mrs Crannon." She grins, waggling her left hand at me. Her engagement ring has a Dwayne Johnson of a diamond on it, and an elaborate wedding band sits next to it. "I'm gay. *And* married. Which, as a combination, is apparently difficult for a lot of the population to comprehend."

"Oh! Awesome. But let me get this straight." [Or should it be "let me get this gay"? Honestly, what a minefield.] "You're both called Mrs Crannon? Does that not get confusing?"

She laughs, cracking heartily into the packet of peanut butter cups I've plonked in front of her. "Yes, in hindsight we probably should've kept our own names. But I had to do something to keep my traditional Catholic parents happy."

I grin. "Aren't you tempted to write some sort of farcical sketch about two wives with the exact same name?"

Mrs Crannon smiles warmly. "Which leads us nicely onto your writing. Mr Rosenqvist told me you've been writing your own scripts? That's great! Tell me more about that." She leans back in her chair [a delightful padded malarkey, you'll be pleased to know, if you're at all concerned about the well-being of my drama teacher's backside].

Suddenly I feel a little embarrassed, mainly because I can tell I'm expected to hold a normal adulty conversation at this point, not one that's peppered with inappropriate gags and self-deprecating humor. And I've sort of forgotten how to do that.

Mumbling idiotically about Nora Ephron, I reach into my satchel, which is decorated with an assortment of pins and badges to give the illusion that I am halfway cool, and pull out the sample screenplay I brought along. It's a feature-length film I wrote over the summer. The logline [i.e. a one-sentence pitch] is this: a broke male sex worker falls for a career-obsessed client with commitment issues. Basically, it's an updated *Pretty Woman* that challenges gender stereotypes while also telling an impressive array of sex jokes. [Be honest. You would *so* see this movie.]

"You've already written an entire screenplay?" Mrs Crannon gapes at me, clapping her hands together like a performing monkey. "Izzy, that's fantastic! So many aspiring screenwriters struggle to even finish one script, and they're professionals who've been to film school. When I was a working theater director I used to despair of writers who seemed incapable of seeing an idea through to the end. You should be very proud of yourself. Writing 'fade out' is quite the accomplishment."

"Really?"

"Really!" She takes the script from me, examining the professional formatting and neatly typed title page. [My best friend Danny pirated the proper software for me on account of my severe brokeness. Don't tell the internet police. Or, you know, the *actual* police.] "I'd love to take it home with me to read. Can I?"

This show of unbelievable support catches me way off guard. "You'd do that? Spend your own free time reading my work?"

"Of course I would!" She crams another peanut butter cup in her mouth, tossing the paper in the overflowing trash can behind her. It's full of empty candy wrappers and soda cans. Obviously she is just as nutrition-conscious as me, which is precisely not at all. "I know how talented you are through working with you on school plays. You have me in stitches with your clever ad libs and witty improv."

I blush fiercely. Again. "Thank you. It irritates the living hell out of most people."

"Well, most people aren't budding comic writers in the making. Have you given much thought to what you'd like to do after leaving school? College? Internships? If you wanted to do both, USC is incredible for screenwriting – Spielberg is an alum – and you could intern during spring break and summer vacation while you're in LA. Best of both worlds."

I fidget with the zipper on the fake leather jacket I picked up at a thrift store last fall. This is the part I dread: coming clean about my financial situation. For the second time this afternoon. It shouldn't be a big deal, and in day-to-day life it doesn't bother me that much, but now that it's actually having an impact on my future decisions, it's kind of uncomfortable to discuss.

But like I say, Mrs Crannon is good people. So I tell her the truth. "Actually, I'm not sure I can afford college. I figured I'd just get a job here to support me and my grandma, and write in my spare time. Film a few shorts if I can scrape together the cash."

She frowns. The sound of her computer putting itself to sleep whirs through the quiet room. Even technology has zero interest in school after the final bell. "Have you looked into loans? For college, I mean." Figures that'd be her next question.

"Kind of. But the idea of being in that much debt scares the crap out of me. Especially with no parents to fall back on."

She rolls up the purple sleeves of her wild tunic, revealing a set of black rosary beads triple tied around her wrist. Another peanut butter cup bites the dust. She's plowing through them with such velocity I can only be impressed. If consuming chocolate was an Olympic sport, Crannon would be on the podium for sure. She's practically Simone Biles at this point.

"I get it," she says, in a way that entirely suggests she doesn't get it at all. "I do. But you have to think of it as an investment. In yourself, in your future. It's so cliché, and I know you'll have already heard it all with Rosenqvist, but you're young, you're bright, you're ambitious. You have to go for it."

I nod, but I feel a little deflated. It always leaves me feeling kinda empty when people preach "follow your dreams" to those with "do what you gotta do" kind of lives, even though I know their hearts are in the right place. Maybe being reckless and risk-taking is an option for them, but for me it just isn't.

Mrs Crannon senses the shift in mood, even though I try my best to hide it from her. Showing vulnerability is about as appealing to me as sticking my face into a bucket of mealworms. But she picks up on it nonetheless.

Wiping a smear of chocolate from the corner of her mouth,

she says, "I'll help you in whatever way I can, Izzy. Dig out old contacts, keep an eye out for paid internships, recommend some places to submit your work to while you're still a high-school student. USC would be great, but traditional college education isn't the only way into the industry." She smiles at me, and I can't help but smile back. "We'll figure it out. I promise."

When I leave twenty minutes later, stuffed full of Reese's and silently praying Mrs Crannon actually enjoys my screenplay after all that hyperbolic encouragement, I realize that I don't just like her in a Stockholm Syndrome way. I like her in a human way.

So I do have a heart. Who knew?

7.58 p.m.

"And so, it transpires, I do in fact possess an organ of the cardiovascular variety," I finish, triumphant.

I'm chilling at the diner with Ajita and Danny, my two best friends in the world. We have a mutual love of nachos and making fun of everything.

Martha's Diner is super old school, with neon signs and jukeboxes and booths and checkered tiles. It's massively overpriced and you have to take out a small mortgage to afford a burger, but their fries have been cooked at least eighteen times and are thus the most delicious substance on earth. Honestly, you should've seen the hype all over town when Martha's

15

opened. Largely from those people who post Marilyn Monroe quotes on social media and go on about how much they wish they were born in the 1950s. Like, calm down. We still have milkshakes and racism.

Incidentally, Martha's is also where my grandmother Betty begrudgingly moonlights as a pancake chef. I mean, it's not exactly moonlighting when it's her only job. But it sounds more glamorous if you say it that way. In reality she works twelve-hour shifts on bunion-riddled feet and is in almost constant pain because of it, but there's just no way she can afford to retire. That's why I can't go to college. Not just because of the tuition fees, but because I need to stay in my hometown and work my damn ass off to give her the rest she deserves after so many years of hard graft. It's my turn to support her for once.

Anyway, I've just filled my pals in on my chat with Mrs Crannon, and explained how I'm not as dead in the soul department as previously thought.

"Interesting hypothesis, but I reject it unequivocally," Ajita replies, tucking a lock of black hair behind her ear and slurping her candy apple milkshake. The henna on her hands is beginning to fade after her cousin's wedding last month. "I mean, it's pretty off-brand for you to care about people. In fact, short of an alien parasite feasting on your brain, I'm not convinced you have the capacity to like more than three individuals at any given time, and those slots are already filled by me, Danny and Betty."

"Valid point," I concede. Smelling burnt pancake batter, I peer past the server station into the massive chrome kitchen, trying to see if Betty's knocking around. There's no sign of her. She's probably swigging from her hip flask out back while telling dirty jokes to the naive dishwasher. [To clarify, the dishwasher is a person. Not an appliance. My grandma may be nuts, but even she doesn't engage kitchenware in conversation.]

"That's cool of Crannon to read your script, though," Danny says, stirring his salted-caramel banana milkshake with three jumbo straws. He's wearing a grubby Pokémon T-shirt I got him for his twelfth birthday, which still fits due to his scarily low BMI. "She didn't have to do that."

I nod enthusiastically. "Right? And she was so complimentary. She even likes it when I spontaneously ad lib during rehearsals. I did attempt to show some self-awareness and reference the fact it renders most people homicidal, but she was adamant. She genuinely likes my banter."

"Clearly the woman needs to be sectioned under the mental health act," Ajita points out helpfully. I flick a blob of whipped cream at her face. It lands on her nose and she licks it off with her freakishly long tongue. She's Nepali and about three feet tall, but her tongue is like that of a St Bernard. If I spilled my entire milkshake on the floor, for example, she could just vacuum it right up with her tongue without even bending down. It's truly remarkable.

"Well, I think Izzy's funny," Danny mumbles, disappearing under his unruly platform of matted hair.

Aghast, Ajita and I exchange looks. Danny has literally never complimented me at any point in his life. Even when I was five years old and my parents had just died, ours was a friendship built on good-natured antagonism.

"To look at?" Ajita suggests, mentally flailing for an explanation.

"Shut up," he says, not looking at either of us. "I'll go pay for these milkshakes."

And then he slides out of the booth and walks up to the cash register, where a large-of-breast freshman greets him with as much enthusiasm as she can muster for minimum wage.

"What on earth was that about?" I whisper to Ajita, too shocked to crack a joke. "He thinks I'm *funny*? What's next – he thinks I'm also a fundamentally decent human being?"

"Let's not get carried away," she says hastily. "But wait, he's paying for the milkshakes? Danny. Buying us things. Why? Has he been hustling us this whole time? Is he the Secret Millionaire? I think the last thing he bought me was a box of tampons, and that was just his pass-agg way of telling me I was overreacting during an argument."

Having forked over the moollah, Danny walks back across to the booth, tucking his wallet back into his jeans pocket and looking rather pleased with himself. The Pikachu on his shirt smirks obnoxiously as he almost collides with a waitress carrying three club sandwiches. She shoots him a dirty look, but his gaze is fixed so intently on me that he barely notices. Then he smiles this weird, bashful smile I've never seen before. *Smiles.* Danny. I mean, really.

What, pray tell, the fuck?

Wednesday 14 September

7.41 a.m.

The universe is weird. My parents were perfectly healthy and happy when their car was hit by a drunk truck driver [and obviously the truck too, not just the driver himself – that probably would've ended differently]. Boom, dead in an instant. But my grandmother, Betty, the woman who raised me from that day forth, is repeatedly told by doctors that she's going to die soon, on account of her significant BMI. And yet she's still kicking ass and taking names.

Anyway, even though the doctor repeatedly tells her she has to cut down on fat/sugar/carbs/basically everything fun, Betty makes French toast for breakfast this morning. She's absolutely incredible at it, due to making delicious batter-based goods 807 times a day at the diner. Our tiny kitchen, full of ancient fittings so retro they're now back in vogue, smells of sweet cinnamon and maple bacon. The old radio is playing a tacky jingle-based advertisement in the corner.

"What's on at school today, kid?" Betty practically whistles, ignoring the fact I'm feeding Dumbledore under the table. [Dumbledore is our dachshund, by the way. I'm not hiding the ghost of the world's most powerful wizard in my kitchen.]

"Oh, the usual. Feigning interest in the periodic table. Pretending to know what a tectonic plate is. Trying and failing to be excused from gym class for the thousandth time this semester." I stir sugar into the two cups of coffee perched on the batter-splattered counter [try saying that five times without giving yourself a tongue injury].

This is our morning routine: she makes breakfast, I make coffee, and we chat inanely about our upcoming days. It's been this way as long as I can remember.

"Would you like me to write a note?" she asks. "I'll explain how your parents just died and you're having a hard time."

I snort. "Considering that was thirteen years ago, I'm not so sure they'll buy it."

"Besides," I continue, "a couple of teachers have actually been pretty cool about my career potential lately. That's kinda motivating me to show up to class a little more often, even if it's just to show them I care about my future."

We sit down at our miniature wooden table, tucking into stacks of French toast which slightly resemble the leaning tower of Pisa. She listens intently as I tell her all about my meeting with Mr Rosenqvist yesterday, and about how delightfully Swedish he is, and also about his excitement re my sketches, which I have categorically told Betty not to watch and yet she does anyway. Then I brief her about the subsequent awesome session with Mrs Crannon, and about how the enthusiasm from them both has made me feel slightly more optimistic about my strange brand of social commentary combined with dozens of dirty jokes per page.

"They're right to be excited, kiddo," she agrees. "You're hilarious. But how come you've never mentioned this screenplay of yours?"

"I guess I was just embarrassed," I admit. "Like, what does some random teenager from the middle of nowhere know about writing movies? I feel like a fraud."

I almost confide in her about my fears of sticking out like a sore thumb in New York or Hollywood, if I ever make it that far, but I don't want her to feel bad or anything. She knows deep down I don't care about our lack of money, and it's not like I blame her for our predicament. But if she knew it was a big obstacle in my career path, she'd only end up feeling guilty. And that's the last thing in the world I want.

"If your mom were here, she'd say . . ." Betty trails off, blinking fiercely. She almost never manages to finish a sentence about my mom. As predicted, she fixes a neutral expression back onto her face, and I let it slide. "You shouldn't feel like a fraud. Everyone starts somewhere, right?"

Right. But for most successful people, somewhere isn't here.

"Maybe we could look at buying you another camera," Betty suggests, slurping her milky coffee through a straw. "I've been working so many doubles at the diner lately that I'm not actually behind on rent for once. You may notice, for example, that the bacon we're currently consuming is actually within its use-by date. We are practically living in the lap of luxury here. So I'm sure I could scrape together the cents for a secondhand DSLR and a lens or two. You know, if you want."

The suggestion sends a pang through my chest. Earlier this year, when I'd begun to realize how much I wanted to make it as a comedian, Betty bought me a nice camera and a light box so I could start up a YouTube channel. I filmed a couple videos, and I loved it. People responded pretty well too. One went vaguely viral. But it was a long, cold winter that stretched all the way into early April, and Martha's was so quiet there wasn't enough work for Betty. I ended up having to pawn the camera to cover our gas bill. It sucked, but you do what you have to do.

"Nah, it's all right," I say to Betty. "I'm just gonna focus on scripts for a while. All you need for that is a working computer, and if worst comes to worst I can always use the library." I smile gratefully. "But thank you. I promise I'll pay you back when I sell out Madison Square Garden with my standup special."

We chat about my weird brand of comedy for a while longer – I get my wildly inappropriate sense of humor from her. She also tells me about how back when she was a young woman, it was considered unattractive for a woman to tell dirty jokes or do ridiculous impressions of political figures. And how that made her want to do it even more.

Every time I catch myself moping about my general lack of parents, or our dire financial situation, I just remind myself how lucky I am to be raised by such an incredible human who's always taught me how to laugh, no matter what's going wrong in my life.

I love my grandma. Especially when watching her feed crispy bacon to a chubby wiener dog and singing her own special renditions of popular nursery rhymes. Today it's: "Little Bo Peep has lost her sheep and doesn't know where to find them, largely because Little Bo Peep is fucking irresponsible and should not be in charge of livestock." It's tough cramming all those extra syllables into the last two lines, but she really makes it work.

8.16 a.m.

Danny meets me at the gates of my housing community so we can walk to school together, as we've done every weekday for a decade. I decide to forget all about the weirdness of last night in the diner and write it off as a strange anomaly that will most likely never be repeated.

"Morning," he chirps, like a cockatoo or something similar, I don't know. Like most people with better things to do, I'm not that clued up on bird species. And then – THEN! – he hands me a paper coffee cup with steam billowing out the top. "Picked you up a mocha."

He doesn't have one for himself. Only for me.

And just like that, any attempt to overlook his sudden and deeply disturbing personality transplant goes out the window.

"Oh. Um, thanks." As I take the cup from him, my fingertips brush his, and he leaps back so far it's like I've driven an electrode into his groin. His satchel plummets to the ground, and it takes him roughly ninety-eight minutes to pick it back up again, that's how hard he's fumbling.

"Don't mention it," he grins. As he stands back up, I catch a whiff of new aftershave on the breeze. Another bashful smile before he turns away.

Sorry, but WTF? Danny and I have been friends since forever, and I've never seen him like this before. And we've been through a *lot* together. Especially right after my parents died. While the court was deciding who to grant my custody to, I spent a lot of time over at his house, since his mom is my godmother and all. We played outside in his family's sprinklers, running around in just our underwear and spraying each other with water from the hosepipes. I remember liking it because nobody could tell I was crying almost constantly.

For a while we all thought I'd end up living with them, since the government had concerns over Betty's ill health. Let the record show that I'm eternally grateful they chose her instead of the Wells. I mean, they're amazing people, don't get me wrong. But I can't even imagine being with anyone but Betty.

All I'm saying is that if anyone's gonna pick up on Danny being weird, it's me. And he's definitely being weird.

Regardless, the rest of the walk is fairly uneventful. We chat about the geography homework we both struggled to complete without slipping into a comalike state. We discuss plans for tonight – torn between filming a skit or binge-watching *Monty Python* for the gazillionth time – and speculate about what movies will garner the most Academy Award nominations in a few months' time.

He's forgotten to pick up a cardboard sleeve for the coffee and it burns into my palm as we walk, making it impossible to forget. As usual, we meet up with Ajita halfway to school, and she eyes the coffee like it's a grenade with the pin pulled out. Neither of us address it, but I know she's thinking exactly what I am:

What's going on with our best friend?

10.24 a.m.

Geography is, as suspected, a snoozefest of epic proportions. I think if you offered me $500,000 right this second to tell you what it was about, I couldn't, and that is saying a lot because for half a million dollars I could both go to college and pay to have

Donald Trump assassinated. [Apparently this is an illegal thing to say, so it's important to clarify: I AM JOKING. In fact, it is fair to assume that any legally dubious sentences at any point in this entire manuscript are jokes. I'm not sure if this gets me off the hook or not, but I'm hoping so because otherwise I'm almost certainly going to jail, where I will rot forever because I do not have the patience for a Shawshank-style escape. In fact, without Netflix it's perfectly possible my general will to live would just evaporate within the week.]

At some point when Mr Richardson is droning on about, well, drones, I make eye contact with Carson Manning, who's sitting in the next row. He's a professional class clown so I instantly know I am in trouble because my ability to resist laughter is non-existent.

Carson smirks and holds up his pad of paper, revealing a ballpoint-pen doodle scribbled in the margin of his sparse notes. Immediately I suspect the drawing to be a penis because teenage boys love nothing more than sketching their own genitals, but I'm pleasantly surprised to see a charming caricature of Mr Richardson. Doodle Richardson has giant jowls and a tattoo of an alpaca on his arm. This is funny not because our geography teacher actually has such a tattoo, but because he reminds us at least once every thirty seconds about the time he went trekking in Peru and climbed Machu Picchu.

As expected, I snort with ugly laughter, but Mr Richardson

is too busy reminiscing about the alpaca who stole his protein bar to scold me.

Carson looks genuinely pleased with my seal of approval and smiles broadly, tiny dimples setting into his smooth brown skin. The black shirt he's wearing is tight around his arms and shoulders – he's the star player on the varsity basketball team and is in tremendous shape – and his blue beanie hat is slightly lopsided.

Even though we haven't talked much, I feel like I already know Carson. Like, as a person. Is that weird? We have a ton in common – we'll both do anything for a laugh, and if the rumors are anything to go by, his family isn't exactly rolling in cash either. In fact, I think I might remember seeing him at the soup kitchen a few years back, when Betty had the shingles and couldn't work for a bit. [That was a dark time for our dental hygiene. When you're super broke, toothpaste is the first luxury item to go. Ajita blessedly snuck her tube into school with her so I could do damage control before first period.]

So yeah, Carson Manning. He's good people. And not exactly terrible to look at.

Interesting development.

11.58 a.m.
On the way to our last period of the morning, Danny, Ajita and I stop by my locker to grab a textbook I dumped there last week

and haven't looked at since. The halls are pretty busy with people shoving their way to different classes, and the general squeak of sneakers on linoleum echoes around.

We reach my locker, and I'm barely paying attention as I enter my combination since I'm too busy trying to figure out what the hell's up with my lifelong pal. But as soon as I open it, something soft and dark red tumbles out and hits the deck. Baffled, I reach down to scoop it up off the floor. It's a sweater I've never seen before, though immediately recognize the embroidered logo on the front. Gryffindor. My Hogwarts house.

"What the hell?" I murmur. "Who put this there? Have I got the wrong locker?"

Then I see the bow ribbon gift tag lying next to my sneakers on the floor. It's a gift.

Only two people other than me know my locker combination: Danny and Ajita.

Danny shifts his feet and stares at the ground.

Ajita puts two and two together almost as quickly as I do. "Hey, Danny," she says, a mischievous grin on her face. "Remember that time in fourth grade when you got so excited over the new *Harry Potter* movie that you vomited all over yourself?"

Instead of retorting with a quick-fire clap-back like he usually would, Danny goes all weird and bumbly, muttering some solid curse words that'd definitely get him and his entire family thrown out of their church.

Frowning, Ajita nudges his shoulder. "Come on, I was only kidding. Well, I wasn't because you actually did that. But there's no need to drop so many f-bombs."

Danny looks homicidal. He just huffily folds his arms and stares at his feet. Jeez. Where's his sense of humor gone?

1.25 p.m.

It's Danny's turn for a careers session with Rosenqvist this lunchtime, so while he's off justifying his plan to become a hotshot surgeon, despite his mediocre GPA, Ajita and I take the opportunity to talk through his erratic behavior of late.

[Okay, so now that I'm turning this into a book I know I'm supposed to describe everything in great detail in order for my readers to be able to visualize the scene, but really, it's a school cafeteria – you all know what they look like and, if you don't, I really don't think it's on me to educate you. It's loud and plastic and smells like old microwaved cheese.]

Ajita bites into her veggie hot dog and studies me intently. "I have to say it, dude. And I know it'll make you cringe, and I know you'll disagree vehemently on account of your fundamental distrust in my judgment, but I think it's fairly obvious what's happening here."

"It is?" My own meat-filled hot dog is slathered with enough hot mustard to kill a small horse. My nostrils sting fierily.

"The guy's blatantly harboring a newfound crush on you. It's thrown him way off guard since he's known you for, like, a million years, but now he's developing The Feels and is unclear how to proceed."

I mull this over. "So he just keeps buying me an assortment of beverages and novelty sweaters, and complimenting personality traits he's previously expressed extreme disgust at, all in the hope that I will somehow fall in love with him in return?"

The sweater sits in my lap like a warm cat, but I feel guilty every time I look at it. Danny and I used to watch *Harry Potter* movies all the time, whenever I stayed over at his house. Ajita didn't arrive on the friendship scene until middle school, and in those early days it was just Danny and me against the world. And *Harry Potter* was our thing. We escaped to Hogwarts whenever we could.

"Look, I never said he was particularly subtle with his tactics," Ajita says through a mouthful of hot dog. Pieces of bun spray everywhere as she talks. It's delightful. I wish I'd brought some sort of umbrella or shield-type object. "I just think he's in trouble in the romance department."

Before I can express my complete disgust and horror at the situation, an extraordinarily tall girl I don't recognize plonks her tray down next to Ajita and smiles familiarly. She's got insanely curly auburn hair and freckled white cheeks.

"Hey, Ajita," she says cheerily. "Hey, Izzy."
Pardon me?

"Iz, this is Carlie," Ajita says, suddenly staring intently at the ravaged remains of her hot dog. I can only assume this ashamed expression translates as: I am so sorry, dearest Izzy, for having people in my life you do not know about, for I understand how rude and inappropriate this is considering we're meant to be best friends, and I can only endeavor to be a better pal in future, one who keeps you abreast of any and all new friendship developments as and when they unfold, lest I be condemned to an eternity in geography class a.k.a. hell.

You know, something like that.

But really, WTF? Ajita and I inform each other of every single minor thing that ever happens to us, including but not limited to: bowel movements, disappointing meals, new and freakishly long hairs we find on our bodies. So it's utterly implausible that she knows mysterious tall and pretty people and just forgets to mention it to me.

[On closer inspection, it is possible I have friend jealousy.]

"Hi, Carlie," I finally reply, once I've gotten over the unspeakable betrayal of the situation.

She smiles, all straight white teeth and naturally pink lips. "Nice to finally meet you."

FINALLY????

I repeat. WTF?

"So, Ajita," she says, spearing some lettuce on her fork and crunching into it loudly. Seriously, she is eating a salad. I'm not kidding. An actual *salad*. I was not aware this was a thing people did in real life. "Are you looking forward to tennis trials later?"

I absolutely die laughing at this, to the point where I am so hysterical I fear a little bit of fart might slip out.

Both Ajita and Carlie stare at me as though I'm having some kind of seizure. Without, you know, making sure I'm not in any immediate physical danger. All I'm saying is they're not the sort of people you want around in a potential medical emergency.

Once I finally wipe my tears away, I splutter, "Ajita? Sports? *Tennis??* You must be new here."

"Actually, I am new here," Carlie replies, popping a cherry tomato in her mouth. A fucking cherry tomato! Can you even imagine!

Ajita clears her throat. "Erm, Iz, I actually . . . I thought I might go and try out. I think I might quite enjoy tennis. Serena Williams makes it look like an excellent thing to do." A sheepish smile. "Carlie's the new captain."

And then they exchange the strangest moment. It's like I'm not even there, nor is the rest of the cafeteria. They just look straight at each other. [This might not sound weird on the face of it, but think about it. How often do you actually do nothing but LOOK at the person next to you without saying anything? It's unnecessarily intense for most scenarios.]

I swallow the last mouthful of hot dog and resign myself to the fact my best friend has been replaced by someone who likes *sports*, of all things, and that I am but a mere distant memory thanks to the sudden arrival of a Victoria's Secret model into our lives, and that Ajita undoubtedly has absolutely no interest in me or my existence now that she has a new best friend to collude with.

Both of my best friends are behaving way out of character. I always thought I'd know if the alien apocalypse began with those closest to me, but now I'm not so sure.

It really has been a WTF? kind of day.

3.46 p.m.

I feel a little jittery all afternoon, due to the seismic shifts taking place in my beloved friendship tripod.

For one thing, I really, really hope Danny isn't infatuated with me because I don't feel the same. At least, I don't think I do. I've just never thought of him that way. When you grow up knowing someone your whole life, they feel more like family than a potential suitor. [Suitor? Who do I think I am, a princess in a magical kingdom governed by frog princes?]

But for now I can cling to the hope that maybe this is just a blip, and Ajita is hugely misreading the signals. Maybe these gifts are just his way of showing that he's proud of me for the screenplay stuff? And the smiles are him finally growing out of the sullen teenage boy phase? Here's hoping. Because I have no idea how I would deal with an unrequited love situation. Have you met me? Have you seen how awkward I am? Exactly. It's just not feasible that I could navigate such a dilemma with my dignity still intact.

Then there's the Carlie/Ajita thing. Obviously I know it's irrational to be jealous, but I can't help it. I think it's human nature to feel vaguely territorial over your best friend. Not in a canine pissing-all-over-them-to-mark-your-patch type way, but more in a childish not-wanting-to-share-your-favorite-toy type way. Yes, it's selfish. Yes, I'm immature. But is it so wrong to simply want a monogamous friendship? [Yes, past me. Yes, it is very wrong.]

Anyway, I very much prefer when things stay the same. What's that biological term? Homeostasis? Does that apply here? Can we please find a way to make it apply to friendship circles?

4.32 p.m.

Alas, all is not lost! Mrs Crannon called me into her office at the end of school. Her computer is wearing several of the 1920s wigs she sourced for our *Gatsby* production, and she's combing them as I walk through the door. Before I've even taken a seat in the Iron Maiden chair of doom, she offers me a cup of coffee and a triple chocolate chip cookie, which is how I know my instincts were correct and she is in fact a fantastic human being on all fronts.

"So! I finished your script," she says, all warm and friendly.

Through sheer nerves and stress, my stomach almost plummets through my asshole. [I realize this is a hideous thing to say, but you all know exactly what I mean, and I shall not apologize for vocalizing the sensation.]

"Oh, did you?" I sip the coffee, immediately giving myself third-degree burns, and try to resist the urge to flee the room, banshee-screaming, with my arms flailing in the air and a trail of cookie-based destruction behind me.

She abandons the wigs and leans forward onto her elbows in a very teachery way. "Izzy, I promise you I'm not just saying this because you're my student and I'm trying to be encouraging. You have an unbelievable talent."

"Really?" I grin insanely, like an insane person.

"Really! I fully planned to only read the first ten pages last night and make some notes for you, but before I knew it, it was after midnight and I'd finished the entire thing. *And* I'd completely forgotten to make any notes. That's how good it is. It's smart and funny, and your social awareness really shines through. I didn't feel like I was reading the work of a high-school senior."

The cynical side of me feels like she's laying it on a little thick at this point, but I'm so happy I just don't care. I beam even more. "Thank you, Mrs Crannon. That means the world."

"I'm glad," she says, smiling back just as proudly. "Now, I've been thinking about next steps for you. You're unsure about college, which is totally fine, and you're not in a position to take on unpaid internships just yet. Again, that's okay. But I did have a few ideas. Firstly, I really think you need to get this script into industry hands, whether agents or producers."

I sigh. "Right. But no agents or producers accept unsolicited submissions. I already looked into it."

"Maybe not," Mrs Crannon agrees. "However, there are a lot of screenplay competitions out there that have judging panels made up of exactly those kinds of people – agents and producers and story developers who're looking out for fresh new talent. I did a bit of research over lunch, and there's a fairly established competition running in LA, aimed specifically at younger writers. It's heavily development-focused, so as you progress through the various rounds, you get a ton of feedback from people who really know their stuff, plus meetings with industry executives if you make it to the finals. And guess what the grand prize is?"

I shake my head, hardly believing what I'm hearing. How could I not have heard about this? It sounds like a dream.

"A college scholarship!"

I blink, wondering if I heard her right. "What?"

She hands me a printout of a web page [literally something only old people ever do] which has all the competition info on it. Across the top is bold branding: The Script Factor.

But my eyes land on one thing.

Entry fee: $50.

"This is great, Mrs Crannon, but . . . I can't afford it." My voice is all flat and echoey. "The entry fee, I mean. I could never ask my grandma to give me fifty bucks. That's like seventeen hours of work at the diner." [I did mention math not being my strong suit.]

Without a trace of condescension, she replies, "I thought you might say that." And then the unthinkable happens. She reaches into her purse, pulls out a leather wallet, and hands me a fifty-dollar bill.

I stare at it in her hand, stunned. "Mrs Crannon, I . . . I can't take that. No. Thank you so much, but no. No, I can't."

"You can, Izzy. I want you to. My father recently passed away, and he left me some money. He was a teacher too. English literature. He'd love to know he was helping a talented young creative find their way."

Her crazy tunic is all orange and pink and yellow flowers, but all the colors blur together as my eyes fill with hot tears. I'm used to having emotional support from a select few people, but to have a near-stranger take such a massive leap of faith in me? It's overwhelming.

"I don't know what to say. Thank you. Thank you so much."

"I'm glad to be able to help. Just remember me when you're famous, won't you?" She grins and boots up her ancient computer, which still has an actual floppy disk drive. "Now, let's fill in this entry form together, shall we? The deadline is tomorrow, so we have to move fast."

11.12 p.m.

Hung out with Danny and Ajita tonight (you know, once she'd finished tennis trials with SATAN PERSONIFIED, i.e. Carlie) and unfortunately the sequence of events that unfolded gave credibility to her theory that Danny is madly in love with me.

We're in Ajita's basement, which is bigger than my entire house, playing pool and watching this obscure Canadian sketch show we all love. The conversation drifts toward school gossip, as it so often does, and I just happen to mention finding Carson Manning hot in a sexy-yet-unintimidating way.

Danny is incredulous. "Carson Manning?" He gapes at me, pushing his thick-framed glasses up his nose so he can actually see the red ball he's trying to pot. His mousy brown hair is doing that weird frizzy thing he hates.

"But he's . . ."

"Black?" Ajita snaps, aggressively chalking up her cue. Blue dust hangs in the air around her, giving a vaguely satanic vibe. God, is she fierce when calling people out on their problematic bullshit. Reason number 609,315 why I adore her.

"No," he backtracks hastily. "He's just . . . well, he spends his whole school day pretending to be an idiot just for laughs. I didn't think feigned stupidity was your jam."

I try explaining that finding someone hot does not necessarily imply a deep emotional connection, but he's too pissed. Ajita and I just eat our nachos and ignore his pet lip, and continue to systematically destroy him at pool for what must be the seven millionth time this year. Ajita goes on an impressive potting spree and buries four stripes in a row. I whoop delightedly. We complete a complicated fist-bump routine we devised in freshman year. Our aversion tactics seem to be working, and Danny almost talks himself out of his emotional crisis, until . . .

Ajita: "So, Izzy, I heard a rumor today." She pots a fifth. Danny is almost apoplectic. He's not great at losing.

"Yeah? Did Carlie tell you?" Petty passive aggression aside, I try to act disinterested. But Ajita knows I am deeply nosy, and while I don't like to be directly involved in conflict itself, I must know absolutely every detail about other people's drama or else I will spontaneously combust.

"Zachary Vaughan wants to ask you out."

Soda exits my nose in a violent manner at this point. My brain is fizzing. Is that a thing? It feels like a thing.

Now, it's important for you to know how utterly despicable Vaughan is on practically every level. He's pretty, but he knows it, he's rich and he flaunts it, and his right-wing daddy is so racist he probably has an effigy of Martin Luther King on his bonfire every year.

The effect on Danny is nuclear. "That's ridiculous. What a joke! Has the dude ever even spoken to you?"

I say nothing, flabbergasted by his vitriol. [Good words. Well done, past me.]

But Danny can't let it go. He takes aim at the white pool ball and misses entirely. He sighs and thrusts the cue angrily at Ajita. Instead of catching it she just leaps out the way, which if you ask me speaks volumes about her tennis abilities.

Danny scoffs, all haughty and such. "I don't get it. His dad would freak. What's he trying to pull, asking a girl like you out?"

This pisses me off a bit, but because of my previously described aversion to actual conflict, I let Ajita fight my corner.

"What do you mean, a girl like her?" Ajita's awesome when she's in battle mode.

"Well, he's a senator's son," Danny mumbles in his awkward Dannylike way. "A *Republican* senator."

I snort. "And I'm poor. Forget my above-average face and rocking rack – no guy could ever see past my lack of money?"

But instead of biting back on the defensive, Danny does look like he feels genuinely bad for throwing my impoverished state in my face. So even though it stings, I let it go.

Ajita clearly shares my train of thought. She pots the black ball, securing our utter annihilation. "*Aaaaanyway.* Whaddaya fancy doing for your birthday this year, D?"

It's Danny's birthday next month, and while mine is usually

a subdued affair, due to my lack of funds, Danny always does something cool for his. He's an only child, so his parents don't mind forking out for me to tag along too. Last year we went paintballing, the year before it was go-karting.

"I was thinking maybe zorb football?" Danny says, pushing his glasses up his nose for the thousandth time. "You know, where you run around in inflatable bubbles and attempt to kick a ball around a field while crashing into each other like dodgems. It looks hilarious. And is the only circumstance in which I would consider participating in sports."

"Oh yeah, that looks incredible," I enthuse. "I've seen some YouTube videos. One of us will almost certainly die a gruesome death, but I'm game."

Ajita pipes up. "Speaking as the person who will most likely die that gruesome death, I'm willing to take one for the team."

Danny grins. "Perfect. And I think your brother would love it too, Jeets." Ajita's brother, Prajesh, is thirteen and already an amazing athlete.

"You wouldn't mind inviting him along?" Ajita asks, plonking herself down on the sofa. I nestle in next to her while Danny racks up the pool balls to practise not being awful. "That's so sweet of you. He would love that."

"Of course," he says. The balls spread and rattle around the table as he strikes the white ball in the perfect break. Two plop into pockets, and he smiles with satisfaction. "I think he's having a rough time at school at the minute."

Ajita looks crestfallen. "He is?"

I share her concern. Prajesh is like a little brother to me too.

Danny backtracks somewhat. "I mean, it's nothing sinister. I don't think he's being bullied or anything. But the last few times I've seen him in the hallway, he's been by himself, looking a little lost. And I know what it's like to be a slightly awkward and nerdy thirteen-year-old. So I don't mind taking him under my wing for a while."

"Thanks. I'd appreciate it." Ajita smiles, but it doesn't reach her eyes. I can tell she's going to worry and obsess over this. Her big, tight-knit family is her whole world.

A flash of envy catches me off guard. Fleetingly, I wonder what it must be like to have so many people to love and care about, but I shake the thought away like I always do. Self-pity isn't my style.

[Hold that thought, O'Neill. The worst is yet to come.]

Thursday 15 September

1.23 p.m.

Carson comes up to our table in the cafeteria at lunch. Ajita kicks me under the table because of what I confessed last night, and in response I throw a boiled potato at her perfect brown face. Seriously, how are anyone's lips that full and skin that smooth and eyes that dark? It's possible I'm kind of in love with my best friend. She's ridiculously attractive.

[It's funny that the horny teenager stereotype tends to refer only to boys. Things I have been aroused by lately: cherry-flavored lip balm, a fluffy blanket, a particularly phallic lamppost.]

Anyway, Carson. He loves the potato-throwing incident because it's a good ice breaker, and he begins to hypothesize what other vegetables would make suitable weaponry, until Danny rudely asks him what he wants, which is an act of douchebaggery not often associated with Danny Wells – at least, not before any pool-table confessions of attraction occurred.

I try to flutter my eyes seductively/apologetically at Carson, but Ajita kicks me again, which I assume means "Izzy, stop doing that, you look like you're standing in front of that torture device at the optician's that blows air into your eyeballs" so I immediately cease and desist. When you've been pals with someone for basically your whole life, you learn to decode their secret messages based on the severity of their physical violence.

"Soooo," Carson says, "there's a party at Baxter's this weekend. BYOB. You guys in?"

"Sure," Ajita replies on behalf of us all. I'm grateful because I suddenly feel like my tongue is glued to the roof of my mouth. I take a desperate gulp of orange soda and pretend to be disinterested in the entire conversation, watching as a gaggle of freshmen attempt to circumnavigate the complex seating hierarchy in the cafeteria.

When I catch his eye, Danny looks like he might combust with rage. Remembering the Gryffindor sweater now stashed at the back of my wardrobe, I do feel sort of bad. But what can I do? Never speak to another male in front of him again?

Carson, unperturbed by the intricate melodrama unfolding, grins. "Awesome. See y'all there."

And then he disappears, and I'm free to resume normal respiratory function. I'm kind of disappointed by Carson's lack of eye contact with me, especially after our alpaca-based hijinks in class the other day, but I figure I'll be able to dazzle him with my unbelievable wit and sarcasm once we've both had a few beers at the party. [Sorry, lawyers. I meant Capri-Sun. The best of all the conversational lubricants.]

Afterward I ask Danny what his beef is, even though I quite clearly do not want him to answer, but he just mumbles incoherently about history homework and disappears to the library for probably the first time in his life.

Ajita and I go to the bathroom so she can examine her eyebrows for potato shrapnel and I can text Betty about the party. Not for permission – I can't think of a time she's ever prevented me from having fun [perks of being a tragic orphan] – she just likes to be kept in the loop about my social engagements so she can plan when to get drunk herself.

Betty says this in response:

Cool . Baxter, is he the arrogant mofo with the micro-penis complex ? I met his mom at parent-teacher night, think her doctor injected her lip fillers with a cattle syringe !

Honestly, the one thing I hate about my grandma is the space she somehow finds between the end of her sentences and subsequent question/exclamation marks. Though at this point I just have to be grateful she gave up on text speak, and calling me hun. Shudder.

I show Ajita the reply as she's wiping away rogue mascara smudges in the bathroom mirror, and she cackles her witchy cackle. "I'm so jealous," she says. "I want to be raised by your grandma."

I helpfully tell her that if she wants I can arrange for her entire family to be killed in a terrifying road accident, but despite all her big talk she doesn't seem too keen on the idea.

Anyway, after much discussion and speculation, Ajita reckons senator's son Vaughan made Baxter invite us so he could seduce me with his egotistical banter and ultimately convince me to drop my pants. But I'm crushing on the dude who delivered the invite himself: Carson. So this could be *sehr interessant*.

Like the true high-school cliché I am, I immediately begin to plan my outfit and strategize on how to convince the boy I like of my brilliance, pushing all thoughts of Danny to the back of my brain.

8.48 p.m.

Danny's hanging out with Prajesh tonight to make sure he's doing okay. I think he plans on showing him his collection of vintage Nintendo consoles and having a *Mario Kart* marathon, so he rain-checks on me and Ajita. To be honest, I'm pretty glad for the girls' night. With everything that's going on with Danny's newfangled feelings toward me, I'm finding myself monitoring my jokes and general behavior around him. It'll be nice to just relax and not have to worry about making things worse.

We're chilling and eating junk food in Ajita's basement, and I decide to fill her in on the latest developments in the screenplay competition and Mrs Crannon's unbelievable generosity. I mean, fifty bucks. *Fifty bucks.* I've never been in possession of fifty bucks in my life. I'm practically Bill Gates.

"Ajita, consider this. What if – and hear me out, please, because I know this is going to sound absurd – but what if not all teachers are Dementors in human clothing?"

"You're right, that does sound absurd." She tosses a Pretzel M&M into the air and catches it in her mouth. This sounds impressive, but you forget her ridiculously long tongue. She's basically like a lizard catching flies.

"I'm kinda scared, though," I admit. "About entering this competition."

"Why?"

I pick at some stray lint on the sleeve of my sweater, despising the admission of vulnerability, but needy for my best friend's reassurance. "I just keep thinking that I'm too working class. Too 'common'. They'll write me off as trash. These opportunities are not for People Like Me, you know?"

Ajita issues a funny kind of smile as she pours the remaining M&Ms down her throat straight from the packet. "I'm Nepali-American. Trust me, I know."

"Right," I agree. "And I know your experiences of marginalization are much worse than mine. But do you ever just feel like the deck is stacked against you?"

"All. The. Freaking. Time." She crumples up the packet and shoves it down the side of the sofa for her parents to uncover in about a year's time. "And I think I'll feel that way as long as I live in this country. But what are you going to do – not even try? What's the worst that can happen if you enter a competition and it doesn't pan out?"

I properly think about this, and my fear really comes down to this. "I'll be laughed at. And not in the good way."

Turning to face me head on, Ajita replies, "So what?"

I smile. I know what's about to happen. "So I'll feel stupid."

"So what?"

"It'll be embarrassing."

"So what?"

When one of us is scared to do something for fear of rejection, this is how we talk each other around it. By asking "so what?" and forcing ourselves to justify the fear, we soon realize there's rarely anything to actually be afraid of.

I'm already struggling to come up with more answers. "So it might make me want to give up writing."

One more time: "So what?"

Watching as she tucks her legs smugly under her butt, I concede, "All right. You win."

"No, *you* win," she grins. "No matter what. Just by putting yourself out there. Look, it's human nature to shy away from situations where we might experience shame, especially in public. There's something primal about wanting to avoid embarrassment at all costs. Not to get too academic on you, but from a psychoanalytic standpoint, it's about preserving your ego – and thus your sense of personal identity."

"Calm down, Freud," I say. "Spare a thought for the idiots in the room."

"Sorry, I forget about your below-average IQ. All I'm saying is that self-preservation and resistance to shame is natural. But it's also not logical. And because it's not a logical fear, it can't be countered with a logical response. You have to face emotion with emotion. So channel all your passion and bravery and wildness, and shove them in fear's face, okay?"

"Okay." I grin back even harder. "You're the best. Even though you're far too intelligent to be my best pal."

"I know. I tell myself this on a daily basis. And yet *I'm* the one who has absolutely zero idea what to do with my life. Figures. So what are you going to focus on next?" Ajita asks. "You have to be working on something else so you don't go insane waiting for the results of the competition."

"I'm not sure," I say, digging my fist into a bowl of salted popcorn. [It may seem like we're always eating, but that's because we're always eating.] "I had an idea for a short film about a couple in a failing marriage, and one of them – an extremely extroverted individual who never listens to their partner – loses the power of speech to a rare brain disorder. And it, like, totally changes their entire relationship. It upends everything they thought they knew about love and communication and humor. It forces the dominant one in the relationship to swap roles."

"That sounds cool."

"Right? But I can't figure out whether the extrovert who loses their speech should be the man or the woman, because either way the underlying message could be considered problematic. If the man is the outspoken, domineering type, and the wife is super submissive and meek, it feeds into a relationship stereotype you see so often. But then if it's the woman who ends up losing the power of speech, the message is kind of like, you can only have a successful marriage if the woman sits down and shuts up. You know?"

Flabbergasted, Ajita looks at me as though she's genuinely shocked I'm capable of posing thought-provoking questions. "That sounds like an exhausting internal debate to have, and I'm quite frankly surprised I can't smell your brain burning. Why don't you try and plot out both versions and see which feels best?"

"Good plan, Kazakhstan. Can I borrow your laptop? I'm in the mood to word vomit onto a blank document and see what happens."

"Sure thing." She tosses me her sleek MacBook, which makes my decrepit laptop with the H key missing look like some sort of prehistoric tombstone. "Or why don't you make it a same-sex couple? Two women, one extrovert, one introvert. Seriously messed-up relationship dynamic. What's not to love?"

She's not looking at what I'm doing when I open up her browser, which is good. Because as soon as I do, the first thing I see is an open Facebook tab.

The last thing Ajita looked at online was a photo of Carlie on a beach in a tiny bikini.

Kissing a girl.

Friday 16 September

6.17 a.m.

Am I reading too much into this? Was Ajita casually flicking through Carlie's Cancún photo album and just happened to land on that particular picture before I arrived?

But I remember the weird stares and the familiar welcomes in the cafeteria. I remember how surprised I was that Ajita hadn't mentioned her new friend to me until that moment.

What if she's not just a friend?

How have I never considered this before? Yeah, we've gossiped about guys for God knows how long, but looking back . . . is it always just *my* drama we're analyzing? Does she ever discuss guys she likes? I'm actually not sure she ever has – at least not in a romantic way. I wrack my mind for the last crush she told me about, but I come up empty. I always thought she was a virgin just because she was waiting for the right guy, but what if there *is* no right guy?

God, I'm a self-involved mess of a friend. I mean, I'm never going to be a detective, but my lack of observational skills is truly astounding, especially in the context of something so significant in my best friend's world. What else have I missed?

If Ajita is gay, what's she going through right now? How long has she known? Is she terrified to come out because of what her family and friends will think? What *I'll* think? Of course I would be nothing but proud of her, and happy that she's embracing her sexuality, and I hope she knows that. But still, it can't be easy having to guess how people will react. To gauge responses before they even happen.

All I want is to be there for her, but I don't know how best to do that. I keep thinking about what I would want if the situations were reversed. I'd probably wish she would sit me down and be like, dude, I know what's going on and it's fine, I still love you, okay? I'll keep this a secret for as long as you need me to.

But no matter how close we are, Ajita and I are different people, and I can't treat her the way *I'd* want to be treated – I have to treat her how *she* wants to be treated. It's an important distinction. What's best for one person is another person's worst nightmare. And right now it seems like she'd rather keep this all quiet while she figures it out. You know, if there's even anything to figure out. I might be reading too much into it, as I have a tendency to do.

Riddle me this, dear reader. How does one ask one's best friend if they're gay when said best friend clearly isn't ready for one to know?

2.45 p.m.

I'm writing this post in incognito mode from computing class because I am a fearless rebel who cannot be tamed. Usually I would wait until I got home and was safely in my cardboard-box-sized bedroom with a small mountain of peanut butter cups, but this is a legitimate emergency.

Spoke to Danny at lunch. It's true. He's in love with me. Which is catastrophic on a number of levels. The conversation went like this:

Me: Dude, what's going on? You've been so weird lately.

Danny: What? No.

Me: Danny.

Danny: It just bugs me when you and Ajita gossip about guys all the time.

Me: Ajita and I have gossiped about guys since the age of eleven. It's never bothered you before.

Danny: *long silence while blushing*

Me: *reciprocates long silence because of aversion to conflict*

Danny: Well, it bothers me now.

Me: Why?

Danny: I don't know.

Now, I know you may think this doesn't sound like your average declaration of love, and yes, while I was typing out the exchange I began to wonder whether I'd misunderstood the whole situation, and perhaps I am simply an incredible narcissist, but I'm sticking to my guns. He's in love with me. Let's examine the evidence.

Article A: When I confronted him about being weird, he replied defensively at the speed of light. Which means he pre-empted the question. Which means he knows he's being weird. And then when I applied the tiniest little bit more pressure, he folded like a poker player with a pair of twos. Trust me, I am fluent in Danny. This means he is hiding something.

Article B: He blushed. Danny has never blushed in his life. In fact due to his immense paleness, I have kind of been operating under the assumption that his blood is colorless, like IV fluid.

Article C: He said, "I don't know." Let me tell you, Danny is the most opinionated son of a preacher man on the planet. Possibly in our entire solar system. So for him to utter the words "I don't know" is utterly implausible. Of course he knows. He just doesn't want to say it.

I'm not sure how I feel about this development. I think at the moment I'm mainly sad because anything that jeopardizes our friendship is not okay, and everyone knows unrequited love is the cancer of friendship circles. And I do not even a little bit love him back. I don't think. I mean, I love him, like an annoying cousin or particularly needy hamster, but I am not *in* love with him. I don't think.

Or maybe I am in love with Danny? Maybe I'm just missing the signs. Maybe the fact he often makes me feel queasy when he burps the national anthem is not a symptom of disgust, but deeply rooted infatuation. Maybe the fact we're so comfortable around each other, to the extent where I often FaceTime him from the toilet, is actually a sign we're soulmates. It's not exactly how I imagined my first great romance would unfold, but is it really realistic to expect an epic *Notebook*-style love story in this day and age?

How doth one know that one doth be in love? [I'm unconvinced by the accuracy of my "doth" usage in this sentence, but am leaving it in for authenticity.]

9.16 p.m.

It's quarter past nine on a Friday night, and instead of headbanging at a gig and/or participating in recreational drug use, I'm chatting to Betty in the living room over a mug of hot cocoa. Rock and roll.

Our living room is the size of your average garden shed. The walls are covered in that weird textured wallpaper most commonly associated with old folks' homes. We found the velvet sofa on the street, had it examined for termites, and then promptly covered it with blankets and cushions from a thrift store. My grandma's child benefits and Martha's wages don't quite stretch to IKEA, which Mr Rosenqvist would probably be horrified to hear on account of his proud Swedish ancestry.

We also have one of those old TV sets, fatter than it is tall, without cable. Honestly, the battle I had to go through to get Betty to have Wi-Fi installed. Like Vietnam but with more waterboarding.

We're both piled on the velvet sofa in our sweatpants, and her wrinkly feet are in my lap as I give her a much-needed foot rub while she knits. This is her first night off in ten days, and I can tell she's feeling it. She groans as I bury my thumb in the pressure points caused by her bunions. For the thousandth time, I wish it was me working so hard instead of her. But when I got in from school, I rang around all the places I'd dumped my résumé, and none of them showed any interest in hiring me. Not even Martha's.

Once I've moved onto painting Betty's toenails a vivid shade of fuchsia I tell her about the Danny situation, and she doesn't even have the common decency to act surprised. Even Dumbledore also looks at me like, "Duh, it's been graffitied on the kid's face since the start of summer; now give me one of those peanut butter cups or I'll *avada kedavra* your ass." She asks me how I feel about it, and I reiterate the thing about unrequited love being the cancer of friendship circles, and how maybe I am actually in love with Danny, but I've been mistaking it for a mild stomach flu. At this she is mortified.

"Izzy O'Neill, you are absolutely not in love with Danny Wells."

"No, I didn't think I was." I wipe a rogue smudge of nail polish from her skin with a cotton bud. "How do you know?"

"Do you want to kiss his face with your face?"

"No."

"Do you want to marry him and grow old with him and help him tie his shoes when his arthritis gets the better of him?" Her knitting needles click together at the speed of light, which makes it sound like there's a cicada chorus occurring in our living room.

"Not even a little bit. The thought is vaguely horrifying."

"Do you want to let him enter you?"

"Gross. No."

Apparently this is all the evidence she requires to deliver her final verdict: Danny's love is unrequited. She then proceeds to give a long anecdotal monologue on how she's always liked Danny and how this is not a surprising development, which I am going to paraphrase for you here:

"You and Danny have always been close pals, especially in the beginning, when it was just the two of you. Ever since you brought Ajita home in the third week of sixth grade, cramming on this sofa with giddy excitement over your first play date, I knew you kids had something special. He's an only child, so he struggled a bit when he first had to share you, but he soon got over it. You all bounced off each other. Always cracking jokes, inventing games and acting out elaborate stage shows with no solid plot arc whatsoever. Danny doted on you even then, but you always kept him at arm's length. He's always been infatuated with you – I think he just finally worked that out for himself this summer. Poor kid."

"Well," I say. "Shit."

"Shit indeed." She tsks at a dropped stitch in the scarf she's knitting, examining the damage between her thumb and forefinger. "Hey, has he talked to you much about his parents lately? Danny, I mean."

I frown, swiveling the lid back onto the nail polish and admiring my handiwork on her toes. They look vaguely less horrific. "No, I don't think so. How come? Everything okay with them?"

She shrugs. "Word at the community center is that their marriage is on the rocks. Could just be small-town gossip, but who knows?" As she talks, Betty ditches the knitting needles and rubs her temples with her thumbs, round and round in circular motions. At first I think she's trying to summon the Holy Spirit, but judging by her pained expression, she's not feeling so great.

"Another tension headache?" I ask.

"It's those damn strip lights in the kitchen at work," she grumbles. "Staring at fluorescent tubes sixty hours a week would give anyone a migraine."

There's a weird internet phenomenon, born around the same time as BuzzFeed, glorifying sassy older women who work until they're a hundred years old. Look at them! Throwing shade at snarky regulars and serving day-old coffee grounds to their ruthless managers! So hilarious and inspiring! But *this* is the truth. More and more vulnerable old people can't afford to retire, and so they keep working at grueling service jobs because they simply have to. It's a matter of survival. They work through sore feet and headaches and bone-deep exhaustion, illness and injury and grief. It's sick.

Anyway, after the pep talk with Betty my general sadness over the Danny situation has made way for crushing guilt. What am I supposed to do now? [I am asking this purely rhetorically. I almost never follow the advice of others due to my insane stubbornness.]

I would love to be brave enough to take matters into my own hands, like a soldier who proudly charges to the front line and faces enemy troops head-on. But alas I am instead going to hide out in my soggy trench until the problem passes, or I'm brutally murdered by a rogue grenade. Either way I am fundamentally a coward and not the kind of person you want on your side in a battle zone. [There have been a lot of war metaphors in this post, which I think is a beautiful representation of my emotional turmoil and deep inner conflict. Imagery and whatnot. What a poet I am. Like T S Eliot but with better boobs.]

Unreasonable though it may be, I feel a bit cross with Danny for messing up a perfectly good friendship, even though I logically know it's not his fault.

Is it mine? Is my raw sexuality, infectious personality and awe-inspiring modesty sending out the wrong message?

11.59 p.m.

Update: just looked at myself in the mirror. My blonde hair is more "terrifying scarecrow" than "glossy shampoo commercial" and I have raccoon eyes from three days worth of mascara and eyeliner gradually building up and soaking into my skin. The bra I'm wearing doesn't fit properly, on account of me never having any money, so I have a slight case of quadruple-boob going on. My thrifted Hooters T-shirt [shut up, I bought it ironically] has cocoa stains all down the front, and also a patch of Dumbledore drool shaped like Australia.

It might not be the raw sexuality thing.

Saturday 17 September

1.30 p.m.

Party day! Danny and I are spending the afternoon trailing Ajita around every clothing store imaginable in search of the perfect outfit for tonight, both of us providing helpful and educational commentary on her selections. So far we have vetoed the sequined overalls [like a cabaret show vomited onto a hillbilly], the high-waisted mom jeans [she's three feet tall and they come up to her nipples] and the distressed faux-vintage band tee [when challenged to name any song or album by Pink Floyd, she mumbled something about us being assholes, which is offensive yet accurate].

I'm super excited to wear my outfit for tonight – a gray silky shirt I've had for years and years, but I still feel like an absolute queen when I wear it. It's an original Armani with these silver studs all around the collar, and it's the only piece of designer clothing I own.

When I was fourteen and just starting to be painfully aware of how badly I dressed compared to everyone else, I found it on a weekend shopping trip with Ajita [I could never afford to actually buy anything, but I enjoyed hanging out with Ajita enough to tag along]. It was in Goodwill for $40, which is a lot of money for Goodwill, and I had nowhere near enough to afford it. I went home and begged Betty to loan me some cash, and she agreed to put aside a little money from her next paycheck to buy it for me. I spent every single night praying nobody else would buy it in the meantime. By the time we went back to get it, it had sold, and I was heartbroken.

But who'd bought it? Ajita, who had got it for my birthday. I honestly nearly cried when I tore open the carefully wrapped tissue paper and saw the silky gray material I'd fantasized over for so many weeks. I still only wear it on special occasions because I never want the magic to fade.

Anyway, back to our preparty preparation. The mall is absolutely packed, and I keep subconsciously hoping we'll bump into Carson and Co. There's a group of basketball dudes hanging out at the wishing fountain, laughing raucously at something on one of their phones, but Carson isn't among them. In fact, on second glance, I'm not even sure they go to our school. By the time we finally sit down for hot pretzels, I'm pretty sure I've given myself repetitive strain injury in my neck.

I guess it's a good thing we don't see Carson since Danny might just expire in sheer fury if we did. Though to be fair to him, he's acting pretty normal today. Making witty observations about dumb fashion trends and such. Long may it last, I say.

Still, thinking about what Betty told me about his parents, while Ajita's ordering our cream sodas and pretzels, I nudge him on the shoulder. He's doing anything he can not to look at me, staring up at the fake palm trees which shade us from the strong September sun currently beaming through the mall's vast skylight.

"Hey, everything okay at home?" I say, quietly enough so the table of snooty-faced soccer moms next to us don't hear, but loud enough that it's not weird or conspiratorial.

Regardless of my volume policing, he immediately tenses. "Why wouldn't it be?" He sweeps stray salt granules off the table with his hoodie sleeve, then rubs at a dried condensation ring with his thumb.

Message received. "No reason. Forget I asked."

The plan for tonight is to get ready at Ajita's, as her house is a stupidly beautiful mansion and also just around the corner from Baxter's place. Her parents are super-rich neurosurgeon geniuses, and fully expect Ajita to follow in their footsteps, which is hilarious because Ajita has flunked every biology class we've taken over the last two years. Not because she's dumb [she isn't], but because Danny and I are dreadful human beings who lead her astray on a daily basis, like annoying parrots sitting on her shoulder and chirping in her ear about how much more fun it is to perform a silent film for our classmates than it is to learn about plant-cell structure.

Besides, I have it on good authority that in the real world, nobody will ever question you on the function of the mitochondria [THE POWERHOUSE OF THE CELL! See, I know things] or the vacuole [nah, I got nothing]. By good authority I obviously mean my grandma.

[Man, you really just cannot predict where my tangents are going to take you next! From fashion advice to cell biology. What a narrative rollercoaster. I really am incredibly versatile and insightful.]

Then, armed with our crates of beer [Capri-Sun], we'll get a lift to Baxter's empty house at like seven thirty this evening. The party starts at eight, and I know it is borderline tragic to arrive so early, but you remember how I told you I need to know everyone's drama and business? Yeah, I have FOMO when I miss a significant portion of a social event. Ajita does too. So we just sit in a corner watching everyone and eating popcorn, like *Big Brother* but more intrusive.

6.24 p.m.

Writing this from Ajita's ensuite bathroom, because DANNYYYY.

About five minutes ago, after I'd dragged a brush through my scarecrow hair and done my makeup to the best of my ability [smoky charcoal eyes and nude lipstick if you're interested]

I pulled my party attire out of my duffel bag and started to get changed in front of Ajita and Danny, as I have a hundred million times before. Seriously, they have both seen me in so many different stages of undress that they could probably do a pretty accurate life drawing of my naked body, with freckle location accuracy down to a fraction of a millimetre. Since I'm not body conscious, and because we've all known each other for so long, I've never felt weird getting changed in front of them. It just wasn't a thing. Before tonight.

Ajita's sitting at her vanity table, trying and failing to get fake eyelashes to stay on her face, and has accidentally glued one eye shut as a result, while Danny's sitting on the edge of her bed and flipping through his phone. Honestly, he's barely even paying attention to either me or Ajita. I kinda get the feeling he'd rather be playing video games with Prajesh, but Ajita's athletics prodigy of a brother is away at some sadistic training camp in another state.

So then I whip my tee off and I'm just standing in jeans and a bra, *as I have a hundred million times before*, and before I can put my fancy Armani shirt on, Danny groans, covers his eyes emphatically with his hands and says, "Jesus, Iz, do you have to do that here?"

Ajita's glued eye pings open in shock. "What are you on about, dude? You've seen her shirtless before. Hell, you saw *me* shirtless about ten seconds ago. What's the big deal?"

He drops his hands into his lap and stares at his grubby fingernails, cheeks burning as fuchsia as Betty's nail polish. But before he has to reply, I save his awkward ass.

"S'all right," I say quickly. "I'll go next door."

He shoots me a grateful look that tells me everything I need to know.

Shit. We're in trouble.

10.53 p.m.

Update from the front line: Danny is off chatting up one of the cheerleaders, who looks like Michelle Obama's younger sister, but he keeps glancing over at me to make sure I'm witnessing his superb flirtatious finesse. I just nod encouragingly for lack of anything better to do, trying to ignore the fact that to the untrained eye I look like a creepy uncle lurking on the edge of the dance floor and supporting his lecherous nephew's efforts to get laid for the first time.

Ajita and I are chilling on a lime-green sofa in the living room. The house is rammed with sweaty teenage bodies, which are completely incongruous with the immaculate decor. The lighting is low and the music is loud, and everyone's drinking beer out of plastic cups, spilling it all over the wooden floorboards. That's gonna stink in the morning.

My best friend, bless her heart, is completely unperturbed by the fact I'm updating my blog while at a party. At this point in our friendship she's pretty used to me tapping furiously on my phone's touch screen as she chugs her beer and observes the teenage drama unfolding in full flow around us.

Baxter's house is actually super nice, probably because his mom launched this tech start-up a couple years back and it's really taken off. They used to live in a low-income housing community like mine, with metal bars over the windows to prevent break-ins, but now they're firmly in the fancy part of town, where every mansion has at least three cars in the driveway. One of which is usually a Range Rover, let's be real.

Inside, the house is like something out of an interiors magazine, with bold printed wallpaper, metallic sculptures and glass coffee tables. They've mixed it with that industrial chic look that's so big now, all exposed brickwork and factory-style lighting. I'll give it to them, it looks pretty cool. And thanks to my fancy shirt I don't feel as out of place as I usually do.

"Fancy a game of beer pong?" I ask Ajita, who's curled into the corner of the sofa with her shoes kicked off, hugging a black-and-white chevron-print cushion. She's pretty buzzed after just two beers, on account of her severe tinyness.

"Nah, that requires moving," she practically yawns. She's a sleepy drunk. We haven't seen either Carson or Carlie yet, but it's possible they're in another room. Judging by my best pal's apathy toward the concept of physical activity, I guess we shall never know.

"Good point, well made," I concede. "In that case, can I get you another bottle?"

"Now you're talkin'." She winks at me like some sort of gangster. I mean, gangsters probably don't wink at each other all that much. But you know what I mean.

Oh God, Vaughan just arrived with his oily entourage. His hair is slicked back and his Abercrombie shirt is way too tight, and he has a swastika tattooed on his exposed chest. [I made that last bit up as I have a tendency to do.]

And now he's scanning the room, probably scoping me out like those birds that hover in the air above their prey until they're ready to strike. I don't really know what kind of bird this is, but I swear I saw it on some nature documentary, or in real life, or on one of the rare occasions I was paying attention in class. It's hard to distinguish at this point. Anyway, the analogy made perfect sense when I started typing, and I've committed now so I'll stick to it.

I'm a worm. Or something. A drunk little worm trying to wriggle away from its gross predator.

BRB, off to dig a hole in the dirt and stay there until he goes away.

11.48 p.m.
Yeah I slept with Vaughan.

Sunday 18 September

9.18 a.m.

Last night went up in flames. Seriously, I make such unbelievably bad life choices. Can I blame this on the tragic orphan thing again? No?

Sigh. Here we go.

So Vaughan tracks me down in my little wormhole, a.k.a. the sofa, because I'm not sufficiently committed to my role as a creature of the dirt, and offers to get me a drink. I oblige on account of the fact our crate of beer is running low and I'm losing my buzz quite rapidly, and I think we have established at this point that I am utterly shameless in an impressive spectrum of ways.

En route to the fridge, he makes some actually rather astute observations about our surroundings, such as: "Wow, there are, like, so many people here," and "Baxter is an embarrassment at beer pong," and "If Kenan Mitchell were green, he would basically be Shrek." I agree good-naturedly because I am very thirsty. [Not like that. Stop snickering.]

Of course my respiratory system chooses this precise moment to start evicting a metric fuck-ton of phlegm from my body, and I cough like a maniac for several decades. Vaughan says, "Yeah, it's really smoky in here. Let's get some fresh air." Literally not one individual is smoking a cigarette or any other substance in our immediate proximity, which does seem statistically unlikely and yet is true at this precise moment, but like an idiot I follow him outside anyway because a) he is carrying my beer and b) fresh air doesn't actually sound too horrible thanks to the general scent of teenage boy in the living room.

We sit on one of those fancy swinging bench things only rich people ever have. The garden is pitch-black, meaning I don't have to look at his overgelled hair, which is perhaps why I temporarily forget I'm talking to Zachary Vaughan (don't call him Zach; he gets upset for reasons I cannot begin to understand). I half expect there to be long stretches of awkward silence, but he just hands me my beer and asks me a nice question about my grandma. This is one of many signs that I have somehow fallen through a wormhole and landed in an alternate universe, and thus cannot be held responsible for my own actions. Or something.

"So how's your dad's campaign going?" I ask him, once I've finished telling him about how, when Dumbledore the Dog dies, we're going to get another dachshund and call it Voldemort, and pretend to our house guests that the Dark Lord has risen once again and killed all our other pets, including Luna and Neville the goldfish and Hermione the hamster (none of which ever existed, but the story works best if Voldemort commits mass homicide as an opening act). Betty and I both feel this is exactly what Dumbledore the Dog would want. Vaughan appears completely unperturbed by this idea, which you sort of have to admire.

But at the mention of his dad he immediately stiffens. [Again, not like that. What's wrong with you?]

"Do we have to talk about it?" he snaps, swigging from his plastic cup. We can almost hear the babble of laughter and the low pounding of house music, but the double glazing is doing a pretty good job of keeping the garden quiet. Which is unfortunate because right now I could really do with something cutting through the awkward silence.

Hastily I explain how I don't give one singular shit about his father's campaign and only brought it up because conversational protocol dictates that I ask him a question, and I know absolutely nothing else about him.

"You're cute when you babble," he says to my total horror and disgust, because unlike the popular noughties rock band, cute is never what I aim for.

"So tell me something about yourself that has zero to do with your family's controversial political stance," I say. I regret adding the word "controversial", but I think he's a bit drained by my challenging social skills at this point because he lets it go.

"All right. I'm the oldest of four siblings. I want to go to law school, preferably as far away from here as possible."

"That's cool," I say. "Have you always wanted to be a lawyer?"

"No," he admits. "It's just what my parents want me to do. They're both defense attorneys. Or they were until my dad got into politics. God, why does every conversation always swing back round to my dad?" This last sentence is laced with a bitterness I wasn't expecting.

There's another lull in conversation. Looking around the rose-smelling garden I can just make out a koi pond, plus the silhouettes of some creepy gnome-type things in a nearby flower bed. One is brandishing a fishing rod like a weapon.

"Er. Right. So. Here's a question," I mumble, in a desperate bid to ensure there's no possible way his dad can crop up again. "What's your patronus?"

This is in fact a sly test disguised as an interesting point of conversation. If he doesn't know what a patronus is, I know immediately that there's very little point in proceeding with the bench-based festivities.

But without even hesitating, he replies simply, "A duck-billed platypus."

I'm quite taken aback by this. It's not at all the answer I was expecting. Most dudes go with something obvious like a lion, but this is quite unique. "Oh really? Why's that?"

He swigs his beer again. Despite the speed of his drinking he still seems pretty sober. "They're just awesome and unique. Like, did you know they're the only mammal that has a sense of electroreception? They hunt their prey by detecting the electric fields generated by muscular contractions. So basically they're super smart, but in their own way." He shrugs, like he can relate. "And they're the only venomous mammal on earth. I like that they can strike back and defend themselves if they have to."

What. The. Hell. He's genuinely given this some thought. Like, Zachary Vaughan has put some serious time into considering his patronus. If there is any surefire way to win my respect, this is it.

I smile, observing his silhouetted profile. He's really not terrible to look at – one of those cute dimple chins and a ski-slope nose that tilts up at the end. His father may be a fascist dictator, but he obviously has good genes.

"What about yours?" Vaughan asks.

I've had my answer prepared for over a decade. "A sloth."

He spits beer everywhere as he laughs. "That's hilarious. It's so perfect. Cute and sleepy and highly entertaining. Yep, you're a sloth, Izzy O'Neill."

I grin. I can't help it.

"Okay . . . what else can I tell you about myself?" he muses, looking around the garden as though waiting for divine inspiration to strike. He clocks the gnomes, and looks as perturbed as can be expected.

Then, borderline surprised like it's the first time the thought has ever crossed his mind, he goes with: "Oh, I know. I'm a virgin, ha ha ha."

???

[Yeah. Not what I was expecting either. I'll give you a few minutes to process this.

. . . You good? Okay, so you recovered faster than I did.]

I have zip/zilch/zero/*nada*/nil problem with the fact he's a virgin, I just was not anticipating this plot twist in the slightest.

So, very supportively and insightfully, I say: "Oh."

Then the awkward silence kicks in. And all I can think to add is, "Why are you telling me this, of all people? We've never spoken before tonight, even if we do know each other's patronuses now. How do you know you can trust me? I mean, I assume this is a secret."

He shrugs and says, "I like you, Izzy. You're funny and stuff. And I knew you were wary of me, so I told you something personal in the hope you'd see I'm not the jerk everyone thinks I am."

Now, I personally find this logic quite flawed because I could very easily have turned out to be a vindictive psychopath and leaked this information everywhere. Obviously this is not the course of action I actually choose to take, but really, how did he know I'm not fundamentally awful? Also, being a virgin and being a jerk are not mutually exclusive, so the whole thing is quite hard to wrap my head around.

"Thank you, Vaughan. I feel kind of . . . honored? I guess?"

He just smiles and says nothing.

Mainly because I have no idea what to do or say next, I down the rest of my beer and then instantly start kissing him. Yes, I instigate it, for no other reason than: I wanted to. Which is a mistake, because if you've ever downed three-quarters of a can of fizzy liquid in six seconds, you know what happens next.

burp

Fuuuuuuuuuucccccckkkkkkkkkkkk –

My cheeks start to burn with the fiery magma of Mount Etna as I pull away, mortified.

Next plot twist: he is not an asshole about this horrifying bodily development. He just laughs and says, "I guess now we both know something embarrassing about each other."

Then I get all serious, which shockingly I am capable of on occasion. "Being a virgin is not embarrassing, Vaughan. You know that, don't you?"

"Try telling that to the rest of the basketball team."

And then he's kissing me again, and it's actually not terrible, actually it's really good, like really good, and he smells like fresh laundry, and his lips are so soft, and sweet Jesus of Nazareth –

You know what happens next. Yes, I take his virginity on the garden bench.

Izzy O'Neill: keeping it classy since never.

12.42 p.m.

Betty just came knocking on my door with a bacon sandwich and a glass of extra pulpy OJ like the true legend she is, and demanded to know everything. I told her the abridged version. She laughed so hard at the burping incident she almost gave herself a hernia.

[Most of you probably find it really odd that I tell my grandmother about my sexual conquests, but she's just never been weird about it. She's of the general opinion that my mom (her daughter) led the life of a saint and she still ended up dead at the age of twenty-four, so I may as well enjoy myself because this could all be taken away at any moment, and do I really want to be at heaven's gates/hell's trapdoor thinking about all the things (read: people) I wish I'd done?]

[In hindsight, it's possible my grandmother is partially to blame for the sex-scandal situation.]

Okay. So remember Carson Manning? Hot-yet-unintimidating, class clown, alpaca doodler? Yeah, him.

Vaughan and I come in from outside, and it isn't like in those cliché movies where people who've just had sex look very obviously like they just had sex. There are no tree branches in my hair, for example, or dirt on my knees.

Much like Vaughan thirty seconds ago, the party seems to be reaching its climax. There are several people passed out in corners, several people making out against kitchen counters, and the music is now some sort of soft remixed reggae I don't actually hate. The windows are steamed up with sweaty condensation, which is quite gross, and there are plastic cups scattered all over the floor.

I disappear to find Danny (oh shit, Danny!!) and Ajita, leaving Vaughan in the kitchen with Baxter and some of the other basketball guys. Vaughan doesn't do anything gross, like squeeze my ass as I walk away, which I appreciate because catcalling-construction-worker-style romance is not really my idea of a good time. I know some of you may find this unreasonable and absurd, but it's true.

Ajita is in exactly the same spot on the sofa, playing on her phone and looking generally bored when I track her down. A quick scan of the room shows me Carlie is still MIA.

"Where's Danny?" I ask, only mildly terrified of the answer on account of his inevitable wrath.

She cocks an eyebrow, knowingly, like Buddha or some other wise religious figure, and points.

Huzzah! Danny is playing tonsil tennis with Michelle Obama

Junior! This is excellent news. He can no longer go all Judge Judy on me for my romantic escapades. I celebrate with another beer and plonk myself down on the sofa. Ajita and I play a game of Shut Uppa Yo Face, whereby we watch other people's conversations from a distance and improvize what we think they're saying, each of us taking a character. The loser is the one who can't think of anything to say and stalls, ultimately conceding with the words, "Shut uppa yo face." I will admit this is a very niche game and not suitable for most social situations.

We're right in the middle of an epic duologue – a big-issue argument over whether shredded cheese tastes different to its blockier counterparts [obviously I prefer shredded because of my fundamental laziness] – when Carson approaches us. As Ajita and I are both deeply competitive souls, neither of us wants to lose, so we just keep going and going and going, debating heatedly about the merits of grated cheddar. Carson finds this difficult to respond to. Interestingly he does not contribute to the conversation, given he has no idea it is part of an elaborate improvization contest. Maybe he just doesn't have strong opinions about cheese, which I have difficulty wrapping my head around.

Eventually I lose the game because my beer-marinated banter is not on top form by this stage. Ajita politely excuses herself, disappearing in the direction of Baxter's hotel-like bathroom.

"O'Neill," Carson says. His voice is amazing, all warm and gravelly. "Can I sit?"

I resist the temptation to sarcastically reject him and say, "Sure."

He seems genuinely pleased as he sinks into the sofa next to me. He's close enough that his arm is pressed against mine, and I can feel his muscles bulging. The smell of his cologne makes me want to lean in even closer, but I manage to control myself for once. The soft remixed reggae continues to play in the background.

"This music's pretty cool," I say, bobbing along idiotically to the laid-back beat. I wish I could stop myself from looking like such a moron at all times, but alas I cannot. I'm actually pretty nervous, though I hate to admit it. It's rare for me to like someone for more than sex – I'm no virgin, but I've never been in a long-term relationship. Or, you know. A relationship, period.

"Thanks!" he grins. "It's actually my iPod." Again he looks genuinely pleased with the compliment. He's peeling away the label on his beer bottle and not actually looking at me, though, which makes me think maybe he's feeling the same nerves as I am. I hope.

We chat idly for a while longer. I would love to give you a play-by-play of this conversation, but frankly it's a little fuzzy. But what I do remember is . . .

"So, hey," he says, slurring his words slightly. "I found your blog."

Any blogger in the history of the internet will understand the sheer horror and humiliation associated with this sentence. It is the stuff of nightmares. It is legitimately enough reason to load yourself into a cannon and fire yourself into the ocean, clutching your laptop to your lifeless chest.

I start scanning my mental archives for any and all mentions of a) periods, b) other bodily functions, or c) Carson himself. Ding ding ding. Pretty sure I've covered all the important shame bases with my now-not-so-hilarious anecdotes. I'm about to excuse myself to go and immediately change my URL and install a password [which you will be relieved to know I have now done] and swallow a liter of bleach [have not yet done this, but give it time] when he adds: "So you like me, huh?"

"No," I say matter-of-factly. "I just think you're hot in a sexy-yet-unintimidating way."

He grins wolfishly. "Always the goal."

I think I might as well just tattoo perma-blush to my face at this point because the amount of time I've spent in a state of embarrassment tonight is unprecedented and deeply concerning. I should just save my blood the hassle of having to rush to the surface of my skin and have red ink injected into my cheeks. Fortunately for my Corona-addled voice box, Carson picks up the conversational baton once again.

"And I think you're hot too. In an entirely intimidating way."

Then he kisses me!!!

Lest you think I am an even worse homo sapiens than you

already do, let me just say that I am fully aware of how inappropriate this is. I can't even enjoy the moment I've fantasized about endlessly through classes on trigonometry, because I'm scanning the room for Danny and/or Vaughan through the corners of my eyes. For a minute I wonder why I am so concerned about Vaughan, and it's not just that I don't want him to tell people about my gas problems. I think it's maybe the fact I've recently learned he's not a grade-A asshole and actually has a soul? Who knows?

Clearly I am not ashamed enough to stop the Carson-kissing and such, but just so you know, I do have a conscience, although it is perpetually buried under several liters of beer and an abnormally high sex drive.

The music is very loud and most people are very drunk, and I'm very dizzy like I've spun around in circles for eleven days, so eventually I just relax and let myself enjoy it. Surprisingly Carson is not as good a kisser as Vaughan – too much Dorito-flavored saliva for my personal taste, although I am sure others are into that particular sensation – but he's kinda cute in the way he keeps pulling away and smiling bashfully before diving in for another round of tongue hockey. Don't worry, he won't read this review of his snogging technique. Like I say, I've password-protected my blog now. [Which should have really been my first move upon its creation, but you live and learn.]

I'm in a slight quandary.

Part of me – the biggest part – wants to get it on with Carson. He's cute and funny and, well, I want to, which should not be too hard for you to grasp.

Then there's the annoying, niggling part of me that worries what people will think of me if I do. If the school population discovers I banged two dudes in one night, the girls will call me a bitch and a slut, and the guys will high five and call me easy while flinging their own feces at each other.

Anyway, due to that abnormally high sex drive I mentioned earlier, I'm soon following him upstairs to Baxter's parents' room, where we proceed to have a lovely time. Ten out of ten would recommend having sex with Carson Manning. You can do it at least three times in one commercial break, and I sometimes think brevity is an underrated quality in coitus. I'd rather have short and sweet than cross over into slightly-boring-and-chafey territory.

[I know you're probably reading this thinking, *Oh my god, what an unbelievable whore!* even though you generally consider yourself to be fairly progressive, but don't worry. Later in the book I plan to address your problematic concerns about my promiscuity in a personal essay titled "Old White Men Love It When You Slut-shame".]

Monday 19 September

5.47 a.m.

I know! Look at that time stamp! While I am generally of the opinion that one should not rise before the sun unless one has been roused by a swarm of locusts, I can't sleep. Not only because I find out whether I've made it to the next round of the screenplay competition this week – have already refreshed emails six thousand times this morning, despite the fact it's still 1 a.m. on the West Coast – but also because even more shit went down last night, and my metaphorical tail is well and truly between my legs. I did a Really Bad Thing. I'm too ashamed to even tell Betty, which gives you some indication of its magnitude.

After I finish typing out the full recap of the party yesterday afternoon, Ajita texts our group chat and invites Danny and me over for a full debrief and twelve tons of extra-jalapeño nachos. This makes me slightly nervous because I'm not sure how much Danny already knows about my sexploits at this point. By slightly nervous, I mean a herd of rhinos are stampeding my guts. But like the brave soul I am I abandon my physics homework and head over on my rusty deathtrap of a bicycle.

Five treacherous miles later I arrive at Ajita's, and Prajesh greets me at the door with a berry and spinach smoothie. Because he's one of those student athlete types he's always talking about The Daily Grind, and also lecturing me about the fact I'm probably vitamin deficient in basically everything. [Do not fear, I did not have sex with him, for he is thirteen and even I draw a line somewhere.]

"Hey, Praj," I say as warmly and big-sisterly as I can. "How you doing?"

He zips up his hoodie. "Yeah, I'm cool. You?"

I want to ask him how school's going, but at the same time I don't want him to feel crappy about the fact we've been discussing his lack of friends behind his back. So instead I say, "All fine and dandy. I hear you've been hanging out with Danny. Playing video games and such."

He nods. "Yeah. He's a cool guy."

There's a weird silence I've never really experienced with Praj before. He's definitely going through an awkward adolescent phase. His voice broke over the summer, and he still looks uncomfortable with the way it sounds.

I take a sip of the smoothie to be polite, and even though it looks like sludge it tastes pretty good. I thank him for looking out for my arteries and wave him off as he heads to practice.

Heading down to the basement I spot Danny's sneakers by

the door, and the nerve-rhinos start mating in my large intestine. Logically I know I don't owe him a damn thing, but guilt's a funny and unpredictable beast.

Sometimes Ajita is not a good person to have in the room during a time of tension. She's a master of manipulation and orchestrates the most wonderfully uncomfortable situations and conversations, which is quite entertaining when you're not on the receiving end of her shrewd witchcraft, but not so much when you are a mere pawn in her game of distress chess.

She's curled up in the armchair like a smug python, leaving Danny and me to sit up close and personal on the two-seater sofa. The beanbag has conveniently been tidied away. I bet she paid Prajesh ten bucks to take it to his room and fart on it, thus rendering it useless for the purpose of this debrief. All I'm saying is if she ends up with pink eye I will not offer her even the slightest bit of sympathy.

My first clue that Danny knows ALL THE THINGS is that he doesn't look up when I "accidentally" trip down the last three stairs. Ajita snorts like a wild boar. Danny sits rigidly. I flump into the seat next to him.

"What's up, guys?" I ask, cheerier than Mrs Cheery during National Cheeriness Week, helping myself to a handful of nachos from the table. They've barely touched them, which is another sign that it's not just my imagination – there is definitely An Atmosphere.

Ajita eyeballs me, and without the handy indicators of physical violence, I'm struggling to translate. Probably: tread carefully, he's pissed. Which makes me pissed, to be honest, as he does not have ownership of my vagina by any stretch of the imagination, and really what right does he have to make me feel like shit for acting on said vagina's natural urges?

So I throw him a trademark Izzy O'Neill curveball. "How was Michelle Obama Junior?" I ask, grinning and nudging him in an old-buddy-old-pal kind of manner.

I feel like this is a strong tactic, focusing the attention on his behavior rather than my own, until he mutters, "How were Vaughan and Carson and the rest of the basketball team?"

As I flinch, Ajita says, "I'll be upstairs," which surprises me because usually she thrives on this quite rare level of severe awkwardness. Even more upsettingly, she takes the nachos with her, and I feel their absence deep in my soul.

The door at the top of the stairs bangs shut behind her, and I hate myself, I really do, but I start smirking. I don't know what it is. Sometimes I think our bodies are hardwired to respond to extreme tension with uncontrollable laughter. It's that thing where your teacher tells you to stop giggling and it just makes you giggle even more and then you get sent out of the room to calm down, and you think you've managed it, but then as soon as you come back in you collapse into another fit of hysteria. Yeah, that.

"It's not funny, Izzy," Danny snaps.

The TV flashes silently in the corner, illuminating the purple velvet on the pool table. There's an abandoned game still set up from before I arrived.

"Why isn't it?" I ask, sincerely wanting to know the answer.

"Do you really want to spread that kind of reputation for yourself?" His voice is colder than the North Pole pre-climate change.

Suddenly I'm not laughing. Deciding to keep at the deflection tactics I've employed so efficiently thus far, I retort, "What's it to you?"

"I care about you, Izzy. I don't like seeing you make a fool of yourself." He's fidgeting with his man jewelry – a leather-strapped watch from some vintage shop downtown, a shark-tooth surfer bracelet that doesn't suit him in the slightest, and a festival wristband from the summer, which all the ink has rubbed off so it's basically just a bit of fraying plastic.

"I had a good time, Danny. I don't see how that makes me a fool. Would you judge one of the guys for sleeping with two girls in one night?"

Now he looks up at me, aghast. "You slept with them both? I thought you just kissed Vaughan! Jesus, Izzy. What's wrong with you?"

I'm getting mad, but am trying desperately to swallow it so I don't drive a wedge even further between us. "Nothing is fucking wrong with me." Okay, so I didn't mean to curse.

"They're both just using you." He looks so sad, and guilt starts building inside me, even though I know it's illogical and futile to regret anything. Actually, I know I don't regret anything. I just don't want to hurt him even more than I already have.

I soften my voice. "So? I'm using them too, Danny. It's not like I'm gonna marry either of them. I'm young. I'm allowed to have fun."

He sighs, still staring at his ragged festival wristband. Pushes his glasses up his nose. "Wouldn't you rather sleep with someone who actually cares about you? Who'll still want to know you the next day? Who likes you for you, not just your body?"

I bite my lip, which is chapped as hell from hangover dehydration. "And who would that someone be, Danny?"

He finally meets my eyes, and the look on his face tells me everything I need to know. Silence floats between us like poison gas.

Breathing is hard. When did breathing become hard? The air is loaded.

Finally, because I am so articulate, I manage to say, "Oh. I'm sorry."

Then I lean over to give him a hug – I mean, what else do you do when your best friend is sad? – and he hugs me back so tenderly and affectionately that The Atmosphere is amplified tenfold. His heart beats against my shoulder, and he's so warm, unlike most skinny people. Something tickles my neck, and at first I think it's his hair, but it's his soft breath, and then my chest starts pounding too.

What's going on? Betty convinced me I didn't want this, but right now my traitorous body is telling me otherwise. But I can't. I can't. The dude's in love with me! I can't lead him on like this! Stop, Izzy. Stop.

No! Now I seem to have pressed my face into his neck too, and oh man he smells good – not like cologne, but just clean, you know, like he uses really good soap probably stolen from a fancy hotel – and WHAT THE HELL, THIS IS DANNY! DANNY! Remember Danny? He's seen you cry snotty tears when you broke your wrist playing hopscotch in the schoolyard, and he's seen you make a complete dick of yourself doing your Kevin Spacey impression, and he's seen you eat an entire sharing platter by yourself at TGI Friday's, and . . .

Wait, why did I ever think that was a bad thing? Isn't it nice that he knows everything and still wants to kiss you? Oh! Now I see what he was getting at. It's deeper, and it feels nice, like home, and even though somewhere in the back of my mind I know it's not what I want, that voice is getting quieter and quieter, and so when he pulls away just a few inches and our mouths are almost touching, I don't move a muscle, and I let his lips brush mine, and I shiver, and then . . .

Then we're kissing and it's not awful and everything I thought I knew is blown out of the water.

Cue my mind becoming stuck on an eternal loop of this-is-wrong-no-it's-right-no-it's-wrong-but-doesn't-it-feel-good? I can't recall ever having thought so much during kissing in my entire life, and I have done a lot of kissing, and also a lot of thinking, just never quite at the same time.

Danny's not a bad kisser. Better than Carson, worse than Vaughan. Is that a really cruel thing to do? Pitting these dudes against each other in some sort of kissing league table? Ooooh, maybe I could create some kind of anonymous online voting system whereby students give feedback on their best and worst kissing experiences, except the results would only be visible to me so I could make smart future smooching choices and nobody's feelings would get hurt.

This is totally going to become the new Facebook. Maybe I should just sell the idea to Mark Zuckerberg so I don't actually have to do any of the work, like coding or design or general administration. He probably has teams to deal with that kind of thing. Or maybe . . .

Christ on a bike, O'Neill. STOP. THINKING.

His hands move down to my waist, then the tops of my thighs, then along the waistband of my jeans, and that's when it starts to feel a bit wrong. Mainly I think I have cognitive dissonance when it comes to kissing. I honestly believe there are not many people on this planet that I would not kiss. It's just not a big deal to me. But even I find sex stuff way more intimate and personal, and Danny's adventuring hands are giving me the willies.

There's a weird expression on his face. Urgent yet tentative, like he knows I will realize this is a huge mistake at any second, and the primal part of him wants to capitalize on the situation before that happens, while the best friend and good guy part wants to make sure I'm ready.

But it just doesn't feel right. It doesn't. Not at all. He's all sharp angles and translucent skin [I apologize if this is offensive to a) angular people or b) vampires] and it's uncomfortable and I want it to stop. And as soon as I realize this, the guilt is crushing; I've made a mistake, I've led him on, and all I can think about is how I'm going to have to let him down.

Hopefulness is written all over his face, and I hate it. Because I can tell this moment has confirmed something for him – just in the exact opposite way it did for me.

That's why, mid-kiss, I start to cry. It starts as a single whimper, and quickly escalates into pathetic sniffles, shortly followed by wracking sobs. All the good stuff.

He knows why. He knows me too well, so there's no point in lying to him. He knows what it means, and seeing the moment it registers, seeing the moment his hopes come crashing down, is like being slammed in the chest with the butt of a gun.

"I'm s-sorry," I stammer.

And then, like the coward I am, I run.

I keep crying as I slam out the front door, and I keep crying as I mount my bike and start pedaling home. The streets are pretty empty, thank God, because I have mascara all over my dried-out face and a stream of snot running from my nose.

Why why why why whyyyyyy –

But I know why. I know exactly why. Such a huge part of me was hoping that I'd kiss him and feel the same way he does. That I'd realize it was right, and that Danny and I should be together, and that I love him too. If it worked out that way, it'd be so much easier than having to tell him no, having to let him down, having to hurt him in a way you never want to hurt your best friend. But instead I've made it so much worse. So, so much worse.

6.24 a.m.

I can't sleep and my alarm is going to go off soon anyway, so I'm rereading texts from last night. There are some from Ajita, some from Danny, and some from both Danny and Ajita in our three-way group chat. I haven't responded to any.

Ajita's:

Babe, Danny told me what happened. Can you call me so I know you're okay and not in a ditch somewhere? I know your crying episodes are invariably followed by half-hearted attempts to drink bleach. I'm worried. Love you xo

I'm getting pissed at you. You know when I'm worried my body temperature escalates, and then I start to sweat, and then I inevitably break out in zits for at least a week. So: fuck you! Love from Ajita's epidermis xo

(I do love you though. And you are not a bad person. Stalin was a bad person. You are lovely. See you tomorrow. xo)

Danny's:

I'm sorry, Iz :(

I thought it's what you wanted. I never would've done it if I didn't.

Please, don't let this ruin our friendship. You're too important to me.

Ajita and Danny in the group chat:

lots of phallic vegetable emojis

I hate them both, and I love them both. And now I'm crying again.

Maybe if we all put our heads together we can invent a Ctrl+Alt+Z option for horrible life decisions?

9.17 a.m.

After about seven seconds of sleep I go to school looking like something out of a zombie movie. Throughout history and economics, which I have without Ajita and Danny, my gut twists so severely I think I might actually have developed bowel disease over the last few hours.

In my head I play out a number of detailed scenarios in which Danny a) burns me at the stake in some kind of tribute to Satan, his lord and savior, while Ajita watches on and cackles manically, b) designs some actually rather impressive posters featuring *Sim*-like versions of us mating on the couch and plasters them all over the school, and c) makes human nachos by covering me in cheese, salsa and sour cream then baking me in the oven like some kind of Mexican Hansel and Gretel.

Judging by these worryingly elaborate hallucinations it's possible that lack of sleep and severe emotional trauma have rendered me delusional and insane.

I mean, I've always been the kind of overthinker who has full-blown confrontations with people entirely in my brain. Sometimes I even imagine myself into a bad mood with a person, even though they're entirely unaware that we fell out inside my head. This usually occurs in the shower, for lack of anything better to do. So I'm no stranger to having fantasy arguments. But the human nacho thing is a bit far-fetched, even for me.

On the plus side, by the time third period has come around and it's time to face the music, it's clear that no matter how terribly it goes, it cannot be as messed up as my daydreams.

Because economics is on the other side of campus, it takes me so long to get to biology that class has already started by the time I flump into the seat behind him.

He doesn't turn around, but Ajita does, and winks at me to let me know she's not mad at me for potentially smashing our friendship group into smithereens. To be fair, she does have an impressive cluster of zits forming on her chin, and I make a mental note to buy her some peanut butter cups to apologize to her ravaged epidermis.

I then proceed to stare at the back of Danny's head for forty-five minutes. Again, maybe it's the lack of sleep, but it feels like I'm looking at a stranger's neck; like our kiss somehow transformed his physical vessel into something I no longer recognize. His pale skin, covered in a thin layer of pale peach fuzz and tiny moles, is strange and unfamiliar.

Guilt presses in on me from all angles, and I'm in real danger of bursting into tears all over again.

The bell rings and it reverberates right through my skull, and the shuffling of bags and squeaking of chairs over the linoleum sparks a fresh wave of anxiety. When he turns to me, I plaster the most absurd grin on my face.

He looks tired as hell. Forget bags under his eyes, they're damn shopping carts, and they're indisputable evidence that he's been obsessing just as hard as I have.

"Iz." He shuffles from one foot to the other, rubbing the back of his stranger's neck.

"Hey." And right then my unfaltering [ahem] situational judgment kicks in, and I innately know this is not the place to have it out, so I add, maintaining the ludicrous axe-murderer smile, "Let's talk at lunch?"

He smiles back, probably relieved not to have to spill his guts all over room 506B. Ajita sees the temporary truce and moseys over to us.

"Hey, kids. Wanna run lines on the way to drama?"

We then skip (sort of) to the theater side by side, reading from our *Great Gatsby* scripts and obnoxiously crashing into lockers/students/water fountains/Mr Rosenqvist as we channel our Academy Award-worthy thespian technique. It's insane really, and I know I've taken it too far when I add a Jamaican accent, but it makes them laugh and honestly, that's the only thing in the world I care about right now.

Like Carson Manning, lunch comes too fast.

Ajita grabs our usual table and enough fries for an entire battalion, then sends us outside to talk it out. There are some woods behind the sports hall, and in our bid to get far enough into them that nobody will hear us, we pass a few fourteen-year-olds smoking a squashed pack of cigarettes, as well as our phys ed teacher jumping through the trees like a chimp to build his functional fitness. I think he's one of those CrossFit douchebags; I don't know.

Eventually we stop in a little clearing, and I'm so exhausted I just flump to the ground and lean back against a tree trunk. "Did you sleep as terribly as I did last night?"

He smiles, despite the fact this situation could not be any less funny. "If by terribly you mean not at all then yeah."

I sigh and let my eyes flutter closed, partly because looking at him is hard and guilt-inducing [not hard-inducing, now is not the time for boners], and partly because I'm hoping I can squeeze in a little nap between now and the next sentence.

"Danny, I'm so sorry. I thought I wanted . . ."

"I thought you did too. Otherwise I wouldn't have . . ."

I grimace. "Our sentence-finishing abilities never cease to amaze me."

He sits down next to me and flashbacks from last night play in my mind. He tugs a handful of long grass from the ground and starts tearing it to shreds. The earth smells damp around us, and the only nearby sound is the phys ed dude grunting manically as he does chinups like his life depends on it. Maybe it does. I don't know his circumstances.

"Hey," Danny says. "Remember when we were kids and we used to find hours of entertainment with just a pack of white chalk?"

I smile, despite the situation, tilting my head back so it's leaning against the tree trunk. "We'd go out onto the sidewalk and draw miniature towns on the concrete."

"Yup. Then populate them with completely bonkers characters, and act out full-blown soap-opera scenes." A funny little snort. "I'll never forget the misogynistic old storekeeper you role-played all the time."

"That guy was a dick," I reply, indignant. "He thought all women owed him something. I'll never forgive him for how he treated his imaginary wife."

We both sit silently for a moment, reliving our screwed-up childhood. Well, mine was screwed up. I just dragged Danny along for the ride.

Weighing his words carefully, he adds, "You're like a sister to me, Iz. Always have been. Which is what makes this so confusing."

I feel like now would be an inappropriate time for incest-themed Lannister jokes, so I stay schtum.

His throat sounds thick as he says, "You know how I feel about you."

"Yes," I whisper.

"I didn't want to pressure you."

"You didn't." I mean it too. I knew exactly what I was doing, and need to own my share of the responsibility. I can scarcely ask the next question, but I know I have to. "What now?"

He runs his hands through his ridiculous hair. I want so badly to hug him, but I can't tell whether that'd make it worse.

Quietly he mumbles, "I know how I feel, but I also know how you feel. And that's okay. I didn't plan for this to happen, and I won't let it ruin our friendship. It's only a matter of time before you do something disgusting and ruin it for me. It'll pass, I'm sure. Like a kidney stone. Might be painful, but it will pass." Another smile, but there's not much strength behind it.

We stand up, and we hug, and we do the only thing we can do: we move on.

Ajita is relieved as hell when we make it back with both of us tear-free and relatively unscathed. "Oh, thank God. For a moment I was genuinely concerned our tripod was about to lose a leg. Now please, eat some cheese fries. Drink some soda. Rub ketchup on your naked chests. It's going to be a-okay."

Tuesday 20 September

4.41 p.m.

The life-changing email comes through in the last period of the day, and I squeal like a pig having a bikini wax. [Do pigs even have pubes? These are the important questions, folks.]

The teacher doesn't notice, but Ajita looks at me quizzically, which is fair given that I don't normally sound like a farm animal maintaining its hair-removal regimen. So I fire off a text riddled with excitement-induced punctuation discrepancies.

I made the screenplay competition longlist!!1!!1!!11!!!!

Seeing her little face light up across the room is the best feeling ever. I did that! My accomplishment made another human being happy!

Shut the front door! Dude!! I am so proud of you. That is not something I ever thought possible, because you are a mess and a joke in every facet of existence, but it's true. I'm proud. What happens now!? xo

I'm grinning harder than a grinning machine in turbo mode at this point.

I receive feedback from the judges, who are like, super-duper hotshot producers and script developers, then I get a couple weeks to make changes. Then I send it back and they decide the shortlist from there! Then another round of feedback! Then the finalists are announced – and those lucky three get MEETINGS WITH AGENTS AND MANAGERS AND GAHHH! Who'd've thunk! My dumb sense of humor is actually translatable to real marketable screenplays!

Ajita smirks as she's typing her scathing response.

It definitely would not have even crossed my mind to thunk. In fact your terrible sense of humor has rendered me completely unable to thunk in any way whatsoever. You are the single least funny person in the northern hemisphere. xo

This may sound horrible and not supportive at all, but our century of friendship has taught me that she makes very little sense when happy and excited. Her confusing usage of the incorrect past participle of the verb 'to think' leads me to believe that actually she might not hate me as much as she says she does. Bless.

Celebratory drinks tonight?

A split second later:

Hell yeah. xo

As soon as the final bell goes, I practically sprint [well, jog, because I think my legs might just eject themselves from my body in sheer shock if I attempted to sprint] to the staffroom and knock on the door.

Mr Wong, our math teacher, answers. "Miss O'Neill. How can I help you?"

I barely have time to register his attempt at banter because I'm ready to burst with excitement. "Is Mrs Crannon around?"

A few seconds later she appears at the door, wrapped up in a raincoat and clearly ready to rock and roll her way out of the building.

Breathless, I manage to say, "I made the longlist!"

"Izzy! That's wonderful!" She throws her arms around me, which teachers are absolutely not supposed to do nowadays for fear of being accused of sexual assault, but neither of us particularly care in that instant because we're just so goddamn happy that something in the world is going well.

It feels good. It feels really, really good.

10.18 p.m.

Betty gives us the green light to have a few tipples at mine, which might sound like lax parenting, but you forget that I am a tragic orphan, so Ajita and Danny traipse over at around eight and we merrily crack open a couple of beers and toast my completely unexpected and quite frankly baffling career success.

We're all piled onto our mangled couch, Ajita in between Danny and me to prevent any awkward bodily contact, and sharing a bag of chips. I've been chewing the skin around my nails too much – nervous habit – and the salt and vinegar flavoring makes the broken skin sting like nothing else, so my chip consumption is nowhere near as formidable as usual.

Licking her fingers with her freak tongue, Ajita sighs. "I wish I knew what I wanted to do in life. You're so ahead of everyone else, Iz. It's awesome. But I'm kinda jealous." She sighs again, rummaging in the bottom of the chip packet. "I just don't understand. How the hell are we supposed to have it all figured out by the age of eighteen? We don't even know who we are yet, and still we're expected to choose what we want to do with the next fifty years. It's madness."

The way she says "who we are" makes me wonder whether she's thinking of her sexuality – whether she's still trying to figure it all out for herself.

Danny shifts on the sofa, and the whole thing groans despite his meager body mass. "We'll figure it out though. All of us. We have each other's backs, right? Jeets, if you wanna hash out some career ideas sometime, I'm all ears." I smile. I haven't heard him call her Jeets, her old nickname, in a while. "I know your parents pressure you and Praj like hell, but there's gotta be something you love doing just for you. We can build on that, okay?"

It's actually really nice to see Old Danny resurface for a while. He's always been a sweetheart when it comes to encouraging Ajita and me. Even though his complex feelings toward me have somewhat damaged the dynamic between us, it's good to see him be genuinely decent and supportive without wanting anything in return. I've missed this version of him. Maybe hanging out with Praj has been good for him – he doesn't have many other guy friends.

"Thanks, D," Ajita says. "There are a couple of things I want to look into, but I think if I told my parents I might want to go into fashion they'd just expire there and then." A sad sort of smile. Again I wonder if she's thinking of other things she has to tell them. "Anyway, maybe we won't have to do anything for ourselves," she adds. "Izzy's gonna be so rich she'll buy us a mansion each."

While Ajita is mid-rant about the potential benefits of having a world-famous comedienne as a best friend, most of which involve her getting free stuff, my phone bleeps with a text message from an unknown number.

Hey, Izzy, it's Zachary. Vaughan. Heard about your scriptwriting thing – 'grats! Remember me when you're famous, won't you?

Slyly, so that Danny doesn't see me engage with his sworn enemy, I reply:

Thanks! Word travels fast. Hope everything's good with you!

Two seconds later, bzz bzz.

Things are awesome, thanks. Can't stop thinking about last weekend.

AND HE ATTACHES A DICK PIC. I shit you not. An actual photograph of his erect penis. I nearly drop the phone in horror and disgust. [All right, you nosy bastards. It's above average in length, below average in girth and bends slightly to the left. Are you happy now??]

I honestly do not know why guys think unsolicited dick pics are a turn on. Like, have they ever seen a penis? Do they really look at their own genitals and think, "Yeah, that looks *good.*" No. Exactly.

At first I think Danny picks up on my absolute horror and disgust because something odd flickers across his face, but thankfully he and Ajita have moved on from the mild success of their sex-crazed best friend and are now discussing a sketch idea based on a surfing shark who's terrified of humans. So I'm guessing they don't notice me turn a delightful shade of salmon.

It takes a few seconds to regain composure, but before I've even mustered a halfway humorous response, he messages me again.

Your turn ;)

Like I know triple-texting is an accepted thing now, which I am very glad about due to my incredibly needy nature, but surely when one of those texts is a photograph of a penis, we should re-evaluate protocol?

I am slightly buzzed from the couple of beers I've necked like a giraffe [I am aware this simile doesn't quite work], but my inhibitions have not been adequately lowered as of yet. So I simply say:

Thank you for the splendid dick show. Really. You should start charging for admission to this world-class event! I confess this would price me out of action due to the fact I am a poverty-stricken orphan, but as your business advisor this is a risk I am willing to take.

Not sure what possesses me to go all Richard Branson on him, but I'm not in the habit of questioning where my "jokes" come from, and I am not about to start while embroiled in a disturbing dick-pic fiasco.

God, you're weird. But also very hot. Just one pic? ;)

Then three milliseconds later:

I'll make it worth your while . . .

Teenage boys really do have precisely zero chill when it comes to nudes.

I leave him hanging for a little while, because I'm very evil and enjoy the idea of him sitting on the couch next to his Republican senator of a father, indiscreetly checking his phone five times a minute, and trying to disguise his lopsided boner with a goose-feather cushion, or whatever posh people use to shield their aroused penises from each other.

But then, once Ajita and Danny have stumbled out the front

door like moderately intoxicated baby deer, I retire to my bedroom, whip off my clothes and take the damn picture, hitting send before I have time to talk myself out of it.

[Yes, gasp, sigh. But are you even surprised at this point?]

Wednesday 21 September

7.20 a.m.

I fall asleep before Vaughan replies, but it's no great loss because he only manages to say "fuck" before I assume making a mess of the goose-feather cushion. And that's that.

11.57 a.m.

Morning recess is spent freaking out in the bathrooms and trying not to get kicked outside by the power-hungry prefects who take their jobs as school police more seriously than the actual US police force. We have to go outside and get fresh air during recess periods, for no other reason than the school authorities want us to be miserable. Fresh air is number three on my top ten list of overrated things in life, which, although constantly evolving, currently looks like this:

1. Sliced bread. It's undeserving of its eponymous cliché "the best thing since sliced bread". Give me a crusty baguette any day. Maybe the cliché-makers chose sliced bread because

"the best thing since a French stick" sounds vaguely sexual.

2. The Super Bowl. Its only redeeming quality is the way we as a nation come together to eat chicken wings and yell at the TV, but you can do that any day of the week, without the inconvenient sportsball.

3. Fresh air. Outside = weather, insects and the chance that at any given moment you may be hit by a car. I also think people who love camping should never be trusted.

4. Shower sex. A logistical nightmare from start to finish.

5. Smoking. At some point it became synonymous with cool. Why? It tastes gross. It makes you smell gross. It coats your lungs in ash. [I'm not sure if that's medically correct. Remind me to ask Ajita.]

6. Reading in the bath. You have to dry your hands every thirty milliseconds in order to turn the page, and you live in constant fear of dropping the book spine-first on your bare foofer.

7. Shakespeare. I personally find it unreasonable that he has the monopoly on inventing words. [For example, I'm sure my copyeditors are going to flag up "foofer".]

8. TV talent shows. But maybe I'm just bitter about having a face for radio.

9. Yoga. Specifically the way in which it is marketed as a relaxing pastime. There is nothing relaxing about twisting yourself into a pretzel and saying "om" a lot.

10. Dubstep. I don't feel this requires further explanation.

Thankfully, word doesn't seem to have gotten out about my controversial sexcapades at the weekend. Earlier in the week, the threat of exposure and ridicule felt very real, but, like the rumored *Friends* reunion, it didn't really come to anything. Sexmageddon remains a secret.

But of course, the universe is a hormonal son of a preacher man at times, and I'm well overdue a generous helping of bad karma, so inevitably I meet both Vaughan and Carson in the hall at the same time on my way to fourth period. They're strolling along together, Vaughan carrying a textbook and Carson a basketball, probably chatting about defense tactics or some other sportsball-related subject I have no hope of understanding.

Despite the flurry of activity around the lockers, they both clock me burying my face into my upside-down copy of *Wuthering Heights*. Ajita smirks dirtily and ushers them over, which is almost definitely a fireable offense as my supposed best friend, but at this point I just have to be thankful that Danny has double AP chemistry this morning and isn't here to witness such an unfortunate coincidence.

I mean, they *are* on the same basketball team, so I should really have anticipated this kind of hideous confrontation, but thankfully it doesn't seem like either of them are aware that I banged the other. These are their reactions to seeing their latest conquest out in the wild:

Carson: Cocky grin, trademark swagger, "Izzzzaaaayyyyyyy."

Vaughan: Fierce blushing, frenzied throat-clearing, not a word. [Probably picturing the goose-feather cushion and getting aroused all over again.]

"Hello, gentlemen," I say ever-so-calmly, despite the voice inside my head screaming ABORT ABORT ABORT. Remember how I love all drama except my own? This definitely falls under the category of drama I do not love.

Ajita grins ecstatically next to me, probably wishing she had a bucket of popcorn and some 3D glasses. Her mocking gaze flits between us all in turn, waiting for someone to break the ice. For a minute there's just the sound of freshmen giggling nearby, and Vaughan flipping awkwardly through his history textbook as though its subject matter is of urgent importance to this non-conversation, then:

"So —"

"D'you —"

Carson and I both start to speak at the same time, then both immediately stop when the other makes a sound, gesturing vaguely to continue, which neither of us do. It is this precise phenomenon that makes me despise phone calls.

Thankfully, Vaughan mutters something inaudible and excuses himself, disappearing in the direction of the chemistry labs. With his history textbook. Very good.

Ajita senses the opportunity for me to chat to Carson and follow through on my teeny-tiny crush, so reluctantly says, "I'll see you in English, Iz." She disappears swiftly, giving my elbow a supportive squeeze on the way.

"So I heard your good news," Carson says, shifting his backpack from one shoulder to the other. "Nice one. Always knew you were funny as hell."

Those last three words have the same effect on me as a certain other three words would have on most normal people. It turns me to mush. Especially when uttered in that ridiculously attractive voice of his.

"Thanks, man," I manage to reply, immediately regretting calling him "man".

"No problem. Long as I can be your arm candy when your movie premieres." He winks, slowly and exaggeratedly, in a way that lets me know he's mainly joking, but also a little bit serious.

I play ball. "What's in it for me?"

He strokes his freshly shaven chin, pretending to consider the options. "Don't suppose the pleasure of my company would cut it?"

"Hard pass," I answer matter-of-factly. "I've gotta get to class, but lemme know if you come up with anything worth my while."

Carson's smile is so massive I can practically see his tonsils, and, to be fair, he has got that movie-star charisma that'd probably make him right at home on the red carpet.

"Will do, O'Neill. Will do."

12.49 p.m.

Holy hell. So we're leaving the classroom after a snooze-worthy session on some idiots called Cathy and Heathcliff, ready to meet Danny outside so we can walk to lunch together, when Ajita stops talking abruptly. She's seen something, or someone, that I haven't. I follow her gaze.

Carson is leaning back against a row of lockers, bouncing a basketball up and down. He must feel our eyes on him, because he stops dribbling immediately – and doesn't pick the ball back up, just leaves it mid-bounce and strolls over.

"Hey," he says, not even registering Ajita's presence because he's looking at me so intensely. He smiles another huge smile. "So I thought of something that might convince you to let me be your red-carpet date."

I smirk. He has specks of red and white paint on his shirt, and the palms of his hands are stained blue. He must've come from art class, which is unexpected in itself. "Oh yeah? What's tha—"

But before I can even finish my sentence, HE KISSES ME!! Right there in the hallway!

He tastes fresh and awesome, like spearmint, and his technique is much better than it was that night at the party. It's not a full-blown tongues affair, more soft and gentle. I like it. I like it a lot. I drop my copy of *Wuthering Heights* and let my hands rest on his chest.

When he pulls away, still somehow maintaining his cartoonish grin, I half expect Ajita to give us a round of applause. Instead she just says in a strange voice, "Izzy . . ."

She's wincing, looking just over my shoulder. I turn around, hands still on Carson.

Danny is standing on the opposite side of the corridor, watching. When I meet his eye, he shakes his head in disgust, slams his fist against the nearest locker and storms off toward the fire exit.

"Crap," Carson says, big smile fully disappeared. "I didn't mean to get in the middle of anything. Are you guys —"

"No," I say quickly. "Not at all. It's . . . complicated."

Carson looks relieved, but not altogether convinced. He rubs the back of his head, uncertain. "All right. Well, I guess I'll catch you later then?"

Somewhat deflated, he picks up his ball and walks away. I turn helplessly to Ajita, who for once does not seem to be enjoying the show.

"It's not your fault," she murmurs, grabbing my book off the floor for me. "Really. Danny's the douche who punched a locker. That was so not cool of him, crush or not. Don't feel bad, okay?"

"Okay," I lie, knowing perfectly well I'm going to agonize over this for several hours. Even though I know she's right, and it was a dick move to cause a scene like that. In fact, I'm kinda mad at *him* for making Carson feel like shit. "Should I text him? Apologize?"

I don't even know whether I mean Danny or Carson at this point, but Ajita assumes the former.

"I don't think so. Just leave him to cool off. Let him come to you. Now, lunch?"

For probably the first time in my life, I don't finish my cheeseburger. From guilt, and from the butterflies lingering in my tummy from the first sober kiss of my life.

7.56 p.m.

Being an astonishing success story is really quite time-consuming. Ajita invites me over to film a sketch later, but I have to tackle the screenplay rewrites if I'm going to make Monday's deadline.

I start by separating the judges' feedback into two sections:

Big Edits [e.g. stuff about character arcs, plot and pace, etc.] and Small Edits [lines that don't quite work, sections that need a bit of TLC, all that jazz]. It's beyond cool having actual professionals give me feedback on my script. At first, reading criticism of your work kinda stings, but I think that's probably because the school environment conditions you to think criticism is inherently negative. And yet this criticism doesn't feel that way at all. It's positive as hell, and actually fun to read and consider. Like, this bit is great, but this bit isn't working so well – why not try this other awesome technique instead? I'm already learning so much.

Tonight I plan to tackle the character stuff [mainly the fact that my male protagonist, the beautiful prostitute, doesn't really change at all throughout the course of the script – my bad], so make myself a giant mug of hot cocoa with extra mini marshmallows and get to work.

Yes! Me! Working! It's absurd on the face of it. But it's weird. When you enjoy what you're doing, it doesn't really feel like work at all. It's difficult, sure, but it's still fun. What a revelation. I've never once felt this way about schoolwork, which is nothing *but* hard work.

I get into a rhythm with Post-it notes on my bedroom wall and actually find myself enjoying doing something other than being an unbelievable waste of space. Then I work up character profiles for both the male prostitute and his client, fleshing them out as much as possible before weaving these new details through the script to make the characters feel more developed and rounded.

In the back of my mind while I write is Carson's kiss. I remember the smallest details – the tingling mint on his lips, the vague scent of paint on his hands, the shape of his chest beneath my hands. The fluttering in my belly.

Like I say, it was the first kiss I've ever had while not under the influence of alcohol. It's not that I haven't wanted to do it sober, more that the opportunity has never really arisen. I've never had a boyfriend, and I've never really gotten close enough to anyone to want to make out with them outside of a party setting.

[Also *whispers* maybe I'm not as confident as I make myself out to be, and I just need the wonderful inhibition-lowering qualities of Capri-Sun to take the edge off – and remove that layer of fear Ajita is always trying to get me to defy.]

Anyway, all I know is that despite the obvious Danny issues, I really, *really* enjoyed it. And would very much like to repeat it in the not-so-distant future.

But back to business. While I'm editing, a few things trip me up, like whether the fact the love interest's career obsession makes her cold or unrelatable, so I start a list of things to discuss with Mrs Crannon when I next see her.

It's all going pretty well until my phone bleeps.

I half expect it to be Vaughan with another close-up of his genitals, or Danny telling me to burn in hell, but it's my main squeeze Ajita.

Um. Iz. I dunno how to tell you this, so I'm not going to. But . . . well. Xo

And there's a link attached: **http://izzyoneillworldclass whore.com/**

What. The. Eff?

Frowning, I open a new browser window and type in the URL. And instantly regret it.

Someone made a blog. With the title Izzy O'Neill: World Class Whore. And it's just pages and pages and pages of posts about how much of a slut I am.

Hands shaking like crazy, I scroll through all the selfies I've taken over the past year – each with a dick Photoshopped into my mouth.

I scroll through anonymous "confessions" about all of the hideous sexual acts I've apparently engaged in.

I scroll through a detailed account of last Saturday night, i.e. Sexmageddon. My encounters with both Vaughan and Carson are on display for the whole world to read.

The worst part? Someone has taken a picture of me straddling Vaughan on the garden bench – judging by the angle, it was taken from the kitchen. You can't see any dicks or va-jay-jays, but it's pretty clear we're having sex.

Bile rises in my throat.

I mean, I know I hardly kept my sexual encounters particularly hidden at the party. I quite literally did it like they do on the Discovery Channel, which the Bloodhound Gang would be very proud of, although I'm not altogether convinced they're my target audience so this may not be considered a win.

But . . . fuck. There are so many details nobody should know.

How does the person who made this account know Carson only lasted thirty seconds?

How do they know I have a nipple piercing?

How do they know every single little detail of what happened that night? I set my blog to private before I posted about any of that stuff.

My blood runs cold. I don't know whether to laugh or cry or throw up all over my stack of Post-it notes.

Who would do this to me? Who hates me this much?

Not even Danny and Ajita know some of this stuff. Stuff I don't think I've ever told another living soul. How is this happening?

My privacy has somehow been violated, but I can't even process the logistics right now. All I feel is a repeated stabbing pain in my chest, like palpitations but ten times as vicious.

I might put on a tough exterior, but . . . nobody likes to be hated.

Ajita texts me again.

Have you looked? Are you okay? xo

It takes me several attempts to type out my response.

No, Ajita. I'm not. I'm the exact opposite of okay.

Thursday 22 September

9.04 a.m.

I've been here less than twenty minutes and school is already a second circle of humiliation hell. Everyone stares.

I walk down the hallway to a chorus of mutterings and whisperings, like those creepy church scenes in *The Da Vinci Code* where the Illuminati are chanting and shit. [Did that actually happen? I might be reinventing the plot for comedic purposes. Regardless, I feel like I should be wearing some kind of dramatic hooded cloak and carrying an ancient torch.]

I'm a performer. I'm used to people watching me. But this feels different, you know? At least when I'm on stage, or cracking a dirty joke, I want to be watched. I want to be laughed at.

But this?

Nothing about this is on my terms.

The low murmuring and conspiratorial giggles make me want to cut someone. Ajita tries her damn best to cheer me up, though her jokes fall on deaf ears somewhat. There's a high-pitched ringing in my head, and the horrible comments play on a loop. *Slut. Whore. Bitch. Ugly. C***.*

Worst of all is the picture of me straddling Vaughan like something out of a cheap porno. You can't see my face, but still. Everyone who was at that party knows it was me.

As we walk, the hallway around me whooshes and swirls. It feels a little like an out-of-body experience, which I've always dismissed as melodramatic until now. I have to snap out of this. I can't let cyber-bullies win. So I plaster a smile on my face and pretend not to care.

Besides, it could be worse, I suppose. It could always be worse. I'm not quite sure how exactly, but Betty often says I am so optimistic it borders on the sociopathic, and now is as good a time as any to look on the bright side. I've been through the death of both parents on the same day. I won't let the words of a pathetic bully leave a scar.

So, like the disturbingly chirpy individual I am, I whistle cheerily as I stroll down the hallway, completely ignoring the hordes of people staring me down. Unfortunately I cannot whistle, so really I'm just blowing silently [behave yourselves], but the effect on my mood is positive all the same.

But then, when I walk into second period, there's a group of girls crowded around a desk, staring at a phone and whispering stuff like, "Oh my God, what a slut!" and "Fucking whore" and "If I was her, there'd be no way I could show my face around here."

They shut up when they see me, but it's too late. I already heard.

2.34 p.m.

Of course. Of course today is the day we have a mandatory sex ed lecture in the sports center. Of course it is.

Hundreds of us pile into the hall, taking up seats on the rows of bleachers. There was a basketball game last night, and there are still plastic bottles and wads of tickets stuffed underneath the benches.

Ajita sits protectively next to me, with Danny on her other side. Other than, "I'm sorry, Iz," he hasn't really said all that much about the website, which is probably justified. It can't be nice looking at pictures of the girl you love having al-fresco intercourse with the guy you hate.

The whole way through the talk, I feel everyone staring at me. Not all at once, but in turn. As soon as one person turns away, another chances a sneaky glance in my direction. It's a constant stream of staring I can't escape from.

For some reason, our Bible-hugging English teacher and all-round abstinence champion Miss Castillo is the one delivering the talk. Because obviously in America the only thing we should be teaching our teens about sex is that they shouldn't do it. Don't have sex because you will get pregnant and die. That sort of thing. It's working out *soooo* well for us.

So instead of informing us about contraception and such, she goes on an epic rant about the will of God and how virginity should be preserved until marriage. This works well for her in theory, because by the time we are all married, we'll be long gone from Edgewood High and she won't have to do any awkward banana demonstrations. I'm pretty sure this is the main reason she preaches abstinence. Banana aversion tactics. [And also it's the law.]

Then come the questions. Oh, the questions. Here's what never to ask a crowd of two hundred horny teenagers: "Do you have anything you'd like to ask about sex?"

A football jock pipes up first. "Is it normal to masturbate over fifty times a week?"

Everyone laughs. Castillo blushes furiously, smoothing down nonexistent creases in her pussy-bow blouse. "I-I . . . masturbation is impure, Jackson, and –"

Another dude from the basketball team interrupts. "Is it normal to have sex dreams about your teachers?" Then he winks at Castillo. She looks like she wants to die.

Amanda Bateman, who has a stellar reputation as a lover of third base, chirps up next. "Is it true guys don't like handjobs because they can do it better themselves? So there's no point in anything but a blowie?"

Castillo cringes so severely it looks like she's giving birth in a similar manner to that scene from *Alien*. "I really wouldn't know, Amanda, but –"

"Maybe you should ask Izzy O'Neill," someone shouts, and everyone cackles. "She's a bit of an expert."

The mention of my name is like an electric shock as adrenaline spikes unpleasantly up and down my arms.

That picture.

My cheeks burn. Then the jeering starts. Another girl yells, "Yeah, how many guys is it now, O'Neill? Or did you lose count at a hundred?"

"And that's just on Saturday night!" another dude shouts.

Never one to cower in the corner, I force myself to raise my voice and call back, "You're just mad you didn't make the cut. A hundred guys and I still won't sleep with you! Gotta hurt." I shout loud enough to disguise the shaking in my voice. Steer into the joke, O'Neill. You can do this.

Castillo toughens up a little at this point, and leaps to my defense. "That's enough! Out. All of you. Class dismissed."

I think she has a soft spot for me, which is extremely baffling on account of my poor moral compass and alleged Sexual Centurion. But I'm grateful all the same.

We all stand up at the same time, and conversation erupts everywhere. No prizes for guessing the topic on everyone's lips.

The muttering and giggling as we file out of the sports center isn't about Castillo's cringeworthy delivery. It's all for me. From behind me, Ajita squeezes my elbow. Focusing on breathing as steadily as I can, I steel myself as much as possible. I can break down later, in the privacy of my own home.

8.17 p.m.

By the end of school I'm really quite miserable, despite my best efforts to power through, so Ajita throws an impromptu "would you rather" party in her basement for our somewhat fractured tripod. This basically consists of us taking turns in asking each other impossibly difficult "would you rather" questions, such as "would you rather have teeth for pubes or pubes for teeth?" and then heartily debating the answers like we're members of the UN.

Danny agrees to call a truce for the purposes of this emergency situation, and although he doesn't apologize for his locker-based violence, he doesn't bring up the kiss either. Which I suppose is a win.

Prajesh joins us for a while, but once the questions become increasingly blue he starts to get more and more uncomfortable hearing his big sister talk about sex so openly. He excuses himself with the general expression of someone who's trying very hard not to be sick in his mouth.

When he leaves, he gives Danny this weird fist-bump and says, "We still cool to hang out after I finish at the meet tomorrow?"

"'Course, bro," Danny replies. It's incredibly cringeworthy

hearing him call anyone bro, but nevertheless Ajita nudges his shoulder and flashes him a grateful look.

After an hour or so, with the aid of a metric crap-ton of nachos, I'm slowly coming back to life and laughing hysterically while listening to Danny justify why he'd rather have penises for arms than a vagina for a mouth. Ajita is insisting that this is just not practical because a) penises can't grip things, and b) there would simply be no hiding your arousal. You would just be walking around the supermarket with your arms in the air, knocking boxes of cereal off the shelves, trying to convince the store assistant that you aren't sexually attracted to Cap'n Crunch.

The website thing is actually falling to the back of my mind, until Ajita asks me: "Would you rather sit on a cake and eat dick, or sit on a dick and eat cake?"

Clearly, because unlike the pube-teeth debacle there is only one correct answer, I reply, "The latter, definitely. In fact, there is literally not any situation I would enjoy more."

Danny then scoffs and mutters, "Jesus. Are you ever *not* thinking about sex?"

I'm kind of caught off guard by his tone, which is nothing short of scathing, but like the talented improv actor I am, I bounce back. "No. One time I thought I might be thinking about the Chinese inflation rate, but I was, in fact, thinking about dogging."

To this he shakes his head and mutters, "Unbelievable. No wonder . . ." and then he trails off.

My nerves bristle at this. Ajita jumps to my defense.

"No wonder *what*, Danny? No wonder someone has set up a vile and intrusive blog dedicated to assassinating our best friend for her sex life?"

He stares into his lap. "Forget it."

I'm honestly just not in the mood for a fight, and in fact I feel like I could burst into tears at any moment, so I just say, "Next question, please." But his bitter expression and disgusted body language haunt me for the rest of the night.

It's only when I'm leaving Ajita's that the dark thought emerges.

Is it possible Danny's behind the blog?

11.24 p.m.

I'm going on a mini internet hiatus this weekend. I need to clear my noggin, and also some time and space away from the place where a full-blown character assassination of me is taking place.

Have also told Ajita not to expect hearty contributions to our group chats for the foreseeable future and, like the horrid creature she is, she informed me that my contributions are not particularly valued anyway, so I wouldn't be a huge loss. I also told her to keep Danny so entertained that he won't ask questions pertaining to my virtual disappearance, and if she's not sufficiently hilarious and endearing, just to tell him that I've joined the Hitler Youth and won't be returning for quite some time. I feel like this is both plausible and horrifying enough that he'll have to just accept it and move on, and hopefully will also have the effect that he falls swiftly and irrevocably out of love with me.

On that note: so long, farewell, *auf wiedersehen*, goodnight, or however that preposterous song goes.

Monday 26 September

6.14 a.m.

Have spent the entire weekend working on my screenplay, sending it back to the judges, walking Dumbledore a combined total of forty-two yards, and attempting to figure out how to confront Danny about his potential involvement in the Izzy O'Neill: World Class Whore blog.

In a feat of willpower one could accurately label superhuman, I've managed to steer clear of the blog itself. In fact, I have become quite content in my vacuum of ignorance, to the extent that I've not even told Betty about this unfortunate development. Not just because the idea of showing her a picture of me having sex on a garden bench is both horrifying and disturbing, but also because I don't want to worry her. While I often share the whimsical and occasionally explicit details of my love life with my aging grandma, somehow telling her about the accompanying shame and fear feels a little too personal. [I know. I'm all kinds of messed up.]

Ugh, shame? Where did that come from? I've never, ever felt

ashamed of my sex life before. I refuse to let those internet trolls do this to me. I refuse.

What I want to know more than anything is the who and the why. I've been obsessing pretty hardcore over whether or not to believe Danny is behind it. It's not the kind of accusation I can leverage lightly, and I'm pretty sure that no matter what happens he will hog-tie me and roast me over a campfire for even deigning to ask the question. But I have to know.

Here are the facts:

1. He's butthurt about being friend-zoned and liable to lash out.
2. He saw Carson kiss me and punched a locker.
3. This is Danny we're talking about.
4. Danny!

I mean, that's pretty much it. On the other hand, there's no way he could've known half of the stuff that was posted on the blog, and the picture of me fornicating was taken at the same time he was necking on with Michelle Obama Junior. In fact, he didn't even *know* I'd had sex with Vaughan until I inadvertently admitted it to him the next night. So logistically there's no way he could've taken that picture.

Also, this might sound insignificant, but the tone just doesn't really sound like him. He's a pretty articulate and educated guy. He spends a lot of time on nerdy alternate history forums, for example. Throwing around unimaginative and rather lowbrow insults like "slut" and "whore" and "loosey-goosey" [no, really] isn't his style.

But yeah. I'm going to confront him at lunch. Is that stupid? We'll soon find out.

The thought of returning to school and having to face not only the relentless abuse of my peers, but also the potential wrath of my best friend, is giving me Nervous Belly. Hardcore. Like, I've had four poops already this morning, all of which had the consistency of oatmeal.

Basically it's D-Day, only I'm fairly sure the troops landing in Normandy were a bit more relaxed than I am at present. In fact, I don't think it's too much of a stretch to say the only person who has ever been less relaxed than me is Jack Bauer in *24*, and he is a work of fiction. I wonder if the Counter Terrorist Unit has any interest in hiring me. Maybe I should send off a résumé? Come to think of it, Ajita would not take it particularly well if I were to up and move to Los Angeles, even if it were in our country's best interests.

Shit! Ajita! I've forgotten to end my group chat hiatus. I fire off a quick message despite the ungodly hour.

Guten Morgen meine Freunde! Had a wonderful time with the Hitler Youth, but found their beliefs a bit liberal for my tastes. So I have returned to the land of the brave. God bless America!

I'm really hoping Ajita has fed Danny the Deutschland story at some point this weekend or the lack of context may lead him to believe I am, in fact, a raving lunatic and also vaguely xenophobic.

[You may be thinking at this point, wow, Izzy O'Neill is such an inspiration for maintaining her sense of humor and wit at a time like this, but honestly it's more that I just don't have the mental capacity to process serious situations. Rest assured, the inevitable apocalyptic breakdown is imminent. Can I just take this opportunity to state: THIS APPROACH IS NOT ADVISABLE. I would love to be your poster girl for squeaky-clean mental health, but unfortunately I am not that chick.]

7.13 a.m.

To kill time before school, I pluck my eyebrows. Unfortunately for myself and others around me, I get a bit overzealous with the tweezers and remove a significant portion of my left brow. Current look: cast member of cutting-edge nineties movie about soccer hooliganism and rival drug gangs. I'm not sure if this is an actual cinematic genre, but you know exactly what I mean.

7.16 a.m.

Don't have an eyebrow pencil, but managed to find a box of crayons. Have filled in the patch of hairless brow with Burnt Umber. The finish is a little waxy for my taste, but that's all the rage nowadays, isn't it? People stupidly pay for two separate products, both powder and wax, and yet they really need look no further than their average arts and crafts box.

7.17 a.m.

Had to wash the crayon off. Think I might be slightly allergic as my entire forehead is now mottled with charming red pinpricks. I'm so glad Danny will be able to take me seriously as I accuse him of ruining my life.

10.32 a.m.

As I walk down the corridor toward math class, a gaggle of thirteen-year-olds point and laugh. News spreads fast.

I almost flip them off, but the idea that they've all seen a picture of me having sex, and that they know I have a nipple piercing, and that they all probably buy into the notion that I am a whore of unparalleled proportions, makes me feel hot and exposed under the harsh strip lighting.

It's a horrible dynamic flip, suddenly having a group of younger kids feel like they have emotional power over you.

1.34 p.m.

Disappointingly my eyebrow does not magically grow back before lunch, which is unfortunate as I was hoping for at least a little five o'clock shadow by now. The look of alarm on Danny's face as I approach him in the cafeteria is cartoonish and hilarious.

He's queuing up for chilli fries, staring intently at his phone. *Très* suspicious, *non?*

"Heycanwetalk?" I mutter from around twenty feet away.

He looks up, baffled, and says, "Pardon?"

I clear my throat and force myself to meet his eye. And actually get within three feet of him. His gaze keeps floating up to my spotted-dick forehead.

Anyway, we arrange to meet in the woods after school. I briefly consider burning the woods down, but decide against it.

5.42 p.m.

Well, that could've been worse. Such as if the dinosaurs had been roused from extinction and ravaged the entire school campus.

It's pretty cold in the woods, even though it's still early fall, and I shiver as I pluck up the courage to say what's on my mind. Danny shuffles awkwardly, kicking at a pine cone with the rubber toe of his sneaker.

"So this website thing," I start incredibly tactfully and eloquently, trying not to meet the gaze of the phys ed teacher who is pole-vaulting with a long tree branch just ten feet to my left. "Sucks."

"Yeah. Sorry, Iz. Sucks."

At this point we have both established it sucks. I can't even be bothered to make a joke about two-way sucking and/or 69s, which is how you know I'm in a poor emotional state.

"I just kind of wondered whether . . . you might know anything about who's behind it?"

Obviously at this point I do not expect him to say, "Yes, of course, Izzy, it was I, jilted man friend and all-round Nice Guy – forsooth, how doth thine know?" [There I go again with my unconvincing usage of medieval lingo.] But I am studying his reaction pretty intensely for flushed cheeks or averted gazes.

He just shrugs nonchalantly. "I dunno." Then, realizing his performance is lackluster at best, he tries to inject some anger. He curls the fist he used to punch the locker, which I noticed is swollen and bruised. "But if I ever find out who did this, so help me God, I will –"

"As much as I enjoy the 'Prince Charming to the rescue' routine," I interrupt, only half jokingly, "I don't need you defending my honor. I can look after myself."

"Clearly," he snarls, with such immediate and unflinching spite I recoil slightly. The two syllables drip with sarcasm.

Snapping back with equal vigor, I say, "What's that supposed to mean?"

He looks conflicted, like part of him wants to backtrack, but he knows I'm stubborn and won't let that comment slide. So he just mumbles, "I've been defending your honor for thirteen years. Protecting you from jerks at school, from social workers." A pointed eyebrow raise. "From yourself."

I cross my arms and fix a firm look on my face. This is difficult, because I have the opposite of Resting Bitch Face. My round cheeks, big eyes and docile demeanor often encourage conversation from strangers at bus stops, which sounds quite pleasant, but has in fact made me consider an acid attack on myself on more than one occasion.

"Saving me from myself?" I retort. "Are you kidding me? Because I'm such a disaster that I can't be trusted to make my own choices?"

He doesn't reply, but from the sarcastic sneer I can tell what he's thinking: if you made better choices, there would be no World Class Whore website. Judgmental prick.

"Look, Danny," I say, eager to get to the actual point of this confrontation. "All I know is you weren't that happy with me after the whole two-one-night-stands scenario. And there aren't many people in the world that know such intimate details about me. That's all."

In the silence that follows, branches crack and snap, and the gym teacher pants nearby.

Danny peers at me with an expression I can't read. Anger, I'd guess, but laced with something else. "What are you accusing me of?"

"Nothing." Everything.

My heart hammers against my ribcage. A thousand cruel

comments repeat on a loop in my head. *Slut. Whore. Ugly bitch.* "I just want to figure out who's behind it all. Because you know my motto: do no harm, but take no shit. And this right here is shit I am categorically unwilling to receive."

He shakes his head slowly, narrowing his eyes. "I can't believe this. I genuinely thought that when you asked to talk to me, you'd had a change of heart. About . . . us. I thought . . ." He swallows whatever he was about to say next. Then: "But no. You're *actually* accusing me of setting up that blog."

The awkwardness-averse cringe-phobe inside me desperately wants to backtrack, to insist I'm not accusing him of anything, but I'm too upset. I won't back down. "Yes."

I'll never forget the quiet venom in his next words.

"Fuck you, Izzy O'Neill."

6.00 p.m.

So he lost his shit? xo

Ajita texting, obviously.

Ajita, I don't think Danny has been in full possession of his shit since 2006. But yep. Totally lost it.

This can't be an easy situation for her to be in, stuck between the two of us. [Actually, who am I kidding? She loves the drama. She feeds on it like a reality-TV-addicted leech.]

You still think he's behind it? Xo

I have no idea. In fact it's frightening how few ideas I have. What do you think?

A pause.

I think the boy is stupidly in love with you on account of his terrible taste in women. But no. I don't think he did it. xo

In fairness, I am starting to feel a little bit bad for asking him in the first place. We've been best friends for so long, and yes, he's harboring an inconvenient crush on me for reasons I cannot begin to understand, and yes, I did accidentally kiss him that one time, and yes, he did see me kiss Carson just a few days later. But surely I know him better than that. Surely he would never set out to hurt me that way.

Doubt creeps in. Did I do the wrong thing in confronting him?

11.04 p.m.

In all the self-loathing and furor, I almost forgot that two other people were sort of dragged down with me on the blog – Vaughan and Carson were collateral damage. Of course, they are not generally subjected to the same level of sexual scrutiny due to their Y chromosomes, but still.

I am essentially a Mother Teresa meets Dalai Lama type figure, so I take it upon myself to reach out to these poor fuckboys and make sure they're okay. I know, I know. Fully anticipating the Nobel Peace Prize anytime now. I mean, anyone can get shot in the head by the Taliban, but it takes a really big person to text a fuckboy. [I am 113 percent being sarcastic here. I firmly believe Malala should be leader of the free world, and also CEO of Hershey's because I swear to God peanut butter cups are getting smaller, which is an act of terrorism in itself.]

Text to Vaughan:

Hey. Assume you've seen the blog. I have no idea how the person who made it knows so much about what happened that night, but I can only apologize – obviously this is the last thing I wanted to happen. Well, not the LAST. The zombie apocalypse would be worse I think. Anyway. Hope you're all right.

Facebook message to Carson:

Hey. Assume you've seen the blog. I have no idea how the person who made it knows so much about what happened that night, but I can only apologize – obviously this is the last thing I wanted to happen. Well, not the LAST. The zombie apocalypse would be worse I think. So would a ruptured bumhole. Anyway. Hope you're all right.

As you can see I utilized the copy-paste function on my phone very well [adding the bumhole comment for the second text because I know Carson's sense of humor is even more vile and misjudged than my own]. You know by now that I am a fan of a shortcut, such as when shaving your legs [nobody cares about anything above your knees], or while performing any other sort of body-hair admin. In fact, I think cutting corners is advisable in almost every physical situation, with the exception of maybe brain surgery.

Because he is by far the superior human being/fuckboy, Carson is the only one who replies.

Yo! Ah, hey now, don't you worry. This kinda thing doesn't really bother me. Are you okay, though? Pretty brutal stuff on there, bro. Sorry you gotta deal with it. Lemme know if you need anything.

I am quite touched by this, to the extent where I am willing to overlook him calling me bro.

I'm doing ok. Trying not to let it get to me. Thanks for being awesome about it.

Against all the odds, I go to bed in good snuff. [This is a seventeenth-century term for "happy" which I firmly believe should be reinstated in the modern vernacular. See, I do pay attention in school when it suits me, such as for picking up entertaining slang.]

Tuesday 27 September

10.34 a.m.

Aforementioned good snuffery does not last as long as one might have hoped.

For one thing, we have math first period. Honestly, what was that Pythagoras dude's problem? Why did he have to ruin the simple triangle for everyone? It's just downright inconsiderate, is what it is.

I think it is perhaps the repeated usage of the word "hypotenuse" that sends most of the class into a state of deep boredom that can only be relieved by taking the ever-loving piss out of someone. Of course that someone is me on this occasion, due to my unashamed sexploits and generally ludicrous nature that invites piss-taking in all its forms. Thus my new nickname becomes Herpes McWartface. Kids really are not very inventive with their mockery these days.

As a rule, I tend to lean into jokes at my expense, like how you're supposed to steer into the swerve when you're driving and lose control, so I marked my homework *H McW* yesterday and promptly forgot all about it. So when Mr Wong hands us the homework back, he frowns and says, "Who is H McW? Do we have a new student?"

The whole class erupts. Because I am sick in the head, I enjoy the laughs. As a comedian I am perfectly willing to throw my dignity under the bus if it means getting a giggle.

But Mr Wong won't let it drop and insists I explain the new initials to him. He's the sort of teacher who quite fancies himself as someone who's pals with his students, but he doesn't really pull it off because he is fundamentally not a cool person.

Always coming to my rescue, Ajita chimes in with, "Sir, I believe it is an allusion to the sexually transmitted diseases my friend here may or may not have contracted according to the website Izzy O'Neill: World Class Whore. Anonymous source. Would you like my bibliography in the Harvard referencing style, or will footnotes suffice?"

Even I crack up at this point. People all around me are just dying, like actually expiring with the utter hilarity of the situation, and Mr Wong tries his very best to muster an "I'm-with-you-comrades" sort of grin, despite the fact he's so disgusted he might possibly shit himself right here and now.

The only guy in the entire room whose face looks like a smacked fish? Danny. He glares as me disparagingly and grits his teeth.

And just like that I'm back to feeling like dirt.

1.04 p.m.

By lunchtime the mockery begins to focus on the garden bench picture. You know, the picture in which I am *literally having sex on a garden bench*. *Wunderbar.*

We're in the cafeteria, which is actually pretty quiet because the entire sophomore year group is off at some careers fair in the city. It's spaghetti and meatballs day, and the kitchen obviously forgot about the mass sophomore absence, so those of us still in school are enjoying mammoth bowls of the stuff.

A guy I half recognize as a member of the cross-country team (which is how I immediately know he is some form of psychopath, as a person who voluntarily runs without a gun pointing at his head) approaches the bench I'm sitting at with Ajita by my side. She is mid-rant about our absurd two-party political system and its failings, so is quite annoyed at the interruption.

"Hey, Izzy," Psychopath Runner says, a nauseating grin combined with a strange fake-concerned expression on his face. "Are you all right? Would you like me to fetch the first-aid kit from the nurse's office?"

I sigh. "All right, I'll play along. Why would I require the first-aid kit?"

He's beside himself with excitement at being granted the opportunity to recite his punchline. "Well, you're bound to have splinters from rubbing your knees back and forth on that garden bench. And back. And forth. And back. And –"

"Yes, yes, very good, thank you," Ajita says, slurping her Capri-Sun. [It actually is Capri-Sun for once. Even Ajita doesn't drink beer at school. Yet. Give it time.] "Goodbye now."

He disappears, receiving a multitude of fist-bumps from his fellow cross-country psychopaths.

Ajita finishes her juice pouch and scrunches it up. "Hey, I made you something."

She attempts to toss the pouch in the nearby trash can, missing entirely, then starts digging around in her backpack until she triumphantly pulls out a glossy postcard.

It's a printout of the garden bench pic, but she's turned it into a work of art! I think she's probably just applied one of those Photoshop filters that makes it look like stained glass, but still. It is funny and very Ajita.

I squeeze her hand. "Thank you. For . . . y'know."

Standing by me. Making me laugh. Allowing me to feel like I might actually survive this ordeal, even though I'm too proud to ever dream of asking for help.

She squeezes mine back. "I know. You're welcome."

4.23 p.m.

A girl I vaguely recognize from math class comes up to me in the hallway before last period. She's in a wheelchair and has mousy brown hair and little round glasses and I think her name is Meg.

"Izzy?"

I try very hard to maintain an air of detachedness, since there's at least a ninety-five percent chance she's about to mock me. "Yes, Meg? May I help you?"

"Erm, I . . ."

"If you are here to crack any sort of garden-bench-based joke whatsoever, please do it in the next five seconds because I'm going to be late for geography, and Lord knows rock formations are the number one thing on my mind right now. The last lesson ended on quite a cliffhanger." [Geddit? Cliffhanger! Rock formations! The best jokes are the ones you have to explain.]

She shakes her head vehemently. "No! I wasn't going to. I just wanted . . . well, I wanted to say that I think you're really cool. And funny. You really made me laugh in math this morning. With the H McW thing. I wish I could be as funny as you." She's blushing furiously at this point.

A huge grin breaks out across my face. I can't help it. The unexpected sweetness catches me so off guard that I completely forget the aloof vibe I was aiming for. "That's such a nice thing to say, Meg! You should totally come and hang out with me and Ajita sometime. We make excellent nachos."

"Ohmygosh, really?" she beams. "I would *love* that!"

I scribble down my phone digits for her and head to geography class, feeling very grateful for the few remaining nice people in the world.

5.16 p.m.

WTF? Danny rocks up to *Great Gatsby* rehearsals carrying a bunch of tulips and a box of my favorite chocolates [Ferrero Rocher. Yes, my taste in confectionery is unreasonably pretentious given my financial situation]. Bearing in mind the last thing he said to me was "fuck you", at first I foolishly think this is but a simple apology. Alas, that is not how the following events transpire.

He waltzes down the aisle between rows of seats. Everyone turns to stare. We're about to start blocking the opening scene so everyone is on stage, and when he walks down, face completely obscured by the obnoxiously large bunch of flowers, an eerie silence falls over us.

Mrs Crannon absolutely does not know how to proceed. So I just slip off the stage and run over to Danny, hissing, "Please tell me these are not for me," silently praying that they are lest I look like a self-absorbed loon.

An innocent frown. "I thought tulips and posh Nutella balls were your favorites?"

"They are. But . . . why?" Here's where I'm hoping he'll acknowledge he was a giant dickwad and will apologize accordingly.

He thrusts the gifts into my arms and awkwardly shoves his hands into his pockets. "Just because. I want to start fresh. Forget the last few weeks, you know?" When I don't say anything in response, he adds, "And . . . well, I wanted to show you how great it could be. If we were together."

And that's when I realize. It's not an apology. It's a bribe. Here, have some gifts. Please be my girlfriend and blow my mind with your sexual prowess. That sort of thing.

"Oh," I say. "Thanks. I guess."

I mean, what else could I say with a whole room of extravagant drama-types watching? Besides, I'm still all kinds of hurt that he said "fuck you" in such a vile way.

Danny smiles awkwardly. "You're welcome. I'm going to win you over. You'll see."

If you ask me, this is very uncool. To the innocent onlooker it might seem sort of sweet. To me it seems like he's saying: "I don't respect your decision not to want to fuck me, and I will manipulate the hell out of your emotions until you change your mind."

But sure enough, one slow clap from Evan Maclin turns into a hearty round of applause as every single one of them [bar Ajita] interprets this as a display of romance and affection rather than a thinly veiled assertion of male dominance and ultimate rejection of his place in the Friend Zone.

I dump my "gifts" on the front-row seats [on account of my complete lack of regard for my personal belongings, my purse and phone and other worldly possessions are chucked irresponsibly backstage at the beginning of every rehearsal] and retake my place on stage, stomach twisting uncomfortably. Danny's got an awful bashful-but-also-proud-of-himself face on, accepting the "awwww"s from girls and shoulder jostles from guys.

Argh. I've told him I don't want a romantic relationship. Why isn't that enough?

8.02 p.m.

By the time rehearsals are over I'm absolutely exhausted and vaguely annoyed, and just want to get home to leftover mac and cheese and a gallon of hot cocoa. But no! That would be too simple!

Vaughan is waiting for me by the school gates, shifting on his feet like a rookie drug dealer. I'm about to inform him that I'm all set for horse tranquilizers when he grabs my arm, hard enough that it's painful, and mutters, "Can we talk in the woods?"

Carrying Danny's obscene gifts in my arms, I follow him until we reach a clearing. "If any detectives happen to be tailing us, this definitely looks like a botched drug deal type situation," I say. He looks at me like I have all of a sudden grown an extra nose. I pat my face just to make sure.

Vaughan grits his teeth. I honestly don't know why his default facial expression is a poor imitation of beef cattle. I would bring it up, but he already looks so unimpressed by my character as a whole. "It's not funny. Stop making jokes."

"I'm sorry. It's because of who I am as a person."

I'm about to ask him what he wanted to talk to me about when both of our phones bleep at exactly the same time. This doesn't sound particularly impressive, but seriously, how often do phones make the same tone in perfect synchrony? Am I just easily pleased? [My sexual track record would suggest yes.]

The joy and merriment of the ringtone situation quickly evaporates when I see the issue.

My nude picture has been leaked.

The one I sent Vaughan.

Every single inch of me. Plastered all over the internet for the whole world to see.

No no no no no no no no no please no.

Whoever posted it has dragged Vaughan down with me, because his name shows up at the top of the conversation.

Which means it's a screenshot.

Which means it was taken from my phone. Because my messages are in blue bubbles. So are his – the begging and the dick pic and everything. But all I see is my own naked body.

Shit shit shit shit shit shit noooooooooo.

[Sorry for the expletives, but I cannot muster anything more articulate right now.]

My boobs and va-jay-jay are out there in the world. I feel disgusting and violated and bare.

Twisting uncomfortably in my chest, my heart sinks. This

absolutely cannot be happening. I'm shaking so hard it's probably measuring on the Richter scale.

Vaughan slams his palm against a tree trunk. He's definitely going to regret that tonight when he can't rage-masturbate.

"It was you, wasn't it? You leaked them. Thought it'd be good publicity for your little screenplay. Nothing launches a career quite like a sex scandal, does it?" His eyes are wide with mania and/or recreational drug use.

"I guarantee I am not that intelligent," I say numbly.

A crazed grin splits his face in half. [Not literally.] "Do you know what my father is going to do when he finds out about this? Kill me. He's going to kill me." He looks like he might genuinely cry. "How do we make this go away? How do I make *you* go away?" He practically spits this last part.

He then grabs Danny's tulips from my hands, hurls them to the ground and starts stamping on them like he's trying to kill a cockroach. He does this for at least thirty seconds before I ask, "What are you trying to achieve exactly?"

Vaughan stops abruptly. "Do you have any idea what kind of pressure I'm under? To support my father, to go to law school, to be successful? To be the perfect fucking model son with the perfect fucking grades and the perfect fucking life?"

"No, I don't," I say matter-of-factly. "Because my parents are dead." Adrenaline is ringing in my ears. "I'm going to walk away now because you're pissing me off. Come and talk to me when you've calmed down and we'll figure out how to fix this mess. I will either be here or in Mexico. It's really anyone's guess at this point."

8.54 p.m.

New plan: go home, talk to Betty about my disastrous existence, maybe purchase and consume a vegetable because, on top of everything else, I'm probably at real risk of developing scurvy at this point.

9.28 p.m.

Betty's pretty weary after a double shift at the diner, and to be honest she smells like old fries, but I still hug her super tight the minute she walks in the door. She's damp from the rain outside, which is nice because when I cry silently all over her woolly yellow cardigan she barely notices.

"Kiddo! What's all this about?" she asks. We're standing in the doorway, her sodden umbrella dumped next to the shoe rack, me clinging to her like a limpet to a rock pool. "Don't get me wrong, I enjoy sudden and alarming displays of affection as much as the next girl. But this isn't usually your style."

"Sorry," I sniffle, finally pulling away. Betty pushes the door shut, locking and chaining it while still looking at me with deep concern.

Her glasses are spotted with rain, but instead of wiping them dry she just peers at me through the kaleidoscopic droplets. "Rough day?"

"You could say that."

She ushers me into the kitchen and immediately gets to work filling the kettle. It's one of those unnecessarily heavy beasts which she inherited from *her* grandma, and she can barely lift it despite the Popeye arms she's developed over decades of manual labor.

Once it's simmering away on the stove, she takes a seat at the table with me. It's still covered in crumbs from our bacon sandwiches this morning. I fill Betty in on the Danny situation, but somehow, when I come to tell her about the leaked nudes, the words get stuck in my throat.

"That's sweet of Danny to buy you flowers," Betty says, missing the point entirely.

"No, it's not."

The kettle whistles on the stove and Betty goes to get up, but I gesture for her to stay seated. She's been on her feet all day. I busy myself making tea in the biggest mugs I can find.

"Why isn't it?" Betty asks, propping her feet up on the chair I left empty.

Stirring milk and a third spoonful of sugar into each cup, I sigh. "It was a way to assert his male dominance over me as a woman by not respecting my decision not to partake in a romantic relationship with him. Did you not read that

Feminism 101 book I got you for Christmas?"

"I don't think this exact scenario was in there."

I bring the tea over to the table and take a seat, propping Betty's feet up into my lap. Dumbledore sniffles around the floor, hoping for some rogue bacon juice or even a mini marshmallow from last night's hot cocoa, even though he's probably checked this exact spot a hundred times today. I scoop him up onto my lap too, so he can act as a footwarmer for Betty. He wiggles uncomfortably at first, but soon settles into the strange sort of cuddle, accepting my gentle strokes of his soft brown fur.

"Anyway, the hows and the whys are sort of beside the point," I say. "I'm just feeling kind of exhausted by it all. School. Danny. And . . . some other stuff." I trail off vaguely.

I'm not sure why I don't want to tell Betty about the website, or the nudes. Mainly I don't want to worry her, especially when she's so damn exhausted herself. In fact, I feel kind of guilty about complaining, given all the sacrifices she makes to her health just to keep me alive and in full-time education.

But it seems like she's not really listening. She traces a wrinkly thumb around the rim of the teacup, staring intently at the steam. It looks like she wants to say something heartfelt, but she often needs to give herself a pep talk before spouting a sentence containing actual emotion, so I give her the space she needs to build up to it.

"Listen, kiddo," she starts, throat hoarse like it so often is at the end of a long shift. "I wish your mom was here to see you now." Her voice catches. "You know your own mind, and you're not afraid to speak it, you know?"

Tears press heavily against my eyes.

No, I'm not, I want to scream. *If my parents were here, they'd see nude pictures of me all over the internet!*

I can't talk about this. I can't. And from the tension on Betty's face, she's too exhausted to see the conversation through to the end. So I shut it down.

"Anyway," I say, swallowing my comparatively meager pain, "how was your day?"

10.01 p.m.

Once I'm alone, I take a deep breath and open the World Class Whore blog. Not in a self-flagellatory way; I just want to wrap my head around what's happening, and the way it went down with Vaughan in the woods made it hard to do that. As much as I'm an insane extrovert and love being around people, when something major goes down I need time to process it alone.

I wash my face and brush my teeth, change into prehistoric PJs, switch the lights off in my room and climb into bed. I then proceed to create a cocoon-type setup with the duvet and some pillows, pulling the covers all the way over my head and curling up into the fetal position. I'm not sure what it is about this maneuver that feels so comforting. If I was in any way academic, I'd probably posit that it's something to do with recreating the atmosphere of the womb. But alas, I am not in any way academic. Remind me to ask Ajita.

The website takes a few seconds to load on my phone screen, but it's still not long enough. Even though I know exactly what I'm about to see, it's still like a punch to the gut when the screenshot flashes up.

My boobs and my va-jay-jay, on show to the world. Just under the pic of Vaughan's above-average length, below-average girth, bending slightly to the left penis. For which I'm 104 percent sure he will not receive anywhere near as much criticism as me.

I stare and stare and stare at the photo of me, gut churning uncomfortably. It's not that I'm body conscious or anything. I'm not. But I am old-fashioned in the sense that I like to give people individual permission to view my boobs and other bits, rather than allowing blanket access to seven billion internet users. That may seem unreasonable to you, but it's true.

Oh my God oh my God oh my God. This feeling of violation is skin-crawlingly terrible. It feels like being on the criminal side of a police mirror, where everyone can see you, but you can't see them. I am an exhibit, laid bare before every single kid in my school – hell, probably my town. And I feel so exposed.

Again, I'm not body conscious. But your private parts are

just so . . . intimate. I have a hard enough time showing them to my family physician. A couple of years ago I had a weird lump on one boob, and even though it turned out to be nothing, I still think about the embarrassment of being fondled by a middle-aged male doctor with stale coffee breath, while I tried and failed to make conversation about the strength of the dollar.

Now that mortification is multiplied a thousandfold. And I still don't know anything about currency depreciation.

1.14 a.m.

Fuck. What am I going to do?

Wednesday 28 September

8.05 a.m.

Feel beyond anxious at the thought of going to school today. I woke up stupidly early again this morning, so decided to write a sketch about a senator and his son who get stuck in a waste incinerator like that hugely traumatic scene in *Toy Story 3*. Not that I am harboring any violent feelings toward the Vaughan family or anything.

At least there is slight progress on the eyebrow front. Ajita lent me her pencil, which is a good five shades too dark for me, and I attempted to fill in the little gap. Because of the mismatched hue, I then had to even up the same spot on other side. So I have a very attractive ombré-caterpillar-type situation on my forehead, a look which I am sure we can all agree will hit beauty vloggers' screens anytime now.

I'm too scared to look at the online reaction to the nudes. The mid-sex garden bench pic was one thing, but this is so . . . explicit. Every time I remember they're out there, which is roughly every 2.3 milliseconds, I get a horrible sinking sensation in my belly, like when you go over a speed bump too fast. I obsess over who might be looking at these pictures of me – bare, exposed, eighteen – and judging me for them. Judging my body; my choices; my life.

I know this will blow over eventually. But until then, it's going to be hell.

9.01 a.m.

Ajita, Danny and I arrive at the school gates to find a cluster of freshmen armed with smartphone cameras pointed straight at me. As soon I get within twenty feet of them, they start to snap pics and hit record, and I hear a couple of them narrating my humiliating entrance to their bazillion followers live on social media. Danny wraps an arm protectively around my shoulders, and I don't really know how to take it in the context of everything else that's happened between us, but in the moment I'm just grateful for the support, both emotional and physical. It steadies me.

Then someone shouts, "Jeez, O'Neill, have you banged Wells too?"

It is at this point that Ajita delves into her backpack, pulls out some overripe kiwi fruits and hurls them straight at the freshmen scum. Green pulp explodes everywhere. It's fantastic to behold. Then she yanks my arm and hauls me and Danny past them without looking back.

When I look at the kiwi juice all over her hands quizzically, she simply says, "We were out of eggs."

9.14 a.m.

In the last thirteen minutes, I have been sarcastically told "nice tits" in excess of 587 times.

9.37 a.m.

Oh shit and *merde* and *scheiß* and every other linguistic variable on the word. Just when he was beginning to swallow his confusing feelings and support me through this ordeal, Danny found the mashed-up tulips in the woods. Of course he did! Why would anything run smoothly! I'm a writer. I should've known the tulips were some sort of Chekhov's gun and were doomed to go off in the third act. [I know this is still only the second act, but who are you, the story-structure police?]

He found them all muddy and smooshed before first period. He just went out to get some fresh air [I have tried to explain to him why this is so overrated but he won't listen. In conclusion, if people just listened to me a bit more we'd find ourselves in far fewer upsetting situations]. To clear his head. And boom, he walks straight into the mangled flower carcasses.

Because he is a highly dramatic individual, instead of just leaving the flowers there and letting me off the hook, he gathers them up in a paper bag, brings them back into school and dumps them on my desk just before chemistry is about to start.

"You left these behind last night."

It's such a petty move, but I'm struggling to be mad due to lack of energy and enthusiasm, and the fact that the only thing I'm capable of thinking about right now is the nude photograph of me on the internet.

"It wasn't me," I explain feebly.

Danny shakes his head at me and flumps dejectedly into the seat in front of me.

Yeah. Like *he's* the one who should be feeling sorry for himself right about now. You'd think he'd be concerned about the emotional stability of his best friend, who's just been exposed in all her naked glory to the entire world, and maybe, just maybe, put his own butthurt feelings aside for once.

But no. This is all about him, like it always is. He's incapable of imagining how situations affect other people, and thinks solely of his own feelings. That's what the flowers symbolize: he was hurt that I rejected him, so he set out to fix it. To make himself feel better. Never mind how *I* felt; that I was content with my decision to stay friends.

I'm getting tired of his bullshit. Unfortunately, right now I need all the friends I can get.

3.56 p.m.

So the entire school has now seen my lady parts. And holy backlash, Batman.

I am essentially Cersei Lannister in that messed up-scene [spoiler alert] where she's walking naked through the streets of King's Landing while the peasants chant "shame" and throw vegetables at her. [This seems hugely unnecessary and quite wasteful if you ask me. These people are supposed to be starving and yet they fling food around like chimps.] At this point I can only be grateful nobody has shorn my hair in a similar fashion because I am the last person in North America who could convincingly pull off a pixie cut. My ears have something of a elephantine vibe to them, so I really need the scarecrow hair to balance things out.

[As usual, I digress. Imagine being able to hold a coherent and logical conversation! What larks!]

The rest of my day at school is an unmitigated nightmare. Everywhere I go, kids of all ages and social standings point, whisper and laugh, the words "slut" and "whore" and "legend" echoing around the corridor. The latter was in reference to the two dudes who bedded me, as that is the way of high school and also the entire world. At one point I pass Prajesh in the hallway. He's by himself, but he doesn't say hey to me. He just tucks his chin into his chest and barrels past as though I'm not there.

I get it. I do. If he's already feeling like a bit of a pariah, the last thing he wants to do is associate with an *actual* pariah and alienate himself even further. But it still stings.

Vaughan's dad arrives at lunchtime and practically drags his son out of the school gates, probably to prepare his press statement about how Vaughan is an innocent party in this debacle, and the rumors surrounding his involvement are nothing more than high school hearsay. Honestly, I don't even care. After his flower-stomping and woe-is-me performance I'd be quite glad not to be sexually associated with him.

I was sort of hoping a bunch of other girls in school might rally around me in a show of feminist support, but alas, this is not what happens.

When I'm using the bathroom just after lunch, some horrid creature with an incredibly unoriginal sense of humor says loudly to her pal: "No wonder she's peeing. Being pregnant makes you pee a lot. Ha ha ha!" Seriously. How is *anyone* so unfunny? It is truly beyond me.

To be fair, her friend promptly fact-checks this lackadaisical attempt at humor and says, "I don't think she's pregnant. She's just a whore. With lopsided boobs and love handles." More giggles.

Delightful.

In all seriousness, I don't really blame the other kids for their excessive reactions. After all, it's human nature to experience a kind of dark thrill whenever Something Happens. It's like me and my love of other people's drama. I think anything that helps pass the time in a slightly more interesting manner is always going to become a topic of conversation. So yeah, I don't blame them for their fascination.

And then, if you delve even deeper into your own psyche, you realize that you still experience the dark thrill even when the Something is happening to *you*. You get that jolt of excitement, especially in those first few moments before reality sinks in. When I first scrolled through the website – before it felt real – I felt a strange kind of . . . buzz. Tragedy is stimulating, you know?

I don't know why this is a thing. Maybe because, as a species, humans are generally just bored. That's why we keep inventing new technologies, in the hope that this will finally be the thing that cures our boredom forever. It's why we love smartphones so much, I reckon. And I'd bet a lot of criminals – serial killers, arsonists, hackers – are probably at least partially motivated by the dark thrill they experience when Something Happens. Hell, it's probably why someone created World Class Whore. Restlessness. A desire for entertainment.

Anyway. I'll stop arguing that murderers are just bored. I clearly have a tendency to rant incoherently when I'm upset. Moving on.

I'm hanging out with Ajita and Danny tonight. I wonder just

how mad he is about the flower thing. Maybe witnessing my brutal public shaming will have made him feel a tad sorry for me. Usually my toes would curl at the idea of such sympathy but like I say, right now I'll take any kindness I can get.

Speaking of which, Ajita did something very thoughtful for me earlier. She made me laugh again! Yes, I am still capable of such jubilance. She arrived at my house with a beautifully wrapped package and a gift card written in her brother's calligraphy pen. It read:

For when times get really tough. Love, A xo

And it was a bottle of bleach for me to drink!! She just gets me on a soul-deep level.

[I apologize if my bi-chapterly references to death-by-bleach are in any way triggering. You may have noticed this, but I use humor as an emotional crutch. Only twice have I ever considered actually drinking toilet cleaner, but we shall save those stories for another time. I am just a goldmine of hilarious yet emotionally wrought tales. You lucky devils. Good job on your decision to purchase/pirate this tome.]

4.08 p.m.
Text from Carson.

Hey, Iz. Sorry for dropping off the radar lately – family

stuff. Anyway, if you wanna meet up and chat about anything that's going on, give me a shout. Playing b-ball this afternoon, but free all day tomorrow. Let me know. C

Why is my chest fluttering like some sort of lovesick teenager? Seriously. This is Carson Manning we're talking about. Class clown! Brisk fornicator! Why is my ridiculous crush on him escalating despite everything that's going on?

There's another part of me that's relieved. After the debacle with Danny punching a locker, and then the sudden appearance of the WCW website, and *then* the leakage of my nude photo, an insecure part of me wondered if Carson would tap out of . . . whatever he and I are. I know he's a generally good dude, but even so, it's a lot of drama to willfully be associated with. And also it can't be nice having the whole world know you only lasted a few seconds during a drunken one-night stand. Men inexplicably care about that kind of thing, as if lasting more than an hour in the sack is vital to their masculinity.

Look at me! Enduring a full-blown character assassination and yet still concerning myself with the sexual reputation of a fuckboy! Danny Wells could stand to learn a thing or two about empathy from me. [Oops, right back to sounding arrogant once again. Swings and roundabouts.]

6.21 p.m.

After school we go to Ajita's to film a sketch or two. And, you know, generally take my mind off the hideous state of affairs plaguing my existence.

Our last YouTube upload racked up a dizzying 418 views, so we're feeling quite high on our success and just the right amount of cocky to capitalize on it. We've roped in our fellow theater nerd Sharon, a Chinese-American girl with literally the best deadpanning skills you've ever seen in your life, to help out with a topical sketch I wrote before all the screenplay competition stuff kicked off. It's essentially making a mockery of the "selfie pay" system MasterCard want to introduce – more silly than cuttingly satirical, but sometimes I'm just not in the mood to produce work of *SNL* quality.

It starts off with the following announcement over a bank's loudspeaker: "Issues with selfie pay, up to and including dissatisfaction with the quality of your own face, are unlikely to be resolved in branch. Thank you."

And then in walks a dude with a bag over his head, claiming that he is in fact also having problems with selfie pay. Obviously the branch manager is all, "Well, sir, on first diagnosis I'd say the paper bag over your head might be the issue."

Anyway, it transpires that the disgruntled customer was involved in a cycling accident – a head-on collision with a Crisis Prevention truck. Because plausibility is not a great concern in skit-writing (which is precisely why I love it), this has left him with ISIS imprinted on his cheek. He's all: "I uploaded a photo to my Facebook page and was contacted by an alarming number of admiring jihadis. Next thing I know, the FBI are on my doorstep. For some reason they found the truck story pretty far-fetched. After police tackled me to the ground outside a subway station, I thought a precaution couldn't hurt. Hence the paper bag."

Then the bank manager tries to get him to register a new face to his records, and he gets pretty mad at the whole fiasco. Like: "Will this override my previous face? It's important you understand that I won't be walking around with ISIS stamped onto my cheek indefinitely. Just until the swelling goes down."

She won't listen and he ends up yelling about how he's an upstanding member of this country and how he's fairly devastated that his own face is now a billboard for the gangrene of humanity. It's all very touching stuff.

So as you can see, my brand of humor relies heavily on farcical events. But it actually feels pretty good to do something comedy and writing related in the midst of all the chaos. It kind of . . . centers me, if that makes sense. I know who I am when I'm writing and filming and telling jokes. And it's always nice to have people laughing with you, not at you.

Danny is last to rock up, so I run through lines with Sharon while Ajita messes with lighting – a very professional and advanced combination of desk lamps, overhead chandeliers and one lonely light reflector. Once the set is all sorted [it's in Ajita's father's study and not very convincingly banklike, but what can you do with no budget?] we just have to wait for Danny to arrive with his camera and mikes.

Ajita's phone buzzes and she looks at the name on her screen discreetly. I wonder if it's Carlie. I feel kind of terrible for still not addressing this possible romance with Ajita herself, but it's been a crappy week and I'm so emotionally overwhelmed. I know it's not an excuse, though. I need to be a better friend. She's been so great with me over the last few weeks, and I should repay the favor. I make a mental note to check in with her next time we're alone, even though it might be kinda uncomfortable for both of us. Emotional conversations are not our strong suit.

Eventually Danny arrives, flustered from hauling the tripod on foot, and barely looks at me as we fumble with the equipment. That's when I remember how pissed he is about the mangled-flower fiasco. Should I mention it to him? Should I brush it under the rug? Should I leave for Mexico sooner than first anticipated? There is just no right answer.

Maturely I decide to crack a relentless stream of "your mom" jokes at him until he softens [not like that, stop it]. The genius thing about this tactic is he really cannot crack any back on account of the fact my mom is dead, so it would just be unnecessarily cruel and harsh.

However, the only effect this has is making Ajita laugh so hard a little bit of wee comes out, and she has to go for a shower to sort her life out. Thus leaving Danny and me making small talk with Sharon, who is lovely but deadpan in real life too, so it's hard to tell what she's thinking. It could just as easily be "wow, my new friends are so cool and original" as it could "what a bunch of morons". There is just no way of knowing.

While Ajita's showering and Sharon is changing into costume, I take the opportunity to ask Danny, "How's Praj doing? Anything we need to worry about?"

Danny shrugs, not really looking at me as he tinkers with a mic. "He seems okay. Focusing on his next track meet. Still seems kinda lonely, though. I'm hanging out with him at some point next week, which is helping, I think, but I still want him to make some friends his own age, you know?"

"I do. You're a good friend, looking out for him," I say, and I mean it. There aren't many eighteen-year-old dudes who'd hang out with their best friend's little brother just to make sure he's doing okay. It reminds me why I'm friends with Danny despite all the melodrama.

Part of me suspects Danny enjoys being around Praj too. Like I say, he doesn't have many guy friends, and if things are rough at home it's probably serving as a nice distraction. And he *really* loves *Mario Kart*.

Once Ajita has washed away her rogue urine and hopefully found a diaper to wear, I call action. Despite my love of performing, I do secretly love to direct, even though I have a tendency to whine about it. Mainly I just enjoy bossing people around, but there's something so satisfying about seeing your creation come to life on screen. I get a strange little flutter of excitement at the idea of doing this as a career.

I check my emails for the millionth time today, hoping for news about the screenplay comp despite the fact it's only been a few days since I sent back my revised script. Nothing.

Then it hits me. What if the judges have seen the nudes?

8.50 p.m.

Honestly, what a self-obsessed drama queen I am. Why would hotshot comedy producers and a panel of professional screen-writing judges be scouring the internet in pursuit of teen nudes? If that were the case, surely they're the ones who should be embarrassed, not me.

Get a grip, O'Neill.

10.14 p.m.

Danny and I cycle back from Ajita's together. Our neighborhoods are pretty close, even though his is so much more expensive it might as well be another world.

We're at the junction and about to part ways when he says, "Hey, why don't you come to mine for a bit? My mom's been nagging me to invite you over for months. It's been so long."

To be a hundred percent honest, I'm super tired and just want to get home to Betty, Dumbledore and my cozy bed, but I don't want to spark another argument by saying no. Plus I remember what Betty told me about his parents' rocky marriage, and the way he dismissed me when I probed him about it. Inviting me back to his is a big show of trust – one our friendship definitely needs right now. And it *would* be nice to see his mom, Miranda. She was my mom's best friend, and she always has the best stories.

Which is how, nine minutes later, I'm sitting in the living room of their fancy four-bedroom house, making polite conversation and wishing I was in the comfort of my own home.

Their living room is super formal. It has stiff Chesterfield sofas with tiny, firm cushions, and the floor is pale marble topped with a giant Persian rug. The fireplace itself is bare and unused, but the mantelpiece bears an antique clock and several miniature statues of Jesus and his disciples.

Miranda Wells is beautiful, but in a plastic surgery kind of way. Her forehead's a little too tight and her lips are a little too plump, but she's always impeccably dressed. It's hard to imagine her and my mom being best friends in college. My mom was apparently a total hippie type, by all accounts, all tie-dye and weed and protests. Maybe Miranda used to be too, but she's been the way she is now for as long as I can remember.

"So Izzy, how's school going?" she asks, folding one leg tightly over the other and taking a sip of chilled white wine. "Have you figured out which colleges you're going to apply to yet?"

Here we go again. "Actually, I –"

Danny butts in. "Izzy's decided she doesn't need to go to college."

Sure. It's because I don't *need* to go. I press my lips together. "I just don't think it's the best option for me right now."

Miranda looks like she might be trying to raise her eyebrows, but it's impossible to be sure through all the Botox. "But Izzy, darling! It's so important to get a good education. I know it's what your parents would've wanted, especially your mom. Did you know she graduated summa cum laude? Political science major." [This comes across badly in writing, but I know her heart's in the right place. She's not trying to make me feel crappy by bringing up my parents. She's just old-fashioned about this stuff.]

Again, Danny speaks on my behalf. "I've tried telling her, Mom, but she thinks she knows best. Standard Izzy." He smiles likes he's simply jesting good-naturedly, but his words feel sharp. Loaded.

Eager to move on, I change the subject. "So Mrs Wells, are you going back to Lake Michigan for Thanksgiving this year?"

"Actually, I was thinking of visiting my sister and brother-in-law in Europe," she replies. She sways slightly. I wonder how many glasses of wine she's had. Or where Mr Wells is at ten thirty on a Wednesday night. She thinks I don't see her checking her watch every few seconds, but I do. "I haven't seen them in so long."

There's something oddly sad and vacant about Miranda tonight. I wonder if everything's really that terrible between her and Mr Wells. I feel bad for her, I really do. She might be a bit cold sometimes, but she's always been there for me. And she was important to my mom, so she's important to me too.

"What the hell, Mom?" Danny snaps, catching both Miranda and me off guard. "When were you planning on telling me?"

"Sorry, son, I wasn't quite sure what —"

"Why don't you care about what *I* want to do?" Danny huffs, crossing his arms over his chest. "You know I love going to Lake Michigan for the holidays. It's the only thing keeping me going at the moment."

He looks like a petulant only child. Which, you know, he is. It's been so long since I've been to his house that I've forgotten how spoilt he can be sometimes. I mean, sure, we're all different around our parents or various legal guardians. But still. I can barely stand the sight of him when he's like this.

Suddenly the weight of everything hits me. I'm just so tired that I can't bear to be here a second longer. "Mrs Wells, I better be taking off," I say, rising from the sofa. Danny doesn't look at me. "It's been good to see you. I won't leave it so long next time."

With a slight wobble, Miranda stands up too, placing her glass of wine down on the coffee table a bit too hard. Unexpectedly, she throws her arms around me. She smells of expensive perfume and Sauvignon Blanc. "You take care of yourself, Izzy. And you always know where I am if you need anything." It's not a maternal gesture, and for once I don't feel like there are thirty years between us. It just feels like one struggling woman hugging another. Like we're peers.

I smile warmly, giving her a reassuring squeeze. "Right back at you."

Danny doesn't see me out, just stays on the sofa, shooting daggers at his poor mom. I walk through the hallway and toward the front door right at the same time Mr Wells is returning home from . . . wherever. Judging by the smell of Scotch, he's been at the bar opposite his office building.

He clumsily removes his coat and hangs it on the umbrella stand beside the door. His gray hair has gotten so white, and I'm surprised by the swollen paunch belly hanging over his suit pants – it's expanded a lot since I last saw him.

Only when he turns around does he finally see me. A sloppy grin registers on his face. "Izzy! Great to see you. Been too long."

And then, slowly, deliberately, his eyes run up and down my body. And in that heart-dropping second, I know he's seen the photo too.

I feel disgusting. Like I'm being forced to grow up too fast.

Thursday 29 September

1.35 p.m.

Today some delightful human has printed off and photocopied hundreds and hundreds and hundreds of my nudes and stacked them in neat piles all over campus like some sort of visitor information leaflet. They're all grainy and grayscale, but the quality of the printing is not the issue here. The issue is that everywhere I look the photo is tucked into ringbinders and journals and shirt pockets and uuurgggghhhhhh.

As I walk down the gap between benches in the cafeteria, several gorilla boys from the soccer team fling paper airplanes made from the nude printouts at me. Ajita bats them out of the way with her palm like she's merely swatting flies. One stabs me in the elephant ear. Everyone laughs.

But Ajita just sits me down at our usual table, sweeps away a fleet of origami boats also made from the photocopies, and launches into a monologue about the livelihood of barley farmers in Ethiopia. I mean, I wasn't really listening, so it might not have been about that, but let's give her the benefit of the doubt.

At this point I am so ridiculously grateful for Ajita Dutta. If it weren't for her I'd definitely be spending my lunchtimes holed up in a toilet cubicle, or hiding up a tree trying desperately to avoid branch-swinging Tarzan wannabes practising their muscle-ups.

Still, I can't bring myself to ask her about Carlie. It's sheer cowardice really, but I don't trust myself to broach the subject without upsetting her. Because in reality she doesn't know I found that bikini pic on her laptop, and she maybe isn't aware of the blatant attraction floating between her and the red-headed goddess whenever they're together. I don't want to burst her bubble and force her to confront something she might not be ready to confront just yet.

I wish I was better at this stuff. I can crack jokes and tell stories and make my best friend laugh until the cows come home, but I seem to be missing that innate ability to emotionally support someone through something tough. I really need to work on this, because it's not okay. Is there some sort of course I can take? A diploma in being a certified good pal? Remind me to look into it.

4.47 p.m.

Unbelievable. Danny has bought me another gift to apologize for freaking out over the destruction of his previous gift – the tulips – which were also an apology in themselves. I just want to scream at him, "I don't need gifts! I just need you to stop being a Grade-A bucket of dicks!" but I don't think that would go down very well. Preserving his trademark Nice Guy image is very important to him.

Anyway, as we're all walking home together after school – lamenting the bitterly cold wind – he makes the following announcement: "So . . . what are you guys doing on the first weekend in December? Oh, I know! You're going to see Coldplay live at the arena!"

Oh, wonderful. My inner cynic suspects he probably just wants to sing along to "Fix You" while crying and staring poignantly at me.

Ajita squeals and throws her arms around him. "Danny! That's so awesome. Thank you! I can't even think of anything horrible or sarcastic to say right now."

I attempt to muster some gratitude and deliver a well-intended-but-somewhat-lackluster high five. Lackluster due to my emotional exhaustion and general wariness toward the behavior of Mr Wells, which almost seems to have some kind of ulterior motive.

He purses his lips, clearly put out by my lack of enthusiasm. In his defense, they must have set him back a buck or two of his parents' cash since it's been sold out for months.

Again, it kind of rubs me the wrong way, this pattern that's emerging. It feels like every time he wants me to feel a certain way about him, he throws money at the situation. Milkshakes, *Harry Potter* merch, tulips, Ferrero Rocher, gig tickets. Almost as if he thinks he can buy my love.

"I wanted to show you how great it could be. If we were together."

Maybe I'm overreacting. The Coldplay tickets are quite sweet, I suppose. Danny knows Ajita and I love them, and despite the fact he himself is too hipster to allow himself to enjoy their "overrated drivel", he's a big enough person to swallow his own taste in pretentious hipster music and attend the concert with us. He is trying to be a good friend at least. In his own way.

I just can't figure him out at the moment. One minute he's looking after Ajita and Prajesh like they're his own family, and the next he's treating his *actual* family like dirt. There must be some serious shit going down chez Wells; even worse than the affair, if that's possible. The thought alone makes me feel bad enough to overlook his weird behavior.

Plus, things are crappy enough in my life right now. And I have the option to forgive Danny's relentless stream of weapons-grade douchebaggery, and try to rebuild our fractured friendship. All I want is for things to go back to normal, and this seems as good a place to start as any.

So I say thank you and hug him too.

6.58 p.m.

We've been playing ping-pong in Ajita's basement for around

eleven minutes, deftly avoiding the nude elephant in the room, when my phone vibrates. Message.

Since I'm in the throes of a heated tiebreak with Ajita, Danny inexplicably picks it up and reads before I can even stop him. "It's from Carson," he says flatly. "He wants to see you."

Shit! I forgot to reply to Carson's last text!

Shit! Why did Danny read it?

"Oh. Right," I respond, carefully avoiding Danny's stare. He wants to gauge my reaction, obviously, and I want to deprive him of that luxury. I pick up the ball to serve, facial expression set to intense mode as though winning this match means more to me than anything in the entire world, even awesome basketball-playing boys who look like movie stars and make me laugh and don't judge me for screwing up.

"Bow chicka wow wow!" Ajita adds helpfully, despite the fact I've told her twice a day for half a decade that nobody says that anymore. "Manning wants round two. Who could blame him?"

I try to serve, but miss the table entirely. The score's now 22–22.

At Ajita's comment, Danny goes bright red, hurls my phone at the couch, shoves his feet into his beat-up sneakers and mutters something about seeing us later, which I silently pray does not come to fruition. Within three seconds he's gone.

For God's sake. Just when I was ready to move past this confusing episode of unrequited love and emotional manipulation.

I'm so stunned at his departure I allow Ajita to ace me. 22–23. "What. The. Actual. Hell?"

She shakes her head. "I get it. The guy's hopelessly in love with you. And he knows he's taken up permanent residence in the Friend Zone."

"Oh, right," I snap. "And because he's spent enough money and inserted enough friendship tokens, the offer of sex and/or marriage should just fall out anytime now?"

Sighing, she bounces the ball up and down, waiting for me to regain sporting composure. "I know. It's male-entitlement bullshit."

"But?"

"Still can't be nice reading that message."

"Oh yes. Poor Danny. He is absolutely the one we should feel sorry for in this scenario. Did I ask him to read it? No. I know I'm sadistic at times, but masochistic I am not. And this hurts me as much as it does him."

"Does it really?" she asks pointedly.

"Really what?"

"Hurt you." She lays her bat down on the table, perceptively realizing I shall not be calming down anytime soon, and takes a swig of cream soda. "You seem to be taking all of this in your stride. The website, the nudes, the whispers in the hallway. Vaughan. Danny. I know you're a tough cookie, and you'd rather impale yourself on a garden rake than ask for help or show

183

emotion of any kind, but you're allowed to freak out, you know?"

I'm not taking it in my stride! I want to scream. *It's absolutely killing me! But I'm incapable of showing vulnerability and asking for help because I am a TRAGIC ORPHAN WHO USES HUMOR AS A COPING MECHANISM!!!*

Instead I say: "Have you ever considered a career in the counseling profession? That garden rake image in particular is very vivid."

She sighs. "You know what I mean. You don't have to be unflappable all the time. And you're allowed to ask for help."

I do appreciate her trying to talk to me semi-sensibly for once, but honestly, I am just so filled with wrath at Danny's self-pitying martyrdom that I just cannot face it. And also I know she's probably dealing with her own stuff. Figuring out her sexuality and such. So it doesn't seem fair to offload on her.

I smirk. "Can we talk about something else, like how you pissed yourself yesterday?"

Another episode of *Scrubs* starts in the background, with that irritatingly catchy theme tune: "But I can't do this all on my own, no, I know, I'm no Superman." Or whatever.

Obviously Ajita has no self-control and cannot help herself. "You are no Superman, Izzy. And you can't do it all on your own."

Like I say, I'm not in the mood, so I nip this conversation in the bud. "Good talk, coach."

She finally gives up. I feel kind of bad because I know how

painful she finds trying to be a decent human being, but what can I even say? That all of this is like some kind of night terror, and I've woken up paralyzed and can't do anything but sit and watch?

8.21 p.m.

I head down to the outdoor basketball courts after eating five portions of Betty's iconic mac and cheese. Don't tell her I told you, but the secret is she crushes up salt and vinegar chips and mixes the crumbs with the grated cheese topping to make a crunchy crust thing that is basically better than sex, and I should know, because I have had a lot of both.

Because the universe clearly felt bad for leaving me in this cesspool of a situation, Carson is at the courts alone, shooting hoops. Shirtless. Seriously, what have I done to deserve this good karma? Absolutely nothing, that's what.

It's still light outside, but the sky has that kind of late-summer dusty quality, with tiny flies and a slight haze hanging in the air.

Carson stops dribbling [the ball, not from his mouth] when he sees me lurking on the bleachers. I wave awkwardly, i.e. the way I do absolutely everything ever. He slowly makes his way over to me, buff chest rising and falling rapidly from the exertion. Oh, flashbacks.

Flumping down onto the bench in front of me, he grins. "Izzzaaayyyy. Come for round two?"

My eyes follow his dark snail trail, disappearing into the waistband of his yellow basketball shorts. "Ummm."

He winks. He's so beautiful, seriously. "No joke, though. I had a lot of fun last weekend. You're a lot of fun."

Now I'm grinning too. Stop, Izzy! Do not engage with flirtatious banter! I repeat, do not engage!

"Thanks, Carson. If only the entire world did not equate harmless fun with whoredom of the highest order."

His face kinda drops at this point, and I feel bad for lowering the mood so soon. I didn't mean to bring up my woeful personal life, but bam, there you go. I fidget with my keyring – an Indian elephant wearing a top hat. Ajita got me it when she went to Delhi with her family back in tenth grade. She said it reminded her of my ears. Bless.

"Yeah," he nods, wincing. "Sorry, dude. It sucks, the way people are treating you. Like they ain't ever seen titties before."

"To be fair, most of them haven't."

"Yeah." A sarcastic eye-roll as he spins a ball on his index finger. "Virgins."

I'm not sure what point he is trying to make here, but he says the word "virgins" with such vitriol I don't bother questioning it. Boys are weird.

"You got any idea who's behind it all?" he asks as I try and fail to look him in the eye. [Not because I'm ashamed, but because his torso is just so appealing.] "The website. The leaked photo. All that."

"Nah," I shrug, pretending to be nonchalant when in reality my heart rate is roughly one-ninety-two. "Whoever it was had my phone at one point, though. I leave it backstage in the theater all the time. So it could've been anyone who took the screenshot."

He stares at me, utterly aghast, as though I have just announced my candidacy for Prime Minister of Uzbekistan. "You gotta be the only person in the northern hemisphere not to have a passcode on your phone, dude."

I shrug again, because apparently I am incapable of doing anything else. "I can barely remember my home address. Or the fact I have to brush my teeth in the morning. The last thing I need is something else to forget."

A cheeky grin, which does flippy things to my insides. "Well, I don't think I'll be forgetting that photo anytime soon."

Urgh. This does not sit right with me, and I guess my face shows it because he hurriedly adds, "Because you're so hot. Not because, you know, you should be embarrassed or anything. Cos you shouldn't. Not at all."

But I don't know. Making that kind of comment about naked pictures I did not want to be shared just feels kinda skeevy. I mean, he's a teenage boy. They're generally skeevy by nature. But . . . urgh.

Is this just my life now? Fielding skeevy remarks because I

dared to send a naked picture? Will the world now just assume I'll give it away for free all the time, because I did it once?

Do people feel like they own a piece of me, like I'm public property?

I don't think Carson is like that. Not at all. But this whole thing has made me paranoid as hell, and now I have no idea whose intentions to trust. Not after one of my best friends turned on me for not wanting to have sex with him too.

Right then, my phone bleeps. A text message from a number I don't recognize.

Fucking whore.

My heart sinks, I swear to God. Actually sinks. Heat prickles behind my eyes. I don't know why. I don't know why, out of all the abuse and all the public shaming, this is the thing that gets to me. I hate myself for being pathetic, because I pride myself on being anything *but* pathetic.

All I want to do is cry. The need is so sudden and overwhelming that I simply choke out, "Sorry, Carson. I gotta go."

Almost as soon as I turn on my heel, the tears start to come.

I'm not sure why it's an anonymous message that breaks me. Maybe because it reminds me just how many people have now seen me naked. Maybe it's because it perpetuates that uncomfortable sensation of being watched and judged by a faceless entity. Maybe it's because I'm tired and overwhelmed and it's the straw that broke the camel's back. Maybe it's because, even though being hated by people you know is infinitely worse than being loathed by strangers, the combination of both is just crippling on every single level.

Carson calls after me, but I barely hear.

9.48 p.m.
Back in my bedroom I pull out my phone and stare and stare and stare at the nude picture of myself until it's burned into my retinas forever.

I look at it in the way a stranger might, picking out the imperfections and flaws and telltale signs that I'm still just a scared teenage girl. I look at the soft belly I've never hated until now. I look at my boobs, one bigger than the other, one nipple pierced on a reckless whim last summer. I look at my short legs, one crossed in front of the other as I stand in front of a dusty mirror and try to angle myself in a flattering way. I look at my va-jay-jay and want to die, knowing how many people have now seen it too.

I look at a happy, naive kid who has no idea how much she'll come to regret taking that naked picture in a moment of carefree spontaneity. That it'll make her question every single man in her life and his intentions. That, above all, it'll make her question herself in a way she never has.

Betty hears me sobbing and taps softly at the door. I don't reply, so she lets herself in.

"Sweet girl," she murmurs. "What's wrong?"

I sniffle and press my face into the pillow before handing her my phone.

"Please don't hate me."

Friday 30 September

8.47 a.m.

I wait for twenty minutes by my gates, but Danny never arrives.

10.05 a.m.

Ajita is shocked to see me in school. Her parents, who are unbelievable fascists at times, would make her come to school even if her arms had fallen off in the night, but she knows Betty is a bit of a soft touch. She once let me stay home because of a paper cut. To be fair, it was in the webbing between my fingers and thus a deeply traumatic experience, on a par with losing my parents if we're being honest. But still.

Thing is, Betty is generally in tune with what I need. She's amazing like that, like some sort of psychic presence. Such as the paper-cut thing – we both knew I was actually having a horrible day. I'd got my first period the week before, and even though my grandma was great, I really felt my mother's absence that whole week. It just felt like the kind of thing she should've been there for, like riding my bike for the first time, or accidentally getting stoned on pot brownies and breaking into the old folks' home. And so the paper cut became a scapegoat for my grief, and Betty let me stay home.

On the same level, she also knew that what I needed today was not to stay at home obsessing about a nude picture on the internet, wondering how bad it'd be when I eventually did show my face. So she sent me to school.

I somehow make it through first period without having a breakdown, then Ajita grabs me and hauls me into an empty classroom near the cafeteria. This feels a little like stumbling into Narnia, as empty classrooms are like gold dust at Edgewood High.

All the lights are off, and that's how we keep them as we close the door, dump our stuff on the teacher's desk and slip into a few chairs near the back of the classroom. The sky outside is overcast, and after the bright strip lighting of the corridor it takes a while for my eyes to adjust to the dimness.

Ajita's face is covered in zits. She's obviously been stressed about my well-being. "Dude, what did Betty-O say?"

We love calling her Betty-O. It makes her sound like a low-end cereal brand.

I sigh and rub my eyes. They sting from tears and sleep deprivation. "She was actually really great. I expected her to nail me to a cross like that scene from *The Passion of the Christ*, but alas—"

"Like 'the scene from *The Passion of the Christ*'? Izzy, you do know that movie is actually based on the Bible? It's important that you know that."

I feign outrage. "What? No way! Next you'll tell me Santa Claus has his very own testament!"

Faux-exasperated, she replies, "We'll talk about this later. Now, I need deets. What did the old girl say?"

Even though the door to the classroom is shut, some scumbag sophomores have gathered behind the glass, staring at us agog. Without hesitation, Ajita strides up to the window, pounds it with her fist – causing several of them to flinch – then hastily wrenches down the blind that usually stays up until the end of the day. She rejoins me in our seats as though the last ten seconds never happened. Maybe they didn't. Like I say, I'm pretty sleep deprived at this point.

"Honestly, Betty was awesome. For one thing, she didn't bring up my lopsided boobs, which I appreciate. Some grandmothers would express concern at my lack of aesthetic perfection and haul me straight to the plastic surgeon, but not Betty."

Ajita frowns. "I don't think I know any grandmothers who would plausibly take that course of action."

"Ajita, will you please stop taking everything I say so literally. Never in your life have you taken me seriously, why doth thine *haben* started now?" [Oh wonderful, now I'm throwing random

German infinitives into my bastardized medieval sentences. Things just keep getting better and better on the intelligence front. I think my brain cells might actually be falling out of my ears in the night. Remind me to buy plugs.]

Before she can interrupt with another painfully literal interpretation of my strange answers, I add, "No, really. She was all kinds of amazing. At first she was super mad, but not at me, just at the scumbag who made the website and at all the other scumbag minions who do things like make paper airplanes out of my nudes."

"Then?"

"Then she told me to stay calm, hold my head up, all that clichéd crap . . . and she'll figure out what to do next. Whether that's go to the principal, or to the police, since it's harassment and all that, or string every guy on the basketball team up on her washing line by the nuts."

"Hopefully a combination of all three."

"My thoughts exactly, Ajita. My thoughts exactly."

She smiles sympathetically. "Hey, so, um . . . guess what?"

"What?"

Her perfect little face lights up. "I made the tennis team! Turns out my hand-eye coordination is actually quite good thanks to a decade of ping-pong and video games. Who knew?"

"Oh my God! Dude!" I consider giving her a hug, but decide against it because unsolicited bodily contact gives her the willies, and even though I'm like a house cat who likes to be touching people at any given opportunity, I have to respect her wishes. "That's awesome. I'm so fricking proud of you."

And I mean it. I'm really happy for her. But as she skips off to meet Carlie before lunchtime practice, I can't help feeling slightly abandoned. I know that sounds so selfish, and I hate myself for being this petty, but without her by my side, everything just feels so much more overwhelming.

Like I say, I really need to be a better friend. She deserves so much more.

6.58 p.m.
I hang out with Carson at the basketball courts again after school. I love late September. There's all kinds of fall foliage around now, burnt oranges and dark reds and whatnot, and I can smell smoking chimneys on the crisp air. It's almost beautiful enough to make me forget about the hellish implosion of my personal life. Almost.

We shoot some hoops together, even though I have the sporting ability of a concussed hippopotamus, as I fill him in on the latest developments. This time I manage to avoid a full-scale breakdown, which is good for maintaining the illusion that I am not certifiably unstable. Anyway, he seems genuinely concerned about my well-being, which is all new fuckboy territory. He is like a pioneer. A beautiful, beautiful pioneer whose bones I'm in mortal peril of jumping at any given moment.

"Anything I can do?" he asks. "To help y'all, I mean. You and Betty." It's such a small thing, but the fact he remembers my grandma's name warms my heart.

Barely even looking where he's aiming, he gracefully tosses the ball in the direction of the hoop. It makes a perfect arc then slides straight through the net, not even skimming the rim. Even as a nonsportsball lover, I have to admit it's impressive.

He hands me the ball. I bounce it a couple of times, pretending to know what I'm doing, and say, "Nah. Don't worry about us. Everybody has shit to deal with, you know? Even you, I'd imagine, despite your hot-yet-unintimidating demeanor." He grins at this, and I grin back, before adding, "So I'm not in the habit of offloading mine. It isn't fair."

Clearly picking up on the fact I have no idea what I'm doing with a basketball in my hands, Carson comes up behind me and places his hands on my hips, tilting them toward the hoop. My pulse quickens as he angles my body perfectly to make a winning shot, even taking the time to rearrange my feet. I'm not sure why this feels so intimate, given that we've already had sex. But I like it. I really, really like it.

As he works, he says, "You know I have nine brothers and sisters?"

He's back upright now, still behind me, a hand on each

of my arms. I focus on steadying my breathing. "Wow. That's a lot."

"Yeah. A fertile woman, my mother."

I consider this as he runs his hands slowly down my arms until his hands are cupping mine. "You probably know I'm an only child, and an orphan, and an all-round disaster," I say.

He nods. "Yep." I wait for him to continue. I get the impression he's been thinking about this for a while, and as usual I am ruining his flow by stating obvious tragic details about myself.

Both of us holding the ball, Carson takes aim. I can feel his heart beating against my back, even through my sweater. Like he's working a bow and arrow, he gently guides my arms back, then flicks the ball deftly up toward the hoop.

Again, it slides straight through the net.

I whoop, then turn to face him, grinning. He matches my smile. "You're a natural."

See? He is a good guy. Which is very different from being a Nice Guy à la Danny Wells.

Also, for some reason, I don't feel the need to constantly crack jokes and prove how funny I am when I'm around Carson. At first I thought this was a bad thing – like, shouldn't I be bouncing off him and being hilarious? – but it's actually quite nice to just relax and have a normal chat like normal people. So it's weird.

Our faces are so close together that for a moment I think [hope] he might kiss me again, but after a tantalizing moment, he skips off to retrieve the ball.

I take the opportunity to continue the conversation. "So is everything okay at home? You mentioned family issues. I mean, you don't have to talk about it. But you can if you want."

He grins again, bounding back over to me. He really is cute with a capital C. Huge smile, smooth brown skin, symmetrical features, striking eyes like Will Smith's. "Thanks, Iz. It's really okay, though. Nothing compared to what you have to deal with."

"Well, that's dumb," I retort. "I don't have the monopoly on messed-up family stuff. Just ask the Fritzls."

Carson actually recoils a little here. "Izzy, that's awful."

"So is your face."

"Really? Still making 'your face' jokes in this day and age?"

"Look, I don't care what anyone says, your face and your mom jokes will always be hysterical."

He laughs. "Whatever you say. You're the comedian."

But I haven't even been trying to be funny! I want to say. Is it possible that my natural state is entertaining in itself? What a relief that would be!

"Nah, honestly, it's a'ight," he says. We both watch a nearby seagull doing some sort of Macarena dance as it maneuvers its freshly caught prey into its mouth. "My mom's partner of eight years left us a few weeks back. Left us in the shit too, financially.

Eleven mouths to feed and all. So I've been picking up extra shifts at the pizza place downtown."

"That is unbelievably crappy. I'm sorry."

"Nah, don't be. I get free pizza."

I gasp exaggeratedly. "That is the Holy Grail of job perks. I love pizza more than most things, including oxygen."

He lets his eyes drop to the ground. [Again, not literally. That would be deeply uncomfortable for him. Nobody wants gravel in their corneas. I mean, maybe you do. I don't know your fetishes.]

Biting a lip, he finally says, "Then, uh, maybe we should get pizza together sometime."

Wow, he has such long eyelashes. [Good grief, I really need to stop objectifying this poor boy – it is very unfeminist of me.]

I smile. "Yeah. Maybe we should."

After we've finished shooting hoops, Carson offers to walk me home, which I happily accept. There's something about being around him that just makes me feel calm and level, despite everything going on, but also tingly and excited. And that's a sensation I appreciate now more than ever. I can't get enough.

We walk and chat as the sun is setting, casting a warm glow over the town. Carson and I live in the same neighborhood, so I don't have to be embarrassed as we stroll past the beat-up cars and overflowing dumpsters and stray dogs scavenging for food. To be honest, the only time I ever properly see those things is through other people's eyes. Danny and Ajita's mainly, and even though I know they never judge me, it's kinda nice to be with someone who lives in the same world. It's just . . . easier.

On one street I've walked down a thousand times, a woman I recognize sits on her doorstep, smoking a roll-up cigarette as two toddlers run around her ankles. She berates the little boy for pushing the girl a bit too hard, even though the girl looks totally unfazed.

The woman is big and beautiful. Her black hair is swept up into a bright yellow headscarf, and her lips are painted purple. When she sees Carson, her eyes crinkle in recognition.

"Hey, Mom," Carson says, in the same relaxed tone he uses with me. I blink in surprise, but it also makes perfect sense. The woman's skin is the same perfectly smooth brown as Carson's, and she has the same wide smile. "This is Izzy. I was just walking her home. Izzy, this is my mom, Annaliese."

I smile and say, "Pleasure to meet you, Annaliese."

His mom blows one last puff of smoke through her lips, then buries the cigarette in a terracotta plant pot next to the doorstep. Dusting her hands off on her patterned dress, she stands up and gives me a warm hug.

"Carson's told me a lot about you." Her eyes are mischievous, and I know what she's trying to communicate: he's told me a lot of *good* things. I grin conspiratorially.

"Less of that, please, Annaliese," Carson jokes, but his voice is light. Nothing like Danny's when he speaks to Miranda. "Everything cool?"

His mom nods. "Yeah. Scott was gon' come by, but he didn't. Don't know why I'm surprised."

I guess they're talking about the partner who left recently, leaving them in the shit with money.

Carson grabs the little girl by the ankles and lifts her up. She squeals with delight as he dangles her at shoulder height. "It's gonna be a'ight. I picked up some extra shifts this weekend." He places the giggling girl down again and turns his attention to the boy – his brother? "Looks like someone's getting pizza for dinner again. PIIIZZZAAAAAAA!!" He growls this last bit like a pizza monster, chasing the kid a short way down the street. "GRRRRRR!"

His mom and I are both laughing too. Then she says, "That's enough, pizza monster. Time for your prey to have a bath."

"Yeah, he's pretty stinky," Carson says, fanning his nose extravagantly to illustrate his point. His prey laughs hysterically. "Want me to do it?"

"Nah, it's cool," Annaliese says. "You walk Izzy home. I got it."

Despite the crappy situation she's in, she's all twinkly at the sight of me and Carson together.

As we walk back to mine, I don't have to force conversation. It just flows. "So is your coach cool with you skipping practice to work at the pizza place?" I ask.

"Nah, he's a dick about it," he replies. He works a thumb into the back of his shoulder to dig out a knot, wincing a little as he does so. "But what's he gonna do? Cut me from the team? Pfft. I'd like to see 'em win a game without me."

His confidence is nice. It's not arrogant. It comes with a cheeky grin and a jesting tone, rather than a condescending sneer.

"You must be pretty good then, huh?" I ask. "I mean, I've seen you play, and it looks impressive. But I know more about algebra than I do about sports, and that's saying something."

He laughs. "Yeah, I'm not bad. Not like I'm gonna be one of the greats, though."

"No?"

"Nah. I'm too short, for one thing." I shoot him an unconvinced look. He's well over six feet tall. He holds his hands up. "Hey, I don't make the rules. I'm a shortass compared to the NBA All-Stars. So yeah, not tall enough, or committed enough. Or interested enough, to be honest."

This last one catches me off guard. "Really? I thought you loved basketball."

"I do, man, I do. But you can love a thing without necessarily dedicating your life to it, you know?"

The profoundness of this statement leaves me slightly breathless. I feel like it might apply to my situation, to the pressure I'm putting on myself to succeed in this screenplay competition, but I'm too engaged with the conversation to delve into the idea properly. I tuck it away in the back of my mind to revisit later.

"So do you wanna do the whole college thing?" I ask, enjoying getting to know Carson beyond the class-clown image.

He shrugs noncommittally. "I dunno. I figure I'd enjoy it, but am I willing to get into that much debt just to check a box?" Another shrug. "Right now, I don't think so. I'd rather stay home and support my family. Leave my passions as hobbies. Play when I wanna play, read what I wanna read. That'd be enough for me, I think."

I smile, a warm feeling spreading through my chest. Carson's on my wavelength. He genuinely understands that following your wildest dreams isn't the best option for a lot of people. And he's made his peace with it, but not in a depressing way. He's happy. And for the thousandth time since we started talking, I feel refreshed by him. By his personality, his kindness, his outlook.

Uh-oh. I'm in trouble.

"So what other passions do you have? Besides basketball." I find myself genuinely caring about the answer, rather than just thinking about the next thing I'm going to say. As a nervous conversationalist, this is something of a breakthrough.

"I like to paint. Not like hills and trees and shit. More like art as activism. Art that says something about the world." His hand finds mine, but not awkwardly like some teenage boys would do it. Just relaxed and nice. "I never told anyone that before."

I remember how good his alpaca sketch was, and the blue, white and red paint the first time we kissed in the hallway. "Art as activism. Like Banksy?"

"Man, Banksy's some white-ass bullshit. Sorry," he apologizes hastily, as though he might've offended my white-ass feelings.

I nudge his shoulder playfully, trying to show he doesn't even a little bit have to worry about that. "Why's that?" I ask. He still looks wary. "I genuinely want to know," I add, squeezing his hand.

"A'ight, so the dude flew out to Gaza to spray-paint a kitten on a house that'd been destroyed in an air strike. Like, the fuck? Talk about insensitive. Then our white savior has the audacity to call it art, to demand folks listen to *his* views on the atrocities of war, rather than the Palestinians who gotta live through it." He shakes his head, his hand tensing and untensing in mine. "Sorry. Shit drives me crazy sometimes."

"Don't apologize," I insist. "I love listening to you. And you're right. That's some white-ass bullshit."

He laughs. "You're cool, O'Neill. Maybe I'll show you my work sometime."

"I'd like that," I smile back. [There's been a lot of smiling and grinning in this scene, and I do apologize for the unimaginative descriptions. Turns out there aren't that many synonyms for smiling and grinning. Blame Carson; he's the one who's always making me smile and grin.]

Strolling past the dusk-lit windows on Carson's street, I catch our reflections in the glass.

I'll give it to Annaliese – we do look kinda cute together. No wonder her eyes were twinkling.

Mine are too.

10.42 p.m.

Just received a Facebook message from Danny.

Hey, so I just found this cool Getting Into Screenwriting masterclass you can do online. It's with some prolific writing duo I've heard you talk about before.

And he attaches the link. But before I can even click it, another message comes through.

I know you'll probably freak out that it's $120, but I don't mind paying for it as a treat :)

The order of my reactions are as follows:

1. Heart-stopping nausea at the sight of the figure $120. I've had this knee-jerk reaction to large monetary values for as long as I can remember.
2. Disbelief that Danny would offer to pay.
3. Cautious gratitude.
4. Temptation to take him up on the offer.

5. Remembrance that Danny is in love with me.

6. Guilt.

7. Disconcerting feeling that he's still trying to buy my affection.

8. Anger that he's wielding his power as a wealthy middle-class dude to manipulate my emotions.

9. Concern that I'm thinking too much into it.

It just feels, yet again, like he has an ulterior motive. Up until super recently Danny never bought me a thing, and I liked it that way. It made me feel like we were equal. He never intentionally drew attention to the disparity in our situations. And now he highlights it regularly, buying me milkshakes and sweaters and flowers and Coldplay tickets and offering to fork out an eye-watering sum of money in order for me to advance my career.

Is it because he wants me to feel like I owe him something? Or is that too harsh a criticism?

He looks at my life and sees I don't have much money, and he exploits that predicament to manipulate my emotions. Did he learn that from watching his dad buy his mom's affection instead of earning it? The Lake Michigan lakehouse was bought right after the news of Mr Wells' affair came out, back when Danny and I were still in grade school. I was too young to fully grasp what was going on, but looking back it seems like Danny's dad used money to fix a grave mistake, rather than actually repairing the emotional damage.

I remember his comment back when he found out Vaughan liked me. *What's he trying to pull, asking a girl like you out.*

A Girl Like Me. What does he even mean by that? He's never made me feel like I'm any different, not once in our thirteen years of friendship. Until now.

Cautiously, for fear of angering the beast, I type out what I consider to be a diplomatic response.

Thanks for thinking of me! This sounds like a cool opportunity, but I'd never take money from you. I don't want to feel like some kind of charity case, you know?

The three dots showing he's typing a response appear almost immediately.

Wow, bitter much? You're making me feel like a dick for offering to do a nice thing for you. I can't win with you, can I?

Whoa. I'm about to start composing an anti-inflammatory answer when he sends another message:

You spend your whole life complaining about how unfair the movie industry is, how disadvantaged kids with no connections can't get a foot in the door. And now you're turning on me for offering to help? Like I say. Can't win.

Why is this escalating so quickly? I know he's dealing with some confusing feelings toward me, but man, this is too much.

Taking a deep, steadying breath, I reply.

When I complain about how the movie industry prices

poor people out, it doesn't mean I want a rich person to buy me in. It means I wish the barrier to entry didn't exist at all.

Two seconds later . . .

You're exhausting.

I want to scream in frustration. He's so damn transparent. He offered me money so that when I cried with gratitude and told him he was amazing, it'd massage his ego and make him feel good for helping a Girl Like Me.

It didn't cost him anything, not really. His parents are rich. That money means nothing to him. But he knows it means everything to me, and he's manipulating that imbalance with no shame.

I get why he's lashing out. As a privileged white dude, he's used to being able to buy whatever he wants. He lives in a country where even the presidency can be bought.

But he can't buy my love. And that frustrates the hell out of him.

11.07 p.m.

Texting Carson. You know, an actual decent guy, who is nice to me at all times and has never once tried to bribe me into having sex with him. What a revelation!

He messages me first, which is nice, because although I don't subscribe to the sexist notion that girls should wait for potential suitors to make the first move in a heterosexual relationship, it's always nice to feel wanted.

Watching a documentary on the Fritzls. Inspired by you, obviously. This is so effed up.

I grin as I reply.

I don't think they made a documentary about the Fritzls yet. Are you sure it's not *Keeping Up with the Kardashians*? I've never watched it, but understand they have a very similar dynamic.

Lol. You're literally funnier than every guy on the basketball team combined.

That is best compliment I could hope to receive at this point. I was about to cave into temptation and check the online response to my nudes for the millionth time today, but this is enough to distract me for another minute or two.

Well, that isn't hard. Unlike every guy on the basketball team, who are hard at all times. You know, due to raging hormones and constant exposure to each other's penises.

He doesn't reply to this for around half an hour, and I actually start to freak out that I've offended him.

I refresh my emails several times – still nothing from the competition judges. I just want to know if I'm on the shortlist, damn it! And if I do not receive word within the next forty-eight seconds I am at very real risk of causing a Chernobyl-like nuclear disaster through sheer nervous energy alone.

But then Carson:

Hey, is your friend Ajita single? One of my firm-penised teammates wants to ask her out.

Oh, Ajita, you daaaaawwwwg. I mean, I'm not surprised she's in demand because she's a beautiful goddess and all-round hilarious human being, but still. Always nice to hear my homegirl getting the attention she deserves.

She is indeed single! However, I am not sure firm penises are her jam. I mean, neither are flaccid ones. Like, I just don't think penises are her preferred genitalia. But your pal should ask away, for I am not her spokesperson!

I then ping off a text about this new development to the queen herself, and promptly fall asleep with the most absurd of smiles on my face, dreaming of pizza with Carson Manning in the not too distant future.

Monday 3 October

10.13 a.m.

Things that have happened since arriving at school this morning:

1. Danny ignored me in homeroom. Sigh. This animosity is highly inconvenient because I need him to fix my laptop for me. It just will not connect to Wi-Fi no matter how many sacrifices I make to the technology gods, including but not limited to my firstborn child.

2. Ajita is off sick. She has stomach flu from consuming week-old pepperoni pizza, even though she's supposed to be vegetarian. I texted her to tell her that she is an extremely selfish and inconsiderate individual, but she just told me that she hopes I contract the norovirus in the next few hours so I can join her on the sofa for a Comedy Central binge. That doesn't sound awful in all honesty.

3. All the usual jeers and whispers and general assholery. It is

quite baffling to me that people are still interested in my nudes, because as a solid 6/10 I'm painfully middle of the road. This is why I have developed a sense of humor to compensate, so I'm totally okay with my ranking as "above average but only just". However, I am totally *not* okay with the fifteen-year-old Japanese boy who follows me around everywhere asking me to sign the iPhone case he's had made out of my leaked photo.

4. I flunked math. Shock of all shocks, quadratic equations and/or the ancient wanker that is Pythagoras are not top of my list of things I currently give a crap about.

5. Vaughan made a speech in the cafeteria in response to aforementioned jeers and whispers and general twattery. It went something like this: "Ahoy, gossiping fishwives! It is I, grandson of Benito Mussolini, evil dictator and abhorrent human being. I doth shall [again I'm not a hundred percent clued up on doth usage, but hopefully you'll let it slide] make it abundantly clear that I did not have sexual intercourse with this here Izzy O'Neill." I am paraphrasing slightly. The original was far less eloquent. Basically, he wanted everyone to know that despite all the evidence, he has zip zilch zero to do with my situ. And nothing screams "uninvolved bystander" like a public declaration of innocence.

6. I caved and checked the WCW website again. Nice new additions: a sweepstake in which voters guess my weight, bra size and body mass index based on the nude photo [these are weirdly accurate]; a strongly worded post about how decidedly unfunny I am [lol okay sure]; more amateur Photoshop jobs [in one, my face has been superimposed onto a porn screenshot in which the actress is receiving a penis in every orifice].

7. Bumped into Carlie in the restroom and almost as soon as she made accidental eye contact with me, she turned and speed-walked straight out of there. Thank you for the support, dude! I mean, I understand that as a new kid she probably doesn't want to taint her reputation by associating with the likes of me, but still. If she and Ajita do end up going out, I don't want things to be awkward between us.

Sigh. I might go and hang out with Mrs Crannon. She seems to be the last person at Edgewood who doesn't despise every fibre of my being.

2.45 p.m.
Crannon is also off sick. Am slightly concerned about the fact this coincides with Ajita's absence, and ordinarily I would cook up a delicious conspiracy theory about their passionate, clandestine love affair. But I'm just not in the mood.

Ho hum, woe is me, why must I go on? How can things possibly get any worse?

4.56 p.m.

Ha. Ha ha. HA.

Surely, Izzy, you have seen enough movies and read enough books to know that when the protagonist utters that doomed sentence, "How can things possibly get any worse?" things *invariably* get worse.

In my case, much fucking worse.

Someone sent a video of Vaughan's cafeteria speech to a local newspaper reporter, who uploaded it to the publication's website along with links to the gross, Izzy-shaming blog, and a full background as to the involvement of a Republican senator's son in a small-town sex scandal. Ted Vaughan has been approached for comment.

There's also an image gallery containing – you guessed it – the nude pictures.

It's had over 4,000 shares.

11.07 p.m.

Even though she's still sick, Ajita calls an impromptu but highly necessary girls' night to address the catastrophic developments today brought forth.

She answers the door dressed as R2-D2, which is an

unexpected perk of the evening, and I decide it'll be funniest to pretend not to have noticed. So I just greet her as normal and waltz into her house like I own the place. She plays along nicely, adding the occasional *beep-bop* for believability.

Her parents and siblings are all out at some tragic athletics meet [Prajesh is the next Usain Bolt, by all accounts] so we have the house to ourselves. We cozy up in her kitchen instead of the basement. It's really beautiful – sleek refrigerator with an ice machine, massive central island and breakfast bar, fresh lilies in a vase at all times.

She putters around making nachos – spraying grated cheese and rogue tortilla chip crumbs everywhere as she tries to stay in droid character – while I rant.

"I just don't get it," I say from my perch on a bar stool. "Why does anyone care about my sexploits? It's just so absurd."

"Agreed," she replies, sucking some spilled salsa out of the R2-D2 onesie. "I don't care either. I wasn't even listening to what you just said, for instance. You really are a hugely uninteresting individual."

"Right? And yet four thousand people give a crap about the fact I slept with a senator's son. On a garden bench. And sent him a nude. WHY?"

She rams the haphazard nacho tray under the grill and hops up onto the counter, which is where she always prefers to sit given the chance. She insists it's more comfortable than any sofa money can buy. She's an oddball, my best friend. "In all reality, though, how are you feeling about it? Because this cannot be easy."

I shudder. "The worst part is knowing how many actual adults will now see those pictures. When it was just the website, I assumed the damage would be contained to fellow high-school students. Which was far from ideal, but it was easier to stomach than knowing parents and teachers and all sorts are now going to see my foofer." I groan. "Oh God. I just thought of something else. Nobody in this godforsaken town is going to hire me now."

This feels terrible. Betty is going to have to work even longer just because her disaster zone of a granddaughter has rendered herself completely unemployable.

Ajita tries her best to put a positive spin on the situation. "I mean, you don't know that. I feel like you might have a USP among owners of struggling dive bars. From their point of view, your incredible boobs might attract a whole slew of sleazy clientele as they arrive in their hordes to attempt to woo you. Sales of Johnnie Walker will skyrocket."

I groan again, dropping my head into my hands. This all feels like a bad dream. Why can't I wake up?

"So Danny mentioned you guys had a bit of a fight," Ajita says, changing the subject in a bid to distract me from the fact my future is evaporating before my eyes. "Something about a screenwriting course? Care to fill me in on the non-biased, non-Dannyfied version?"

Instead of spelling it all out, I just hand her my phone and let her read the messages herself.

"Jeez," she says, eyes widening. "Hey, Danny, might wanna cover up a bit. Your privilege is showing."

Exasperated, but also hungry, I pad over to the fridge and open it up, scanning for any potential snackage situations. "Do you understand what I was trying to say, though? Did I come off too harsh with all that stuff about not wanting or needing a rich person to buy me in?" I settle on the remainder of the grated cheese and start shovelling it into my face like popcorn.

"Not harsh at all," she says, giving the nacho tray a shimmy and dumping more guac on top. "It's like when I talk about racism, I'm not asking for one single white person to wave their magic privilege wand and fix one single symptom. What I'm saying is that I want the systemic racism to not exist in the first place. I want a cure, not a Band-Aid." She shrugs. "But a lot of rich white guys will never get that. They'll always make it about them. And why wouldn't they? Historically, it always *has* been about them."

Frustration is building in my blood to such a high concentration that not even rapid ingestion of cheddar can take the edge off. "Do you know, Ajita, I'm starting to lose all faith in the world."

"So how do we take your mind off it? I really thought the *Star Wars* costume would do it."

"What *Star Wars* costume?" I ask innocently.

217

"Yes, very good. Har har. Shall we do some karaoke? I've also got a Chewbacca outfit you can wear for the occasion."

It really is incredible how much better singing along to Eminem's [admittedly highly problematic] greatest hits can make you feel. A personal highlight is our rendition of 'Love the Way you Lie'. I perform the rap segments while Ajita takes Rihanna's chorus. Magical.

Unfortunately her parents return at the precise moment Ajita is holding her brother's teddy bear over the gas cooker, crooning "just gonna staaaaand there and watch me burn" as the blackened nachos set off the fire alarm. But you take the wins where you can get them.

[I would show you the video of us dancing on the breakfast bar dressed as a Wookie and a droid, but then I'd have to kill you.]

Tuesday 4 October

6.31 a.m.

Someone posted a condom stuffed with dog turd through our letterbox this morning. Dumbledore got confused, bless him, and thought it was an exciting new chew toy. And that's the story of how we're going to have to get a new couch.

12.58 p.m.

Betty finally let me stay off school today. She's being all cute and protective and bringing me things. She even knitted me a scarf now that the weather's getting cooler, and it is the single most ugly garment I have ever seen in my life – like roadkill really – but I love it dearly.

Still haven't plucked up the courage to check the news again.

2.12 p.m.

Whyyyyyyy???????

Whyyyyyy did you let me check the news???????

The clickbait piece featuring Vaughan's speech has now

amassed over 100,000 shares all across the state, and has been updated to include quotes from Ted Vaughan, whose political beliefs are as wrong as a sultana in a salad [or really just salad as a concept]. He has this to say:

"The accusations of my son's involvement in this disgusting display of teenage promiscuity are outrageous and deeply insulting. His mother and I have dedicated our lives to raising this young man the correct way, and to insinuate his behavior has been anything other than exemplary for the past seventeen years is nothing but a vicious lie. Izzy O'Neill, whoever you are: please take responsibility for your own actions, which are a living embodiment of everything that's wrong with America's youth culture today."

Ted Vaughan is the kind of guy who's probably absolutely thrilled with this handy little PR boost his campaign so desperately needed. He then goes on about abortion policies and what steps he'd take to fix us broken teens, which I can only assume involve systematic castration of the homosexual population and mandatory chastity belts for all unmarried women.

There's also expert analysis on the ineptitude of sex education-professionals across the country, a roundup of all the female celebrities who've had their nudes leaked, someone preaching passionately about abstinence being the only real form of contraception, and a lot of religious bigots condemning me to an eternity in hell.

And the photo of me having sex with Vaughan on a garden bench. Everywhere.

I'm trying very hard to process these developments, with special regard to the fact my name and face and private parts are now plastered all over the internet, but I feel strangely detached and unable to convince myself this is actually happening.

I have six thousand texts from Ajita asking if I'm all right, and predictably zero from Danny. Ajita's most recent:

Look, I know this is a little off-brand, but I am seriously worried about you. My skin is in more of a mess than, I don't know, Lionel Messi, and there are reporters at the school gates asking people for quotes about you, and though I am surprisingly tough there are only so many times I can rugby-tackle our peers to the ground before my shoulder gives out, and FOR SHIT'S SAKE WILL YOU JUST ANSWER ME, WOMAN?? Otherwise I shall be forced to call you and we both know how much you hate unsolicited phone calls when a simple text message would do. xo

I fire off an eloquent and insightful message about my mental state:

Re the reporters: I don't give a fuck. In fact, if you listen very carefully, you'll hear the sound of all the fucks I used to give exploding one by one, into tiny little fucklet particles that

are imperceptible to the naked eye. Stop by after school? Love you.

Then she says:

Love you??? Are you sure you aren't dying?? It sounds suspiciously like you're dying. And I know you're a tireless curator of all the fucks nobody gives, but promise me you're okay? This press field day is on a whole new unprecedented level of suckage. You would have to combine blowjob extraordinaire Amanda Bateman with a high-end Dyson to even come close to how much this sucks. xo

Despite the enticing myriad of innuendo options available to me right now, I don't even have the energy to reply.

7.28 p.m.

Having spent the whole day inside alone, trying and failing to fight the deep, gnawing shame eating my insides, I have to get out. Of the house, of my body, of my mind. I just have to get out.

In an attempt to cheer me up, Ajita insists on taking me shopping for sketch props with her mom's credit card. I have brief concerns over being recognized in the mall – which is where basically everyone from within a 100-mile radius hangs out on evenings and weekends – but aside from the people I actually know from school, no one seems to notice me.

In fairness, most of the WCW website, and indeed the recent

press coverage, has been focused on my body. Nobody is particularly interested in my face, and with my body covered up like it is right now, what else do I have to offer the world? Precisely nothing.

Still, every store assistant who serves us, every cashier who swipes Ajita's mom's card, I wonder if they know. I wonder if they've seen me naked. I wonder if they laughed at me with their friends, or showed their colleagues in the break room. I wonder if they think I got what I deserved. I wonder if they know the intimate parts of my body that are now public property.

I feel powerless. Completely and utterly powerless.

We're now sitting in the food court, drinking milkshakes [I go peanut-butter Oreo because I am very committed to my varied diet and believe in consuming equal quantities of fat and sugar] and planning a series of satirical Instagram posts using an avocado onesie. Although hipster foodies are absolutely harmless and probably very nice people, we can't resist an easy target. In fact, it's often quite physically painful for us to try and refrain from making obvious gags, like the time I tried to give up "your mom" jokes and almost gave myself a stroke, thus it would effectively count as self-flagellation to attempt to control ourselves. This is, both medically and philosophically speaking, a thing. Trust me. I have an IQ of 84.

Once the hilarity wears off over the mental image of me smeared on wholewheat toast and topped with cracked black pepper, Ajita asks me ever so casually, "So have you thought any more about who started that website in the first place? Cos, you know. This is all their fault. Not yours. I don't want you getting big-headed or anything, because your ego is already intolerable, but . . . you are wonderful. None of this is your fault."

Genuinely I almost cry at this, but manage to resist lest Ajita think I actually have emotions. "It'd be nice if Danny was telling the truth," I say. "That he really did have nothing to do with it."

She mulls this over, taking a swig of her s'mores shake. Next to her is a sign that says Your Sandwish Is My Command. [Don't you dare laugh at this. It's the least funny name for a fast-food restaurant in the whole word. Think of all the wasted opportunities! Lord of the Fries. Forrest Rump. The Codfather. I could go on, but I shan't.]

I add, "I think I'm going to choose to believe him, simply because it's too depressing not to."

"Meaning?"

"Well, I'm getting quite tired of people proving themselves to be royal dickwads every other second." I pause meaningfully, fumbling with the straw wrapper. "Did you invite him today?"

"No. I'd rather fuck a fruit bowl than look at his mopey face all afternoon."

I laugh so hard at this I almost vomit.

9.04 p.m.

Sound the drama klaxon! Within the space of the last thirty minutes, the following hath ensued:

1. Vaughan called me [like, an actual telephone call, in this day and age! Who does he think he is??] to apologize for the media shitstorm he accidentally caused by making a cafeteria speech more ill-judged than the 2003 invasion of Iraq. I essentially told him to have sexual intercourse with the nearest cactus, and he called me a bitch and hung up.

2. Danny texted me, kicking off about my secret girl date with Ajita. It went like this: **Thanks for the invite today. It was really great to hear my two supposed best friends were hanging out behind my back.** He is such a man child. Currently researching ancient witchcraft rituals in an attempt to cajole the universe into smiting him. [I do feel like smite is an underused verb, no?]

I don't have the emotional energy to deal with either.

11.02 p.m.

The day has left me feeling grubby and miserable, so I have a long, hot shower in an attempt to wash it all away. The website, the nudes, the press coverage. Danny. Everything.

Usually I'm in and out within five minutes, barely even looking at my body as I slather it in cheap shower gel and drag a razor wherever necessary, but tonight I examine it more closely than I have in years. It's been put under a microscope for the whole world to inspect, and I want to see what they see. It's sadistic, but it's an itch I have to scratch.

Cellulite and stretch marks around my hips and thighs. A giant mole on my left butt cheek. Swollen boobs because of the time of the month.

Imperfections that, up until a few weeks ago, were mine and mine alone. Until I shared them with two boys I trusted. Now the whole world sees them too.

I scrub for an hour but still can't wash away the dirty feeling.

Wednesday 5 October

8.28 a.m.

Just when you think life could not possibly get any more dramatic and palpitation-inducing, a gaggle of reporters flock to the gates of your housing community and bombard you on your way to school. Seriously, big fluffy mikes, cameras, the works. Now I know how that Jenner woman feels when people ask about her lips all the time.

"Miss O'Neill! Miss O'Neill!"

No. Go away.

"Izzy? Izzy, can you talk to us about Zachary Vaughan? Has his father made any effort to contact you directly?"

No.

"How does it feel to have your naked body on display to the entire world?"

NO.

They just want to hear my side of the story, they say. Yes, but so do the other 631 bloggers/journalists/scumbags who emailed me personally to ask for THE TRUTH and THE LIES and THE

SCANDAL and for a verbatim quote on how much of a royal dick Ted Vaughan is.

Vultures, the lot of them. I just cannot begin to understand why they even care about my naked teenage body and unpalatable promiscuity. Aren't there wars happening or something? Are sex scandals really that interesting nowadays, or are we still in 2007? Is that the buzz of Britney's razor I hear?

Honestly, it was like running a gauntlet. Danny was nowhere to be seen this morning, probably goldfish pouting about our fight and how Vaughan is getting more attention than him, but thankfully Ajita, a.k.a. my guardian-angel-come-pit-bull, shielded me from the flashing cameras as best she could. It was a little like an ant trying to protect Hagrid, but I was touched nonetheless.

In related news, in homeroom I'm going to rip off Vaughan's balls and stitch them to a sock puppet, and then I will explain to the reporters, using my innovative new mouthpiece, just how I feel about that unbelievable scumbag.

10.54 a.m.

Outside of Ajita, the only other student who isn't treating me like I have leprosy is, surprise surprise, Carson Manning.

We bump into each other by the water fountain before second period. He sneaks up behind me and squeezes my shoulders. "Hey, you. How you holding up?" He smells freshly showered – he must've just finished practice.

I wipe a rogue trail of water away from my mouth [seriously, is there any way to drink gracefully from a water fountain?] and turn to him, mustering up the most convincing smile I can.

"I'm all right, I guess. Trying not to look at the media."

He's wearing a gray hoodie and black jeans, and I want to rip them right off him. Good to know the whole sex-scandal thing hasn't deterred the insatiable nymphomaniac inside me.

Carson rubs his forehead, looking anxious on my behalf. "Don't blame you. Please don't . . ."

As he trails off, he shakes his head.

"Please don't what?" I prompt him, rearranging my backpack. I have a terrible habit of hauling my books around on just my right shoulder instead of wearing it properly across both, so am therefore a few short months away from resembling the Hunchback of Notre Dame.

He looks around the busy corridor, where kids of all ages and social standings are staring at us, whispering conspiratorially. "Please don't think any of this is your fault, a'ight? Cos it ain't."

A lump forms in my throat. "I'll try not to."

And then, despite all the stares and whispers, he gives me the biggest bear hug I've ever received.

He's so warm and comforting as he whispers in my ear, "You tougher than they are. Hell, you tougher than most people."

Before I can even reply, he pulls away, picks up the textbook he dropped and, after one last reassuring smile, sets off toward his next class.

These past few days have felt like my insides were being shredded with frozen icicles of shame, but Carson thaws them. Because he doesn't treat me any differently. He looks at me the same way he always has: like I'm funny and cool and someone he wants to be around. Like I'm a person, not a piece of meat.

Something in my chest aches, but not in a sad way.

11.35 a.m.

Fuck. Just when a well-timed pep talk from a guy I care about has me feeling like I might actually survive this, BuzzFeed gets hold of the story. I'm global.

Well, the Vaughan family are global, but I'm caught up in the crossfire. Because revenge porn is still legal in my state, and such a high-profile case involving a politician's son has attracted a storm of media attention and debate. And because I'm eighteen, and thus not a child, they're allowed to show my pictures without being accused of child pornography.

Part of me is glad the issue is being discussed. I just wish I wasn't the catalyst.

Checked my Gmail for shortlist news [and to satisfy the paranoid part of me who's still worried the producers will see the nudes and put two and two together]. *Nada*, but I've had an influx of emails from yet more journalists and bloggers asking to interview me exclusively, and a smattering of hate mail, and also an offer from one of those vile tea detox brands asking me to promote their product to my whopping 213 Instagram followers now that I am apparently an international icon for all that is wrong with the world.

Prior to today, all I really received were emails like "Have you noticed how you have become so fat and hopeless?" and generous offers for $1 liposuction in Outer Mongolia, but now that heyday of spam is apparently over.

1.20 p.m.

Though I'm getting used to lunchtime being an unbelievably traumatic affair, today it reaches all new levels, now that I am known internationally as a slut of the highest order.

Kids listen in on my hushed conversations with Ajita and record our mumblings on their phones. We're only discussing which movie we wanna see this weekend, but still. They snap pictures and take videos and look at my nudes for the thousandth time while masturbating into their sloppy lasagna. [Again, I made this last one up, which you will not be at all surprised to learn. If you are currently consuming lasagna or any other baked pasta dish, I apologize for the mental image.]

I know citizen journalism is meant to be a positive movement, and for authentic coverage of protests and police brutality and natural disasters, yes, I can see the benefits, but this? Really?

Teens must send thousands, if not millions, of explicit photographs to each other every single day. Why is mine so damn interesting? Debating the legality of revenge porn is one thing. Showcasing my body for sport is quite another.

And, fellow students, do you really think Fox News is going to pay you for your under-the-bench photo of my crossed-over knees just because I'm having an unwarranted moment in the limelight? Are you really that desperate for a few extra quarters?

Ajita tries her best to distract me and continue with our conversation about whether or not to see the big-budget thriller or the subtitled art-house movie, but eventually we give up and head for the woods to live out the rest of our lunch hour alone and in peace.

Well, you know, except for our phys ed teacher a.k.a. Crossfit Monkey. But I'm starting to find him strangely comforting. He doesn't exist in the same realm of the universe as us mere mortals, always thinking about how many push-ups he can do before he passes out, so chances are he hasn't seen me naked. Always a win.

2.34 p.m.
Ms Castillo goes a bit "oh, captain, my captain" on us in English this afternoon. She's picked up on the air of animosity and flatulence in the classroom and tries to give us all a motivational

speech about the importance of kindness and abstinence, etc. Anyway it was kind of ruined by the chorus of "you don't even go here", but it was sort of sweet for her to try and make things a bit less crappy for me.

But then she corners me after class, waiting until everyone else leaves before sitting me down and smiling in the most patronizing of ways. "Oh, sweet child." In a very adulty way, I resist the urge to start singing Guns N' Roses at the top of my lungs, instead plastering a receptive expression on my face. "You've had a tough time, haven't you?"

I've had this exact conversation with almost every single teacher in school. Soon as I mess up, by their standards, they take me to one side and instigate a long and painful exchange about my orphan upbringing. They take one look at my over-worn clothing and unkempt scarecrow hair and think I'm a tragic Annie-like figure, and usually I don't have the heart to ruin the charade.

Another syrupy-sweet smile. "It can't have been easy, losing your parents at such a young age."

I shrug. What does she want me to say? "I've had thirteen years to get used to it."

Then she goes into full concerned-grown-up-mode and I get a Shakespearean monologue about how the effects of deep trauma like losing parents can often take a while to manifest. Then: "All I'm saying is that nobody blames you for acting up, and you have a large support system around you no matter how this situation turns out, okay?"

There it is. That buzz phrase adults love: "acting up". It's hilarious because they often use it in the context of behavior they themselves also participate in, such as sex and alcohol. One of the reasons I love my grandma so much is that she's never once uttered those three syllables in my direction.

Normally I'd let it go, but for some reason this bugs me so much more than normal. Probably because I'm guessing she hasn't pulled Vaughan to one side like this.

"Sorry, Miss Castillo, but can you define 'acting up' for me? I'm struggling to understand what you mean."

A sympathetic head-tilt. "Our Lord does not support premarital sex, Izzy. You know that."

My ruthless snark rears its ugly head just at the right/wrong time. "Oh! Well, fortunately I'm an atheist, and I have it on good authority that the scientific universe doesn't concern itself with the romantic activity of teenage girls."

Her hand flutters to the dainty cross necklace around her neck, as if it's an inanimate incarnation of "our" Lord himself, whose ears are too delicate to hear such blasphemy. Though I'm willing to bet that if said Lord really is all-seeing and all-knowing, he's witnessed a hell of a lot worse.

"He still loves you, Izzy. There's always forgiveness for those who ask. I hope you know that."

Smirk. "Awesome. In that case, I've got some more acting up to do before I have him wipe my record clean."

I'm taking it too far. I know I am. A little more meekly, I add, "Am I excused?" People in my hometown take religion very seriously, and poking the bear with offensive banter is not advisable unless you want to be chased down main street with a pitchfork.

[Which incidentally is coming my way anyway. Stay tuned.]

2.59 p.m.

In the hallways and the cafeteria I am an A-list celebrity. Kids I don't even know seem to be torn between a) sucking up to me and trying to get all of the goss so they can sell it to the *Daily Mail* and b) standing in front of me and doing impressions of a Labrador humping an Ugg boot. Some even attempt both which I suppose is commendable in its own special way.

While waiting for math to begin, I give in and read one of the more enticingly headlined articles about me: "Why You Should Care About Izzy O'Neill's Nudes." It should be fairly obvious why I chose this particular feature, since I myself am struggling to understand what all the hoo-hah is about.

In a plot twist so obscene it's bordering on implausible, the feature is essentially a defense of me and my actions. Firstly, it opens with an image gallery of all the gross things politicians and journalists and sleazeballs the world over have been saying about me via Twitter. For example:

"Despite what Kim K wants you to think, feminism is NOT flashing your tits and vaj to the world. Have some class, ladies."

"Nothing less attractive than a slut. Put some damn clothes on, girl."

"Those teen nudes are beyond disgusting. How have we raised our young generation so poorly? How did we FAIL so BADLY?"

"I know we're supposed to be outraged about these Izzy O'Neill nudes but . . . HOLY HELL. Thanks for sharing #nicetits"

"Izzy O'Neill and Zachary Vaughan symbolize everything that's wrong with teen culture."

But then this kick-ass female columnist goes on to retaliate against every single one on my behalf, circling everything back to victim-blaming and violation of privacy. Sending nudes as an eighteen-year-old isn't a crime. Revenge porn *should* be.

Hear fucking hear.

3.51 p.m.

I can't believe what's just happened. Except I can, and that's what makes it even worse.

Math class is, as usual, a form of mental torture on a par with those Russian sleep-deprivation experiments. But I keep myself to myself, pretending to have the faintest idea what people are on about when they say sohcahtoa, and generally watching the clock on the back wall as every second slips painfully by. Then, against all the odds, the school bell rings. Everyone has already started packing up, surreptitiously zipping up their pencil cases under the desk while coughing loudly, and I am no exception.

Before I can escape, though, Mr Wong says, "Miss O'Neill, can I see you for a moment?"

At the mention of my name, everyone's heads whip around. They watch me like I'm a sitcom character, eager for a slice of my humiliation. They're hungry for it now. The nude pictures whetted their appetites, and now they want more.

Standing just in front of his desk, I chew the inside of my lip, feeling as trapped and powerless as I have for days. "Yes, sir."

To the dismay of my classmates, he shepherds them all out and closes the door behind him. I'm fully anticipating another Castillo-esque lecture on my abhorrent behavior.

When he crosses back to the desk, he sits on the front of it, leaning uncomfortably close to me and with his legs spread, like the "just call me by my first name" meme that made the rounds a few years back. He is clearly still working very hard on his nonexistent reputation as a cool teacher.

When he doesn't immediately say anything, I ask, "What can I do for you, Mr Wong?"

He nods weirdly, like he's appreciating something funny I've said or done. Smirking in an uncomfortable way I can't quite put my finger on. "You're handling this very well, Miss O'Neill."

"Sir?"

"All the media attention." He stares at me intently. "You're holding your head up high, and I like that." I can smell tuna salad on his breath.

I take a few steps back, putting some much-needed distance between us, and lean against a front-row table. "Umm, thank you, sir."

"You're not ashamed of who you are, are you, Izzy?" A creepy smile that makes the hair on my arms stand on end. "Not that you should be. Not . . . one . . . bit."

Then his eyes drop south, and that's when I know: he's seen the photos. He's picturing them right now. He's staring through my clothes, at the naked body he knows is underneath.

The old Izzy, the girl that existed before this all went down, might've answered back. Might've called him out, or told him to back the hell off. But she's gone now, and all I can do is run from the room, my eyes stinging and goosebumps covering every inch of me. Run down the hallway, run past a

238

concerned-looking Carson, run out of the front doors until I'm gasping in fresh air like my life depends on it.

Standing on the front steps and trying to catch my breath, I want to claw my skin off. Despite all of the things that make me *me* – my personality, my heart, my sense of humor – I've been reduced to nothing more than a grainy filter and a pair of tits. To a mere sex object.

I wonder whether I'll ever stop feeling so dirty.

4.17 p.m.

I feel bad for pushing past Carson in the hallway earlier, so once I've calmed down in the bathroom – slathering lip balm all over my tear-dried lips – I venture back out to my locker in the hope of bumping into him again. I get my wish, but not in the way I wanted. Not even close.

A handful of basketball players are gathered by the lockers opposite mine, and Carson is among them. They're all carrying their kit bags and heading to practice, by the looks of things. None of them see me as I cross to my locker and fiddle with the combination, hands still shaking from my mini-meltdown. I figure I'll try and catch Carson later, when he's alone. I'm not in the mood to deal with the shoulder jostling and inappropriate comments from his teammates.

Turns out I'm subjected to them anyway.

". . . pictures. Like, damn. Girl's got a body on her, right?" a

239

short dude I don't really know is saying. He sniggers and spins a basketball on his index finger while Carson fishes around in his locker.

My ears prick up. Are they talking about me?

Don't be paranoid, O'Neill. Probably just discussing some girl he's dating.

Baxter pipes up. "Seconded. That nipple piercing is . . ." He kisses the tips of his fingers to his lips as he smacks them, like a French waiter complimenting a bowl of onion soup. They all laugh.

"Not that I'd touch her with a bargepole," the short dude chips in. "Not after the whole world's seen her naked. Supply and demand, right? If you're giving it away for free, ain't nobody gonna pay for it. Plus, she's probably riddled, right? Girl that loose gotta be carrying somethin'."

Now I know I'm not just being paranoid. They're definitely talking about me.

My cheeks burn as I bury my head in my locker. But despite being surrounded by empty peanut butter cup packets and untouched textbooks, I can still hear everything they're saying.

Or, in Carson's case, not saying.

He doesn't defend me. Not once. Just listens in silence as his friends destroy me piece by piece.

6.59 p.m.

Finally, after a never-ending *Gatsby* rehearsal, I leave school feeling utterly exhausted. Like, if I do not sleep within the next 5.2 seconds, I will disembowel a bitch very slowly and painfully using a ballpoint pen.

Was followed by reporters on my way home again, but I arrive relatively unscathed.

The more I think about what happened with Carson in the hallway, the more hurt I feel. Up until today, he's made such a point of having my back, of not treating me like dirt because of the photos. But he sat and listened to his friends pick me apart without saying a word.

Does he really care about me the way he says he does? Or is it all just an act? Does he just want me for sex? Or is it more that he's worried his friends will judge him for being with me? I don't know which is worse. That's what this entire ordeal feels like: going from bad to worse and back again.

It's exhausting, and I want it all to stop.

Remembering how refreshed and centered I felt after filming the selfie-pay skit, I sit down to try and flesh out a three-act structure plan for my latest screenplay idea – the lesbian couple with the failing marriage until one loses the power of speech. It's like pulling teeth. Except more painful. Everything I come up with is either dull and boring or incredibly clichéd. Normally I can visualize key scenes in my head, but tonight I have nothing.

Maybe I'm just too tired to focus on a big project. Maybe I should write a skit or two to get my writerly juices flowing.

Again, usually my mind is filled with hundreds of sketch ideas, and I just have to reach out and pluck one from my subconscious and get it down on paper. But nothing funny or clever or imaginative comes to mind.

I scroll through today's news, hoping something will jump out and inspire a satirical idea. I read interviews with athletes and profiles of politicians and coverage from the Middle East, but nothing is remotely funny. Especially since I have to force my eyes away from the Most Read sidebar which shows 'Senator's Son In Sex Scandal' as the fourth most viewed piece of the day.

No. No no no. Shake it off, O'Neill. Do not engage.

What about a parody? What movies have I seen or books have I read recently that I could take the piss out of without much trouble?

Nothing.

My creative resource pool feels as dry as the Sahara.

8.03 p.m.

I text Ajita. I want to tell her about Mr Wong, first of all, and also about Carson not sticking up for me. And, for once, I want to actually open up about how I'm feeling. About the panicky, powerless sensation gripping my very bones.

Feeling kinda bummed. Wanna come over?

It takes her at least fifteen minutes longer to reply than it usually does.

Sorry kid, I'm hanging out with Carlie after tennis practice. Tomorrow? xo

I shove my phone underneath my pillow and curl up under the covers, probably looking as pathetic as I feel.

10.14 p.m.

I'm just taking my makeup off when there's a buzz at the gate. After a few seconds, guess whose voice I hear at the door?

Danny's.

Thursday 6 October

1.02pm

Was so mad last night I couldn't even bring myself to type out the exchange with Mr Wells. In fact, I'm still so angry I'm just lying in bed in a vague state of furious nausea, like how I imagine Melania feels when she watches Donald remove his shirt.

So he arrives all sheepish-looking [Danny not Donald Trump] and asks to come in, and Betty kindly offers him a whiskey hot cocoa even though he drove here. He declines and asks for some privacy with her granddaughter, which is quite hilarious considering our apartment is about six square feet so there's no such thing as privacy [something I discovered around the same time I located the bald man in the canoe]. Anyway, Betty goes to the living room and promptly presses her ear to the flimsy wall, which I know because I can hear her trying to suck a poppy seed out of her false teeth from about a yard away.

"What's up, Danny?" I say in a very traditional and unIzzylike manner. At this point I'm unsure what the tone of the conversation will be, so I play it safe. [In retrospect I wish

I'd begun with, "Hello, you horrid little cretin," but you live and learn.]

Dumbledore watches with interest. Danny runs his hands through his wild hair, which is bordering on dreads at this point. I consider lecturing him about cultural appropriation, but decide against it.

He eventually says, "I just . . . wanted to see you. Make sure you're okay, with everything that's going on."

Better late than never.

We haven't spoken much since he offered me money to help with my career. Even when BuzzFeed first got hold of the nude picture story, he kept his distance. So it kind of feels like this is too little, too late, but I figure he deserves the chance to make it right again. We've been friends for too long not to give him that. He's practically family, and he's going through a hard time too.

"Oh, you know, I'm all right. It sucks a bit. But you know. Fine." This is an understatement on a par with "the political landscape in the Middle East is a little tense", but I'm not in the mood to go into specifics.

Honestly, he looks terrible. His skin is all flaky like a dry bit of pastry, and his eyes are red-rimmed. I thought I had trademarked this esthetic last year when Ajita went away to teach textiles at a summer camp and I missed her so much I couldn't sleep, so it's strange to see it on Danny for a change.

After shuffling awkwardly for a few more seconds and absent-mindedly brushing toast crumbs off our counter [Dumbledore nearly has a seizure with excitement and immediately begins vacuuming them up], he says, "Good. I'm glad. I just . . . um, I just wanted you to know that . . . well, I forgive you, Iz."

I was not even a little bit expecting him to say this. As far as I can remember, I have not wronged him in any way, other than maybe kissing him when I didn't intend for the kissing to be a recurring event. Last time I checked, this was a thing I am entitled to do, and something menfolk do all the time. Maybe not great to do it to your best pal, but still.

"I . . . what?" For once I am actually quite speechless.

"I forgive you. Really. I do."

"But . . . why?"

"Because I don't want there to be any bad blood between us. And I want to make things work between . . ." He trails off at the sight of my furious expression.

Exasperated, I clarify. "No, I mean what exactly are you forgiving?"

He peers at me questioningly through his glasses, which desperately need cleaning. "Everything."

Maybe I'm just exhausted, or hormonal, or my bullshit tolerance levels are out of whack, but I am ready to cut him at this stage.

"Define 'everything', Danny. I dare you."

Wringing his hands together, he says, "Well, you know. Acting up. The whole sleeping around thing. Leading me on. Spending time with Ajita without me. Sending that nude. Rubbing you and Carson in my face. Crushing my flowers. Treating me like shit for offering you money. Do you really want me to make a list?"

"Sounds like you already have," I snap.

"What's up with you? I'm trying to be nice here."

"Right. You 'forgive' me for acting how every guy in high school acts. Because you're just such a Nice Guy."

"What's that supposed to mean?"

"Did you ever think maybe I don't want your forgiveness for those things?" I say. "We're not together, Danny. I can date whoever I like. I can make decisions about my own body without your approval. So shove your forgiveness up your ass."

Part of me expects him to just crumple – head in hands, dissolve into tears, the whole shebang – but he's obviously in fighting mood too, because he just snarls like Remus Lupin at a full moon and says, "You know, after everything I've done for you, you should be grateful to have people like me in your life. Not every guy would put up with this shit, let alone *still* want to be with you. And the others? Well, where are they now? On CNN talking about what a waste of space you are?"

ARE YOUUUUU KIDDDDIIIINGG MEEEEEEEEEE???????

"I should be grateful?" I yell. "To be treated with basic fucking

247

respect? Get the fuck out of my house, Danny. Right now."

I swear I hear Betty whisper, "Oh snap," through the wall at this point, but I could be hallucinating through sheer tiredness and frustration.

To his credit, he leaves.

So now I'm sitting in the cafeteria giving Ajita the full debrief, and she's just as mad at him as I am due to her pit-bullish tendencies, and in real genuine danger of giving him a rectal exam using a bottle of ketchup, when her phone bleeps. She looks down, instantly horrified.

"What? What's wrong?" I ask.

"Don't freak out . . ." she says slowly.

"Always a great start."

She chews her bottom lip, eyes scanning something on her screen. Then, without even looking at me, she shakes her head in disbelief and says:

"Carson Manning sold his story."

The bottom falls out of my gut like a trapdoor opening. "Sold his story? What story?"

Then the worst moment of my life takes place.

Her face crumples. "You told him I was gay?"

4.44 p.m.

Carson spoke to one of the regional newspapers. They asked him for his side, since he's been mentioned a ton of times on the

248

World Class Whore site, and I guess he needed the money, or has no soul, because he did it. He told them everything.

And I mean everything. Not just his opinion on all the shit that's already been covered, like that fateful night at the party [funnily enough, he doesn't mention the fact he lasted less than forty-five seconds] and my nude pictures, but stuff that's happened between the two of us since. Me texting him to apologize for everything, and thus admitting sole responsibility, according to the article. Meeting him at the basketball courts. Telling tasteless jokes about the Fritzl family.

There's a direct quote too. Calling me a whore.

There are screenshots of our text conversations in an image gallery attached to the article.

Hey, is your friend Ajita single? One of my firm-penised teammates wants to ask her out.

She is indeed single! However, I am not sure firm penises are her jam. I mean, neither are flaccid ones. Like, I just don't think penises are her preferred genitalia.

I doubt the reporter particularly cared about Ajita or the guy who wanted to ask her out. The piece is entirely focused on my disgusting manner in general, and the way teenage girls as a whole have lost all class, all self-respect and dignity – basically supporting everything the Vaughan family has been spouting ever since this atomic bomb of horse shit exploded all over my life. In fact, I wouldn't be surprised if the Vaughans paid this reporter to write such a tacky feature, to be honest.

But Ajita was collateral damage. And for that I will never forgive myself.

Carson texted me as soon as the news hit. Insisting it wasn't him, insisting we'd both been screwed over, insisting he's not that kind of guy. Insisting he'd had his phone hacked, and that everything in the paper could've been gleaned from his text messages. It's true, I guess. Maybe he *was* hacked. Then again, maybe he wasn't.

I don't know what to believe anymore. I don't even think I care about Carson right now. All I know is how terrible I feel about what I've done to my best friend.

Why did I think it was okay to joke about it when Ajita herself has never addressed it? Why did I have a lapse in judgment so sudden and severe that I threw my best friend under the bus for the sake of a punchline?

All this time, the media have been talking about my string of hideous mistakes, about how I don't think through my actions, about how I'm so shortsighted and irresponsible that I can't see how disastrous the consequences of the things I do can be.

Until now I've resisted that line of thinking. Until now I've tried to own my actions, dismissing the idea that they were mistakes at all. So I had sex. So I drank beer. So I sent a nude. Those are things millions of other people, teenagers and adults alike, are doing every single minute of every single day. Knowing deep down I'm not a bad person is all I had left to cling onto, like a life raft when I'm drowning.

But this? Ajita? This *was* a mistake. This *was* a lapse in judgment.

This *does* make me a bad person.

I try to call her – my lovely best friend I'd do anything to protect, my lovely best friend who I've hurt so badly, my lovely best friend who might never forgive me – for the thousandth time since she fled the cafeteria in tears.

She doesn't pick up.

8.59 p.m.
I just got an email from LA. My screenplay made the shortlist. And I don't care. Not one bit.

Friday 7 October

7.14 a.m.

The entire world has gone insane. And not like good, quirky insane, like Ajita after two beers or *The Rocky Horror Picture Show*.

Ugh, Ajita. My heart hurts whenever I think of her. I've sent her over a thousand texts and she won't reply.

I don't blame her.

I wonder if her parents have seen it. I wonder if she's currently fielding endless questions about it from her extended family. I wonder if I've ruined everything for her. I wonder if I was so far off the mark that it doesn't matter anyway. I wonder just how much damage I've caused.

Although it's not like I'm getting off scot-free. The garden bench picture was on the evening news last night. The evening news! Seriously, I am just some random teenage girl with a penchant for nachos and peanut butter cups and sexual intercourse. Why would the host of a primetime TV show invite some political analyst into the studio to discuss Ted Vaughan's campaign, and his flawed parenting, and the implications of his son's involvement in this stupid, small-town scandal?

Why would the entire Vaughan clan use me as a launching pad to discuss their wacko opinions on abstinence?

Why would professional journalists use the word "slut" to describe an innocent eighteen-year-old girl?

I have to go to school today because I'm falling severely behind in basically every class. At this point I would rather sit naked on a traffic cone than walk those hallways, but the stubborn streak in me is screaming like a banshee: "Fuck you guys! Fuck you all! I'll never let you fuck with me!" Except they are quite clearly fucking with me, and I'm not handling it particularly well.

For instance, last night I cried so hard onto Dumbledore that his fur became all matted with snot and saliva, and Betty had to run him a bath in the kitchen sink, and I just watched them both and continued to weep hysterically about all manner of things, such as a) the unfavorable press coverage obviously, b) my adorable grandmother and pet and how I would run through the fiery pits of hell and/or a particularly hilly cross-country trail for them, c) Vaughan turning out to be such a prick, despite his inoffensive manner at the party, d) my eyebrow still not recovering from the overzealous plucking incident and how much it accentuates my lazy eye, e) people who attempt to use "jamp" as the past participle of "to jump", f) how my best friend in the whole entire world will probably never speak to me again and it's entirely deserved, g) how I had my very own guardian angel in the form of Mrs Crannon and I've let her down, h) I was starting to fall for Carson and yet he turned out to be just another fuckboy . . . et cetera, ad infinitum.

Anyway. Long story short, I have to go to school and pretend to care about Tudor England. If I see Vaughan, Danny *or* Carson I plan to pull a full Henry VIII on their asses. I know we are not married so the metaphor doesn't quite work, but rest assured I will feel approximately zero remorse following the public beheading of those treasonous goats. I have brief concerns over probably not having the upper-body strength to lift an axe above my head, but Ned Stark makes it look very easy. I'll keep you updated.

8.05 a.m.

As per our usual morning routine, Betty sits me down for a bowl of cereal and a much-needed heart-to-heart before I haul myself to Edgewood for another day of character assassination.

I'm crunching miserably through a bowl of Lucky Charms, and she's slurping the milk from the bottom of her already demolished shredded wheat.

She finishes and smacks her lips. "Listen, kiddo, I know things are rough right now, but I promise you they'll blow over. Do you realize how short an attention span most people have? By this time next month they'll have forgotten all about you. I know weathering the storm until then isn't going to be fun, but you have so much going for you. The screenplay, for example! That's such incredible news about being shortlisted. Mrs Crannon must be so thrilled."

"I haven't told her yet," I mumble.

"Well, what are you waiting for? Get your ass into school, put a smile on that lovely face of yours, and tell your mentor that she has every damn reason to be proud of you. All right?"

"All right," I lie, knowing I'm still far too embarrassed to show my face in Mrs Crannon's office. I'm not sure I'll ever be able to look her in the eye again. Whether I'll be able to look *anyone* in the eye. I'm even struggling to meet Betty's worried gaze, even though I know she loves me unconditionally.

The shame is seeping into my bones. They feel heavy as I leave the sanctuary of my tiny home and out into a world full of people who despise me.

8.27 a.m.

More journalists hound me on the way to school, and it's infinitely worse without Ajita there to protect me. They follow me all the way to the school gates with their fluffy microphones and TV cameras and notepads and flashing Dictaphones, even though I don't say a word at any point. I am even very careful to maintain an alarmingly neutral facial expression, just in case they manage to flash a pic in which I look a) angry, b) devastated, or c) anything other than a stone-cold Ice Queen with no soul, which is how I prefer to appear at all times.

Getting through the school gates isn't any better. Though nobody approaches me, everybody stares. It sounds like a cliché, but seriously. Everybody. Stares. Not one person manages to avert their gaze as I cross the yard. I catch snatches of conversation – the usual buzzwords like whore and slut and self-respect – but don't allow myself the luxury of sticking around long enough to hear the whole shebang.

As much as I despised being chased by the Japanese kid with the phone cover, or approached by sleazy guys complimenting my nipple piercing, at least then I didn't feel like such a loner.

It's the most disconcerting sensation, being looked at but not engaged with. Hot and prickly, like you're an ant being roasted under a magnifying glass.

10.23 a.m.

Ted Vaughan is using the whole nude picture fiasco as a scapegoat for his deeply rooted misogynistic views, and has issued a staunch statement about how he longs for the good old days when women were classy and respectful and served their male masters like quiet little mice servants with no personality of their own. Something along those lines.

It's really so irritating how I have become an icon for all that is wrong with teen America. Some people try so hard to become icons, like those folks who go on reality TV shows and pretend to be completely devoid of brain cells, and yet here I am, minding my own business and having sex on garden benches and sending naked pictures of myself to fuckboys, and somehow the whole country suddenly knows who I am.

There are actual, genuine teenage icons out there. People who fight for equality, fight against injustice, fight for human rights. Give *them* this much attention. I am entirely undeserving.

My newfound celebrity status makes school borderline intolerable. Someone has graffitied "Izzy O'Neill for President!" in a toilet cubicle, which is completely insane and baffling on a number of levels, and then someone else has added "of the Whore Society" in pink highlighter. I will concede this is slightly amusing and far more innovative than most of the abuse being hurled my way, but still.

While I'm peeing and admiring the semi-originality of the libel before me, I hear a couple of girls enter. Their voices sound young – freshmen maybe. Their conversation goes something like this:

"So we were just texting, like, back and forth, you know? Like, the banter was flowing so easily, he's really funny, like, super hilarious, and I was just bouncing off him, you know? He's just so easy to talk to, so different to other guys our age, you know?"

"I know, yeah." At this point I am extremely relieved that we have established the knowledge of Girl Two.

"And then out of nowhere he starts trying to sext me! Like, asking what I was wearing, what I'd do if we were together. It was so awkward, but I just played along because I didn't want him to think I'm frigid, you know?"

Good grief.

"Oh my God, Louise! I can't believe you!"

"I know! Then, you'll never believe this, he asked me to send a picture. I was like, eww, no! I wouldn't want to end up like that Izzy O'Neill girl, you know?"

"Ugh, I know. I'm surprised she hasn't killed herself yet."

The looks on their faces as I exit the cubicle at this point are comedy gold, but for some reason I don't feel like laughing.

10.59 a.m.

Neither Ajita nor Carson seem to be in school. I'm quite relieved about Carson because although I don't want to admit it to myself, I was actually starting to care a lot about him, and I'm pretty devastated that he turned out to be even worse than the rest of them. And I hate, more than anything, that Danny was right.

"*Not every guy would put up with this shit, let alone* still *want to be with you. And the others? Well, where are they now? On CNN talking about what a waste of space you are?*"

So yeah, I'm glad Carson isn't here. As much as I want to tear him limb from limb for what he did, I'm just not really up for a big confrontation.

In fact, I'm not really up for anything anymore. Although usually I am more hyperactive than your average cocker spaniel [this is an absurd and blatant lie: I am and always have been lazy to my very core], these last few weeks have drained the life out of me. Energy is a thing of the past.

This is going to sound really morbid, but lately all I want to do is go to sleep and not wake up for a significant period of time. Not because I want to be dead, or anything. I don't. I'd never give those toilet girls the satisfaction, for one thing. But being alive feels a lot more difficult than it used to, and I'd really appreciate a prolonged stretch of time off, and to be able to wake up when all of this is ancient history.

Oh, the perils of being internationally reviled simply because of who you are as a person.

You know what? I'd stay internationally reviled forever if it meant Ajita would forgive me. I wish she was in school, just because it'd mean she's relatively all right, and that her parents haven't burned her at the stake or sent her to one of those awful correctional facilities for non-straight people.

Why did I do this? Seriously, what was my thinking when I sent that text to Carson? That's the problem. I wasn't thinking. Not at all. And I've done so, so, so much damage through sheer negligence. It's deeply concerning – that I can screw up so epically and irrevocably, and not even be aware I'm doing it until it's too late.

Why am I like this? I know my generally apathetic and humorous nature can be endearing. [At least, I assume that's why you've stuck with me for so long. You're over 50,000 words into my story and you're still here! You deserve a medal, I tell you.] But this is not okay. It's not okay that I'm like this.

I send Ajita one more message:

I'm so sorry. I'm so, so sorry. I love you. And I'm sorry. Please talk to me. Or don't. Because I definitely don't deserve it. But just know how sorry I am. I'm so lost without you xxx

Anyway, Vaughan's in school today, but he's deftly avoiding me. He's probably heard about how I plan to decapitate him in a brutal Westeros-style murder situation.

Then – because everything I thought I knew about myself and those around me appears to have been blown out of the water – I start to wonder whether he's really the one I should be hating here. Yeah, he made that ill-judged speech in the cafeteria that ended up hitting the press, and he has been a bit of a dick to me on several occasions (e.g. stomping on my flowers), but I sort of understand his thinking. It all boils down to the fact he's scared of his dad. And yeah, he does stupid stuff without thinking – in the same way I do apparently – but I don't think there's any genuine malice there. Just fear, and a desperate need for approval.

The person I should really be pissed at is the person who turned this from something personal between Vaughan and me into a fully fledged scandal. The person who made that website. The person who leaked my nude photo. Because that was cold, and calculated, and vicious. That *was* malicious.

I need to find out who it is.

11.45 a.m.

When I'm walking out of biology class after a highly traumatic dissection of a pig's heart, I see the last person I expect to bump into at school: Betty.

She's leaving the principal's office, and looks absolutely furious about something. The principal, a stern fellow with a big gray mustache, goes to shake her hand, but she totally shuns him, flat out ignoring the peace offering and storming away. She nearly knocks over a gaggle of girls gathered at the water fountain like gormless geese. [Check out dat alliteration. In the unlikely event you are studying this book for a high-school English class, please do feel free to point out my astonishing grasp of literary devices. Between you and me it was just a happy accident, but your teacher doth not need to know this.]

Betty finally spots me gaping at her and approaches with a look of wild hysteria in her eyes. "Izzy! Darling granddaughter! Why did you not inform me that your principal is a cretinous goblin with the worst breath I have ever encountered in my life?"

She's speaking so loudly that everyone within a thirty-mile radius can hear, but I'm truly beyond caring at this point. To say my reputation is in the gutter would be an understatement of epic proportions, so really how much worse can a mad, raving loony of a grandmother make things?

"Betty-O. Dare I ask what you're doing here?"

A strained smile. "Well, Iz-on-your-face, I —"

"Hilarious new nickname by the way."

"Why thank you, I do try. Anyway, I thought I'd have a chat with your principal about his complete lack of action in determining the founder of the World Class Whore website, and his apparent disinterest in the way you're being treated in this godforsaken sanctuary for cretinous goblins."

A small crowd has gathered to listen to our conversation, including Mr Wong. To the average onlooker, it appears he's abandoned an AP class just to get a good vantage point for this unlikely scenario: a lunatic grandma set loose on the halls of a so-called cretinous goblin sanctuary. But I know the truth. He's probably just watching his back; making sure I haven't ratted him out. That this dramatic confrontation isn't about him.

"And? What did he say?"

She turns beetroot-colored at this point. "Funny you should ask! He said that while the website is being investigated, the school has limited resources and cannot prioritize instances of a self-inflicted nature."

WTF? "Self-inflicted?! Someone hacked into my phone! That's victim-blaming. And revenge porn is a big deal. It's illegal in at least thirteen states."

"Exactly what I said, Iz-on-your-face, but the twat goblin just made some sanctimonious remarks about self-respect. He also said that while revenge porn isn't illegal in our state, having sex in public *is*, and we should be thankful nobody is pressing charges."

"It was on private property!"

"I know, I know. But he seems to think that I should, I quote, 'lie low and not make this any worse than it already is'."

I puff air through my cheeks. "Shitting hell."

"Yes. Shitting hell indeed."

The murmuring crowd remains gathered around the principal's office long after Betty departs. I just hope my comment about victim-blaming rings true, even to just a handful of them.

I had my phone hacked. I had my privacy violated. I had my personal life broadcast across the country. And I'm tired of feeling like a criminal for it.

When Betty leaves, I head straight for the woods. It's the only place on this godforsaken campus that you can find any space to breathe. And I'm desperate to get away from the eyes, the constant eyes on me, the never-ending stares that follow me wherever I go. It's suffocating.

But when I get to the clearing, Danny's there. He's sitting on the ground, back against the tree I leaned against when we had that first confrontation all those weeks ago, after I accidentally kissed him.

His head is in his hands, skinny shoulders shaking. Is he . . . crying? I haven't seen him cry since we were twelve years old.

A twig crunches under my foot, but his ears don't prick up. He hasn't seen or heard me yet, and all I want to do is to turn and walk away. The last words he said to me burn through my mind.

"You know, after everything I've done for you, you should be grateful to have people like me in your life. Not every guy would put up with this shit, let alone still *want to be with you."*

Just walk away, Izzy. Walk away.

It's not that easy, though. When you've been so close to someone for so long, seeing them hurt or sad breaks you a little bit. It's an animal instinct to protect them. They're your family, and even if you're mad, even if you've been in a fight, it all gets put on the backburner if one of you is upset.

"Danny," I say carefully, not wanting to give him a shock. But he doesn't hear me. Louder: "Danny?"

He freezes, caught in the act. Then sniffs, wipes his nose and says, "Go away, Izzy."

"No," I reply, defiant. I edge closer. "You're upset. We can put the fight on pause. What happened?"

"Why do you even care?" His voice is sad, but slightly venomous. "I mean nothing to you."

"You know that's not true," I say, persevering through his stubbornness. "You're my best friend. I care when you're hurt."

I step forward until I'm right beside him, but he still doesn't look up at me. He just stares straight ahead, teeth gritted.

"What happened, Danny?" I try again. "Talk to me. Is it your parents?"

For a second he looks like he's considering telling me, but eventually he shakes his head, dissolving into fresh tears. "Please. Just go."

So I go.

12.36 p.m.

Lunchtime. Cafeteria. I'm sitting alone on a bench, trying to eat my grilled cheese and tomato soup in peace. I've accidentally put too much salt in the soup so every time I have a spoonful my face resembles a bulldog sucking a lemon, but in the grand scheme of my life at present I'm sure this is not the greatest tragedy I'm facing. Still, it's taken me a good half-hour to even make a dent in the bowl, and at this point it's just all cold and lumpy.

Carlie and her gang of tennis-playing cronies are sitting on the bench behind me, and for the most part I'm barely listening to what they're saying because, for all their chit-chat about balls, it's not the entertaining kind. But then I hear something that pricks my ears up.

". . . that Ajita chick," a white girl with cornrows [no, really] says to Carlie. "Is it true? Are you two having a thing?"

"Ugh, God no," Carlie says, as though she's never heard anything more disgusting in her life. "She's so annoying. She follows me around like a lost puppy. I only invited her to trials to be polite, and now she's on the team I can't get rid of her."

The underlying anger I've been trying to bury for weeks begins to bubble a little hotter.

"Really?" another girl asks. "You seemed to be having a nice time in the woods together last week, and if the leaked texts from that Izzy slut were anything to go by . . ."

The whole table giggles. God, I hate high school.

"Shut up, all right?" Carlie snaps like the stick of celery she's gnawing. "Why would someone like me be interested in someone like her? She's a midget, she thinks she's hilarious, she's got these weird Indian parents –"

As calmly as I can muster, I stand up, pick up my bowl of cold, oversalted soup, and pour the entire thing over Carlie's head.

Gasps and squeals ripple around the table as Carlie screams infernally. Lumps of unblended tomato trail into her open mouth and down her cleavage. It smells like a sauce factory explosion. People all around the cafeteria stop and stare, pointing disbelievingly at the unfolding scene.

Standing over her like a disapproving parent, I sneer at Carlie, whose smugness is now completely obscured by red chunks. "You will never, *ever* be good enough for Ajita Dutta."

And then I storm out. Or at least I try to. Before I even reach the door, someone grabs my arm. Mr Richardson.

"Miss O'Neill. Principal's office. Now."

2.25 p.m.

"You could've given her third-degree burns." Mr Schumer's angry voice is even quieter than his normal voice. He's intimidating in that cold, calm way, like President Snow in *The Hunger Games*.

His office is impossibly neat and orderly, and he never has the radiator turned on, so I can practically see my breath. It's like a morgue.

I sit in front of his desk, refusing to be sheepish or remorseful, because I'm not. "But I didn't burn her. The soup was cold."

"You didn't know that."

I match his calm, measured tone. "I did. I'd been eating it a mere thirty seconds earlier."

There's a silent standoff in which all we can hear is the buzzing of the strip lighting and the vague sound of the road outside.

"Why did you do it?" he asks, but I can tell by his voice there's no right answer. He's just trying to vilify me even more; to prove that I'm some uncontrollable monster.

"Because they were disrespecting my best friend." On the chair next to me is Betty's scarf. She must've left it here earlier. Nothing but a coincidence of course, but it gives me strength. It feels like she's here with me. I pick it up and wrap it around my neck, inhaling her scent – whiskey and cocoa.

An awful sneer. "Oh. I'm surprised you're familiar with the concept of respect."

My anger flares again, but I do everything in my power not to erupt. To prove I'm capable of self-control. "They're bullies."

He leans back in his chair, robotically, not breaking eye contact. "Just because someone acts in a way you don't agree with, doesn't mean you have the right to punish them for it."

I scoff. "See, that's what I'm having a little trouble wrapping my head around, Mr Schumer. Because a few weeks ago I too acted in a way some people didn't agree with. And ever since that moment the world has done nothing but punish me."

Again, our headteacher says nothing. But I don't miss it when his traitorous eyes drop to my chest, even though it's only for a split second.

He's seen the photo too. Of course he has.

I jut my chin out defiantly. Before I can talk myself out of it, I add, "And since it's such an important subject to you, maybe you want to have a word with your faculty about respect. A certain math teacher can't keep his eyes off me. Especially when he keeps me behind after class just to make inappropriate comments." His eyes narrow. The light catches on his expensive watch and flashes in my face, but I don't flinch. I power through. "Don't you want to know which teacher I'm accusing of sexual harassment, Mr Schumer? Or should I just go straight to the school board with my complaints? I don't mind either way."

Sneering disparagingly, he replies, "You can try. But after your antics I'm not sure there's a single board member who would take your allegations seriously. Miss O'Neill, it doesn't escape my attention that all this is a *little* convenient. You're remembering these inappropriate incidents just now, when you're facing disciplinary action? Falsely accusing my staff of harassment will not get you off the hook."

My blood spikes red hot, and I fight the urge to clamber over the desk and tear his face off.

"I should suspend you immediately. But I won't."

I snort. "Let me guess. Because I'm a tragic orphan?"

"Something like that."

We stare each other down for a few more minutes. That doesn't sound like much, but there are certain times in your life when you realize just how long a minute is, such as when waiting for another driver to let you slip into their lane during a traffic jam, or when waiting for a microwave meal to cook. This is one of those times.

I feel like he's waiting for me to apologize, but I won't do it.

Eventually he says, "You may go. But if this happens again I won't be so lenient. Your behavior has already attracted a wealth of unwanted attention to our school, Miss O'Neill, and by continuing to act up you're only making it worse for yourself. I know you've had a troubled upbringing, but there's only so much understanding we can give before we have to take action."

Now I feel like he wants me to thank him for letting me off the hook, but again, I won't do it.

I walk out without a word.

4.47 p.m.

Desperate to have my faith in the world restored, I stop by Mrs Crannon's office after final bell. Instead of candy wrappers, she's surrounded by balled-up tissues and a tube of menthol oil, and her nose is redder than a baboon's behind. Bless her.

And yet, at the sight of my weary expression, she's the one offering me sympathy. "Oh, Izzy. You poor thing. How are you doing?"

My skin crawls. The idea that this lovely, warm and kind woman has seen my vagina is so sickening, so gut-wrenching, that I can barely breathe. But I'm getting used to having the wind knocked out of my lungs, and I try to push past it.

Swallowing hard, I perch on a desk instead of condemning myself to several minutes of torture-chair hell. "I'm okay,

I guess. I just don't know how I'm supposed to respond to it all, you know? Should I be fighting back? Or lying low for the time being?"

She blows her nose like a trumpet, mumbling against the tissue. "Well, I think only you can answer that. There's no right answer. Just do what feels most comfortable, and know that you've done absolutely nothing wrong. Those of us who truly care about you know that too, and don't look at you any differently."

Even though she's being sweet, my cheeks burn with embarrassment as I let it really, truly sink in that my middle-aged drama teacher has seen me naked. You know those dreams you have when you're a kid, that you accidentally go to school without any clothes on, and everyone stares and there's nowhere to hide and you just want to die?

That's my reality.

I can't do this.

I'd planned to chat to her about my screenplay, but I'm too mortified. I leave without even saying goodbye. Maybe she calls after me, but I can't hear anything over the blood roaring in my ears and the self-loathing rippling through my veins.

4.59 p.m.

I almost don't see him.

I'm hurrying down the hallway in the arts and social sciences building, chin tucked to my chest and heart beating wildly, dreaming of the moment I hit the fresh air, but knowing deep down it won't make me feel any less dirty.

Mercifully, there are no other students around. Most are either at team practice – yes, on a Friday night, because sportsball is evil – or cutting loose for the weekend. Feeling excited about the weekend is an alien concept to me these days.

Because it's so quiet, the soft remixed reggae floats out into the corridor even though the door to the art studio is closed. It's so out of place, so incongruous, that it jars in my subconscious. It takes me back to a very specific time and place in the not-so-distant past – to Baxter's party, sipping beer on the soft couch with Carson pressed up against my shoulder. Before . . . everything.

I stop in my tracks. The art studio is just down the hall and, while the door is shut, the blind over the window hasn't been pulled down. Curiosity gets the better of me and I edge closer, the music growing louder as I do. It's not as intense as it was at the party; it has that tinny quality you get when you play songs through your phone speakers. But it's definitely the same song.

Carson has his back to the door as he paints, working on a giant canvas propped up on an easel. As I creep toward the window, I try to get a better look at what he's drawing, but his body obscures the middle of the canvas. Around the edges, in the background of whatever he's shielding, is the star-spangled banner, painted in the same red and white I saw speckled on his shirt back when he kissed me in the hallway; the same blue that stained his hands.

A brush in his hand, he dabs away at something I can't see, leaning close to the canvas and examining his work in painstaking detail. I'm transfixed, but I also feel like I'm violating his privacy. He once offered to show me his work someday, but like I say. That was before.

I'm about to walk away, to leave him to the painting session he's obviously skipped basketball practice for, when he swivels his body to the side, reaching for some more paint. His shirt lifts up as he does, exposing a strip of toned torso, but for once that's not where I'm looking.

Painted in deep turquoise on the center of the canvas is the Statue of Liberty, piggybacking on an African-American slave. The slave is sweating with the exertion of carrying the statue, and bleeding from whip wounds on his chest. Behind him are hundreds of other slaves, getting smaller and smaller as they fade into the background; into the fabric of the American flag. The colors are vivid and textured, and the light and shade are so expertly manipulated that the Statue's torch seems to shine only on her, not the slaves below.

Damn, Carson is *talented*. He's good at basketball – hell, he's great at it – but this? This is another level. It's so good I can barely breathe.

The soft reggae remix ends. Before the next song begins, Carson twists back to the canvas, and he catches sight of me in the corner of his eye. Our gazes lock through the window. Something unreadable crosses his face. My gut instinct is to go to him, to tell him how incredible his work is. How incredible *he* is.

And then I remember. He betrayed me. He sold me out.

As I blink away my awe at his talent, another song starts, and I walk away toward the fresh air I thought I craved. But at the sight of Carson, I know the truth.

All I crave is him.

6.13 p.m.

Betty has gone out to one of her ludicrous evening classes. They run them for free at the community center – I think Friday nights are yoga finger-painting, whereby they have to paint nude pictures of each other while holding impossible poses. Laugh all you want, but Betty now has the flexibility of a double-jointed circus freak, and the paintings get less creepy the more you look at them.

So yeah, she's out all night, meaning I have some time to do some digging around on the internet to see if I can figure out who exactly made my life a living hell – and why – since the school board apparently gives precisely zero shits. Betty's absence is doubly beneficial because a) I can cry all I want in the process without worrying her, and b) I don't have to share the Wi-Fi, which is a bonus because she's always downloading movies illegally, despite the fact she's never once been able to successful open any of the files. She is the world's worst pirate.

I make myself a pumpkin spice latte using bargain-basement coffee creamer, and settle down on the couch with Dumbledore and a box of tissues at the ready [which means a very different thing to teenage boys, I've come to understand]. And then I open the World Class Whore website.

The first few pages of the blog are just links to all the media coverage surrounding the scandal, usually accompanied by charming captions from the site owner such as: "This is what happens when you're such a world class whore!" Even though it still stings, I'm not interested in this. I need to go back to the beginning.

I press "previous page" until I hit pay dirt. The very first post. The picture of me having sex with Zachary Vaughan on a garden bench. Caption reading: "Izzy O'Neill, slut extraordinaire, in action." There are some tags too: #slut #whore #sex #bitch #noshame. Below are 1,704 comments.

Crap. When I first found this site, the picture only had two comments, both from anonymous users and both fairly standard iterations of what a slut I am. But 1,704? How am I supposed to sort through all of these?

I start with the top-rated comments. Trawl through

dozens of posts about how nobody will ever take me seriously after this, about how I've ruined any hope of a career, about how I deserve to burn in hell for all of eternity because I'm having sex outside of marriage. Huh. Maybe Castillo is a prime candidate.

What I'm really looking for are replies from the owner of the WCW blog themselves, anything I can use to glean hints from, but there are surprisingly few. Just the odd "preach" or "amen!" or "God bless" when someone particularly vile says something derogatory about me. So I guess the site founder is on the religious side of things, which is not exactly a surprise, but that's about all I've got.

A quick flip through Facebook shows me Vaughan got his offer from Stanford. There are 403 likes and 189 comments on his status, not one of them mentioning his dick pic. I don't know why I'm even surprised.

I open a new tab: Twitter. I haven't checked it once since this all kicked off, and I'm not sure I'm emotionally prepared for the inevitable deluge of hurtful slander being thrown my way. But then I think, how much worse can it possibly be? Everything horrible that could potentially be said about me has already been thrown out there in the public domain. There's no stone left unturned. It's been well established at this point that my lopsided boobs and I deserve the most painful of demises. So, Twitter, do your worst.

After scanning my tags, searching my name and scrolling through the feed for ten minutes or so, I'm not surprised by the insults. There really is nothing new. Not from the hundreds of politicians and right-wing journalists and religious organizations condemning me, nor from the regular people reacting to the story, nor from the school kids I genuinely believed were my friends. The tweet from deadpan queen Sharon – "Am I the only one who doesn't see the appeal? Girl should rly lose some weight before her next nude leaks" – hurts a bit, especially after I took her under my wing and invited her to appear in our sketches, but I move on as fast as I can.

Ted Vaughan is louder than them all, vehemently posting every hour about me and his angelic son. I'm scum, I'm a whore, I have no self-respect, I'm everything that's wrong with millennials. I'm out to destroy his son's life, to sabotage his future career, to make him look like the bad guy when really I'm the one who has no place on this planet. Blah blah blah.

But what I am surprised by is the sheer number of people defending me. There's support from other teen girls fighting my corner, saying I'm beautiful and unapologetic and deserve respect no matter what. From feminist organizations discussing consent and misogyny. From columnists exploring gender inequality and slut-shaming, demanding that Zachary Vaughan be held to the same level of public scrutiny for his dick pic.

For every negative comment, there's a positive one to match.

It should feel good, but it doesn't. It's too much. This is all too much.

Betty is out. Ajita and Danny both hate me. Even Dumbledore is more interested in licking his own asshole than cuddling with me.

The whole world is watching me suffer. Enjoying it even. Everyone knows who I am, everyone has something to say about me. And I have never felt more alone in my life.

Saturday 8 October

8.15 a.m.

I barely slept last night because of the aggressive palpitations rippling through my chest. I think I finally dozed off at around 5 a.m., and only a few hours later I'm awoken by a knock on the front door.

Bleary-eyed, still half asleep, I strain my ears as Betty pads over and opens it.

A low voice, male, sort of familiar. Not Danny's southern twang or Vaughan's clipped upper-class lilt. It's warm, gravelly, confident.

Carson.

I can't make out what they're saying, but Betty's tone is pretty harsh. I hear the door bang shut again, and a few seconds later she's perching softly on the edge of my bed. I roll over so I'm facing her, aware my eyes are probably all gloopy and gross from last night's tears. She strokes my hair, tucking the most unruly locks behind my Dumbo ears.

"Carson's here. He wants to talk to you."

I groan incoherently.

"He said something about tomato soup, but I might have misheard him."

Betty's all hunched over and sad-looking. This debacle has aged her massively, and I know she has to work today. Just another thing to add to my endless list of things to feel guilty about.

"He insists it wasn't him. That he didn't talk to the press. Do you believe him?" she asks quietly.

"I don't know," I mumble. "I'm losing faith in pretty much everyone. Even myself. Especially myself."

"Don't say that. Don't you ever say that. You're the best person I know, and I love you very much. I'll do anything to protect you." She kisses me on the forehead as a fresh wave of sobs cause my chest to almost cave in on itself. "I'll tell him to go."

"Thank you, Grandma," I croak. "I love you too."

10.43 a.m.

Thanks to the tomato-soup fiasco, which Carlie's parents immediately told the press about, journalists have started making comments about my grandma's parenting abilities, or supposed lack thereof, and Betty herself had to talk me down from heading over to the local radio station and Hulk-smashing the hosts with all my worldly rage.

As many of the most vile insults usually are, these comments are disguised as concern, like when fat-shamers preach to the obese about their health when really they're just judgmental reptiles who don't like to look at stretch marks lest they choke on their meal-replacement shakes. These reporters are framing their comments as concern over the social-care system and its supposed failings, in the context of how an elderly woman with such a meager income was granted custody of her orphaned grandchild, and whether or not she was emotionally equipped to raise me after going through such a trauma herself, and whether it is in fact Betty O'Neill's fault that her granddaughter is such an indiscriminate whore.

You should add that to your résumé. "Izzy O'Neill: talented writer, below-average mathematician, indiscriminate whore." xo

At this point I have to imagine what Ajita's commentary would be. I think I nailed it.

Betty's acting like the public disapproval of her parenting skills isn't bothering her, but I know it's getting her down. Normally she sings upbeat Motown in the shower, and though this morning's rendition of 'Everybody Hurts' with improvized rap segments was beautiful yet haunting, I'm worried.

I read the shortlist email one more time. About how I have three weeks to act on the next round of feedback before they select the finalists. About how I show a lot of promise, and about how the judges are sure that a bright future in screenwriting awaits.

I still don't care.

12.34 p.m.

Holy fuck. I know who's behind World Class Whore. And . . . holy fuck.

The site creator made a fatal error. They set up social-media accounts for WCW and linked them all together. Then they posted the garden bench pic to the Instagram account.

And accidentally shared it to their personal Facebook account.

When I mindlessly log in while I'm eating my lunch, the first thing I see at the top of my feed is the garden bench photo, with the caption "Izzy O'Neill: World Class Whore".

It's on Danny's account.

My former best friend has ruined my life, sparked a national sex scandal, made me feel like a worthless piece of shit – all because I rejected him. All because I put him in the Friend Zone.

"After everything I've done for you."

He thought he'd earned the right to my love. And when I didn't give it to him, he retaliated by tearing me apart.

I think a dark part of me always knew it was him. I believed his denial because I wanted to; because it was easier than confronting the fact my best friend had betrayed me.

No. Looking back, he never did deny it. Not once did he say, "No, I didn't do it." Instead he said:

"I've been defending your honor for thirteen years. Protecting you from jerks at school, from social workers. From yourself."

"What are you accusing me of?"

"I can't believe this. I genuinely thought that when you asked to talk to me, you'd had a change of heart. About . . . us. But no. You're actually accusing me of setting up that blog."

"Fuck you, Izzy O'Neill."

He never denied it. And still I turned a blind eye. Let myself believe that I really knew the guy standing in front of me. That he cared too much about me to let rejection and jealousy stand in the way of our friendship. That he had seen me cry over my dead parents for so many years, and he would never do anything to hurt me.

I should be convulsing with anger right about now. I should be ranting to Ajita, or screaming in Danny's face, or seeking elaborate and brutal revenge on that pathetic prick. But I'm not.

I don't have the energy, or the conviction. I feel hollowed out by his betrayal.

And, beneath it all, bereft. Bereft of one of my best friends. I think of the Danny of even just last year. Funny and smart and protective and loyal. Happy. Lately, there have been glimmers of Old Danny – playing dumb games, taking Prajesh under his wing, supporting Ajita through her crisis over her future, wrapping his arm around me when I was being attacked in school – but there's no denying it. He hasn't been happy for a while. He hasn't been Danny.

Maybe it's because of me. Maybe it's his parents. Maybe something else; something so far below the surface he'll never let anyone close enough to see it. And yeah, that sucks. It sucks that he's going through a hard time. But sadness is not a get-out-of-jail-free card. It doesn't allow you to treat the people around you like human punchbags. Like they exist solely to make you happy again.

All of this is Danny's fault. He's become spiteful and jealous and cruel. I know that, deep down. And yet a dark part of me, the part forged in this fire of hatred, still wants to blame myself.

I loaded the gun. He just pulled the trigger.

4.09 p.m.

I decide to go over to Ajita's and beg her to talk to me. Can you feel homesick for a person? I have a constant pit of guilt and sadness in my gut. I need her. It's selfish, but I need her. I need her to not hate me anymore. There's no way I can survive this otherwise.

I arrive at her house on my rickety old bike, and it takes me a good ten minutes to pluck up the courage to walk up the drive and ring the bell. [What a boring sentence. Where has my sense of humor gone in these blog posts? Maybe Ajita *was* my sense of humor, like that Samson dude who cut off his hair and lost his super strength. Maybe I'm just not funny without her. I certainly don't feel it. Here, have an Izzy O'Neill original joke: Did you hear about the time Shakespeare used IEDs against his literary rivals? They were completely bomb-Barded. Ha. Ha ha. No, Ajita was definitely my comedic lifeblood.]

Her mom answers the door, dressed for celebration in a red sari. She doesn't say anything, just looks at me sternly. She is absolutely terrifying. She's short, as short as Ajita, and incredibly round. Knowing how intelligent she is just adds to the stress. I'm intimidated both physically and mentally.

"Hi, Mrs Dutta," I choke out, through the driest of throats.

"Izzy. What do you want?" The house is weirdly silent behind her. Usually there's so much going on, with Ajita's brother playing super-loud video games and their five cats running around and knocking things over and generally wreaking havoc on the Dutta household. But today it's like a cemetery.

"Is Ajita home?"

"No. She's not."

I don't buy this for a second. "Okay. Do you know where I might find her?"

Mrs Dutta sighs and takes off her glasses, rubbing her eyes wearily. She looks tired as hell. "I'm not sure my daughter wants to see you, Izzy. Not after the lies you've been spreading about her."

Lies. So Ajita denied it to her parents, whether or not it's true – which I still don't know for sure. It makes sense. They're hugely traditional, hugely conservative Hindus. I doubt her coming out at the age of seventeen would go down all that well. [Look, I even managed to resist a joke about people who *do* go down well. I am a reformed human. Sort of.]

"Please. I just want to explain. To apologize. Please, Mrs Dutta."

"What is there to explain? Was it just an attempt to shift the attention off yourself for a minute? Is that it?" A heavy sigh. "Do you really think our community has been blind to your antics, Izzy? Do you really think . . ." She trails off. Her words are harsh but her tone is soft as she holds up her palms. "But it's not my place to judge. You can do what you like. It's your life to ruin. Just don't involve my daughter, okay?"

My heart is shattering into a thousand pieces. "Please," I whisper, more desperate by the second. "Let me talk to her. Five minutes is all I ask."

A strange expression flits across her face. I think it's pity, and I hate it.

"My heart goes out to you, Izzy. It does. You're just a kid, and you've been through a lot. Losing your parents at such a young age . . . I wouldn't wish that on anyone. But it only excuses so much. And this? This is inexcusable."

I'm about to get down on my hands and knees and beg when I hear babbling voices behind me. A millisecond of fear flashes on Mrs Dutta's face before a giant fake smile emerges, I'm guessing for the benefit of whoever's behind me on the driveway.

Turning to see who she's smiling at, I see a group of Hindu women, around Ajita's mom's age, dressed in beautiful saris of turquoise and violet and peach. I wrack my brain for the date. Is it Navratri? Diwali? They're both in the autumn, but I'm not sure which days the festivals fall on this year.

God, I'm such a shit friend. I should know this, but I've been so self-involved lately I've barely been able to look past my own reflection. No wonder Ajita hates me.

Hissing through her teeth, Mrs Dutta mutters, "Go. Now."

I bite my lip to prevent a heaving sob from escaping, and I back away toward the women. They all stare right at me, silence falling on the small group. One of them, wearing a gorgeous sari of cerulean and seafoam, shakes her head and tsks.

Pushing past them with my head tucked to my chest, I can't look them in the eye.

As I'm mounting my bike, limbs trembling as I clamber over the seat, I hear snatches of their conversation from the doorway.

". . . sorry we didn't come by sooner, but what with all the rumors . . ."

". . . it's been such a scandal in the community . . ."

". . . we didn't know if you'd want to see us, that's all," says the woman who tsked at me.

Mrs Dutta's airy voice dismisses them. "All hearsay, I can assure you. Nothing but spiteful lies."

The magnitude of what I've done hits me all over again. One careless text has shaken Ajita's entire world – her family, her community, her life.

Whether it was true or not, this was not something she was ready for. This should've been on her terms. I stole that from her. And I will never forgive myself.

5.36 p.m.

I don't go straight home. Instead I pedal slowly around town in a strange sort of haze, completely immune to what's going on around me. I move on autopilot, only aware of my surroundings in some kind of subconscious way.

I must cycle carefully because I don't get hit by a truck or anything [which I suppose would've been nice in a poetic way, being killed in the same manner as my parents, just as I'm a hundred percent sure I've disappointed them as much as I possibly can in the short time I've spent on this planet], but there's no active thought process behind the cars I swerve to miss, or the pedestrians in the cycle lane I ding my bell at.

"*Do you really think our community has been blind to your antics, Izzy?*"

The noise of the street – engines and brake pads, laughter and gusts of wind and the beep of traffic lights – is just a vaguely muffled din. All I hear is Mrs Dutta's voice echoing vividly through my head.

"*It's your life to ruin. Just don't involve my daughter.*"

My eyes sting from exhaust fumes and tears.

"*This? This is inexcusable.*"

Is it really? Am I really beyond redemption? Surely people do worse things than I do every damn day, and yet they don't feel like this – like a complete and utter scumbag who doesn't deserve the air she breathes. Do they? Do they just do a really good job of hiding it?

A horn blares behind me, but I barely register it.

Once when I was having a low self-esteem moment – just a standard teenage drama about my lopsided boobs, even before they were on display to the world – Ajita said to me, "Izzy, it is not okay that people who wave the Confederate flag feel good about themselves and you do not." Is that still true? Or have I crossed into a realm so deplorable that even they would feel ashamed?

I think I've stopped cycling, but I can't be sure.

If this was happening to someone else, I'd insist they maintain their pride and self-respect. So you sent a nude, and had sex with a couple guys, and kissed your best friend even though you did not wish to let him enter you. So what? You behaved like a standard teenager. It's not your fault that the whole of America is inexplicably interested in your exploits just because one of your conquests was a senator's son. It's not your fault you were not in love with your best friend, and he couldn't handle it. It's not your fault this is happening to you.

Even the things that *are* your fault. The Ajita thing. You messed up. Badly. You didn't think before you spoke. You're not the first person to do that, nor will you be the last. In fact, someone else is doing it right now, right this very second. Forgive yourself.

But somehow those rules don't seem to apply to my situation. Me? I'm a scumbag. A complete and utter scumbag. All self-worth I once possessed has evaporated, and right this second, right here in the middle of a busy road in the middle of town, all I want – all I deserve – is for a sinkhole to open up beneath me and swallow me whole.

Of course, the universe doesn't work like that. Nobody who wants to disappear actually does. It's always the people like my parents, the people who have everything to live for, who get hit by drunk drivers and are eradicated forever.

The thought of my parents jolts me painfully back to the present. I'm sitting stationary at a green traffic light, cars behind me tooting angrily, some jerkwad leaning out of the window and yelling about how much of a dick I am. Yeah, dude. I know. Believe me, I know.

I start pedaling again, unsure where I'm even going. The mall's nearby. Maybe I could go for a cinnabon. The idea seems so absurd, so ridiculously normal, that I almost laugh. Almost.

Instead I round a corner, and the first thing I see as I turn into the street is a stab in the gut.

Ajita and Danny. Together. Without me.

She throws her head back and laughs at something he said. They carry coffee cups, and I know what's inside them without having to guess: peppermint hot chocolate for Ajita, Earl Grey tea for Danny. He's grinning. His hair is clean for once, and there's color in his cheeks like there wasn't last time I saw him.

And then I realize: they're better off without me. Their worlds are better without me in them.

7.48 p.m.

Betty's out again. Ping-pong tournament. You know when Forrest Gump gets back from Vietnam and is suddenly phenomenal at ping-pong? That was Betty after she lost her daughter and son-in-law. Unspeakable trauma, but on the plus side she became very talented at the most pointless sport in the history of pointless sports. [No offense to ping-pong players. But really. What is the point?]

Feeling as hollow and empty as, well, a ping-pong ball, I open up my laptop and boot up Final Draft to start editing my screenplay. I've read the opening pages so many times that I've lost all concept of whether or not they even make sense, but the judges emailed me a ton of feedback with the shortlist announcement, so at least I have some semblance of direction for the revisions. I'm grateful for the distraction, to be honest. It's keeping my tiny pea brain occupied when the rest of my world is falling apart.

I launch my email browser to retrieve the feedback, and the "unread messages (308)" aggressively reminds me of just how many people know about my scumbag tendencies. Sorting through them is too daunting, so I just search for the producer's name. Frown. It still says "unread (1)". I wasn't expecting to hear from them for another week.

Hi Izzy,

Hope you're well. I'm just dropping you a brief email with a quick competition update.

After much consideration and discussion, the judges have made the difficult decision to withdraw your entry from the Script Factor shortlist.

The recent press coverage following some indiscretions in your personal life will likely attract some unfavorable attention to the competition, which is of great concern to us. We've worked very hard over the years to build a certain kind of reputation in the industry, which is why we're so highly thought of today (and thus why reaching the later stages of the competition is still something to be very proud of!). As a result, any threat to that reputation is taken very seriously indeed.

Particularly due to the sexual nature of your screenplay, we've been forced to re-evaluate your position, and regretfully we've taken the decision to remove you from the running.

I understand this is disappointing, but we hope you continue to persevere in the screenwriting world. You have a lot of potential and the judges saw something in your work that we don't often come across.

We'd like to invite you to re-enter the competition in a couple of years' time — once the controversy surrounding your personal life has settled down (which we're sure it will), we'll be more than happy to welcome you back to Script Factor.

All the very best,

Tom

9.02 p.m.

Every time I feel like I can finally catch my breath, like I might actually survive this, something even worse steals the air from my lungs.

Oh my God. Losing everything and knowing it's all my fault is excruciating.

9.06 p.m.

When this all first kicked off I had the fleeting thought that the competition producers might find out about the scandal. But I dismissed it as standard-issue Izzy melodrama. They wouldn't possibly see the nudes, and if they did, it'd be them that should be embarrassed. I distinctly remember thinking that. That *they* should be mortified to be caught looking at a teen girl's nudes.

And yet now the embarrassment and downright shame is enough to drown me.

How the hell do I tell Mrs Crannon? She'll be devastated. I can't stop fixating on that fifty-dollar bill. I know the money is such an insignificant thing, compared to everything else, but I've been raised to appreciate its value. I've been ruled by it. Fifty dollars to me is the whole world. I agonize over that unbelievable show of love and support and confidence in me – in honor of Mrs Crannon's wonderful father. Her dead father.

I've let them both down. But not nearly as much as I've let Betty down. After everything she's done for me, everything she's given up, every last sacrifice she's made. Every extra shift she's picked up, every painkiller she's swallowed, every chance at retirement she's turned down. Every time she's put my needs before her own. She's worked and worked and worked so I can afford to stay in education, so I can afford to write screenplays in my spare time, so I can have shoes and toothpaste and running water. So I didn't have to live with the Wells when my parents died. So I could keep being me against all the odds.

I owe her the world and this is how I repay her.

9.14 p.m.

My phone bleeps. At first my heart leaps, hoping it's Ajita finally returning my messages, but instead a text from a number I don't recognize flashes on the screen.

Kill yourself, slut.

I hit delete as soon as I see it, but it's too late. The words are already burned into my brain.

9.16 p.m.

I've got something special, Tom said. They'd be happy to welcome me back. I should persevere, despite the fact I'm the lowest form of scumbag imaginable.

My conversation with Ajita about how maybe People Like Me don't belong in Hollywood feels like an eternity ago. I was right. People Like Me *don't* belong. Unless you're perfect and classy and perfect and eloquent and perfect and poised and perfect and *rich*, you don't belong. This email confirms that.

Look at Vaughan. He's done everything I've done. He drank beer, had sex, sent a nude picture. And he just got an offer from Stanford. Why is his life worth more than mine, just because he's rich and male?

My heart hurts. Imagine being deemed so lowly and awful that not even your talent and hard work are enough to keep you afloat in the career you want more than anything. Imagine one lapse in judgment stealing everything from you.

One moment can change everything. In the time it takes to send a nude, or in the time it takes to crack a joke about your best friend's sexuality, or in the time it takes for your car to be crushed by a drunk driver, your whole life can come crashing down around you.

One moment can change everything, and that's the most terrifying thought in the world.

How do we even function knowing that? Knowing how tenuous our existence is, how fragile our happiness? It's debilitating when you really think about it. And now that I've thought this thought, I can't ever unthink it.

9.21 p.m.

I used to believe I could handle everything by myself; that I didn't need help from anyone. The last few weeks have shown me how completely and utterly wrong that is. I do need people. I need my friends and my Betty. I need them so much. The irony is that I've learned this too late, and I'm already losing everyone.

I can finally admit that I need help, but nobody has the energy left to give it.

I feel so fucking alone.

9.27 p.m.

As I toss and turn in my bed, agonizing over every second of the last few weeks, my mistakes gnaw at me from the inside. All I want is a time machine.

I've figured it out, why people just sometimes spontaneously combust: regret. It's enough to set you alight.

Too much. This is all too much. And I'd do anything to make it stop.

9.30 p.m.

It's now, in probably the darkest moment of my life, that my phone bleeps again.

I almost throw my phone at the wall because I'm so sure it's more hate, so sure it's another message telling me to end it all. But, just in the vague hope it's Ajita, I look.

Another unknown number, but a different one.

Hey, Izzy! It's Meg. From math class? I hope everything's okay with you. I know you must be having a rough time, but

I just want to say that I think you're so strong and brave for the way you're handling it all. Sorry it's taken me so long to work up the courage to text you . . . I didn't want to come on too strong! Anyway, I'm around next weekend if you wanna hang out at some point? Mx

Some of the tensed-up muscles in my chest relax. I'm not alone. I'm not.

With every scrap of resilience I have left, I force myself to bury the dark thoughts – thoughts about permanent ways in which I could make all of this stop – and keep breathing.

I dry my damn eyes, pull back the covers and climb into bed, knowing tomorrow can't possibly be as bad as today.

Sunday 10 October

7.20 a.m.

I fall asleep cuddling the bottle of bleach Ajita gave me. After crying for roughly eight millennia I wake up with my standard raccoon eyes and scarecrow hair, but I wake up. And things feel a little brighter.

Pulling on a crumpled sweater and some jeans, I deliberately avoid my reflection in the mirror, knowing I probably look a bit Wicked Witch of the West. The apartment is silent. Betty must be out, or still in bed. I grab my phone and purse and head for the door.

I know where I need to go. Somewhere I haven't been since I was thirteen; since Betty let me stay off school because of a paper cut.

Outside it smells of wet grass. The sun is weak and watery, but there's no wind. The streets are that kind of Sunday morning quiet – barely any cars, barely any people, just the odd jogger and dog-walker. And pigeons. Lots and lots of pigeons.

My bike's ancient gears clank and groan as I pedal almost

robotically, staring two feet in front of the handlebars at all times. The odd thought flits into my mind, but I let each one fizzle out, not engaging with it on any real level. I feel tapped out, emotionally and physically, and it's sort of nice just focusing on the slight ache in my legs as I crest a hill I haven't mounted in so, so long.

The cemetery sits on the only hill in our town, which is generally as flat as the Netherlands. There's a tiny church, which seems empty – I think it's too early for morning mass – and one giant oak tree shading the oldest tombstones in the graveyard, most of which are covered in thick moss. They've all been tended to immaculately, though, and the grass is neatly trimmed. One fresh grave near the entrance is swarmed with bouquets of flowers and notes. It makes me sad to look at, so I turn away. I've got enough grief of my own without absorbing a stranger's.

There's a bench I used to come to a lot when I was eleven or twelve and I first got my bike. It was the first time I was really allowed to go out alone, without my grandma with me, and I used the opportunity to visit my parents a lot. I know I could've done it when I was younger, with Betty by my side, but I always got the sense she dealt with things by not thinking about them and just pushing through. Seeing the spot where her dead daughter was buried in the dirt would make it pretty hard to do that.

Overlooking my parents' gravestones – modest and plain, side by side, the exact same death date – is a memorial bench, made of a dark stained wood. It's not covered by the oak tree. Instead it sits with its back to a low stone wall, basking in the low autumn sun. Far enough from my parents that I don't have to read their names and birth dates, but close enough that I can still feel their presence.

Everything looks exactly the same as I remember it; exactly as I pictured it would be. Except for one thing.

Betty is sitting in the spot I used to, right in the middle of the bench where the plaque is. Her white-gray hair is wrapped in a purple paisley scarf, and she's leaning her arm on a walking stick I haven't seen her use in years. I've always suspected she used it when nobody was watching; when nobody could witness her needing help. She's as stubborn as me.

She doesn't look up as I approach and prop my bike against the wall, nor when I perch next to her on the bench. If she's surprised to see me here, she doesn't show it.

"How you doing, kiddo?" she asks, cradling a Thermos of coffee in her hands. She's wearing at least three silver rings on each finger, kooky old bat that she is.

"Concerned that my grandmother is wearing more rings than, I don't know, Saturn. But other than that, fine." [I know, it's incredibly frustrating that I just had an epiphany about needing the people I love, and yet I'm cracking jokes and masking the hurt like I always do. Hey. Old habits die hard.]

The lie is not in the least bit convincing. She snorts. "Right. Sure. And I'm Harrison Ford."

"I wish," I say.

"Me too. Then I could have sex with myself."

Once upon a time, in a land far, far away, this would've given me a laughter-induced stomach ulcer. But not today.

I sneak a sideways glance at her face, on the hunt for signs of crying, but her cheeks are dry and her eyes aren't red-rimmed. She just looks tired.

I sigh. Here goes. "I'm just . . . overwhelmed. So overwhelmed it's hard to process everything."

Preparing for her usual up-by-the-bootstraps, bravado-boosting pep talk, I square my shoulders. But it never comes.

After a long pause, she says in a small voice, "Me too."

And then the unthinkable happens. She lays down her stick and her Thermos, and wraps her arms around me, kissing the side of my head. Then she tucks a lock of my hair behind my ears, and strokes my cheek with her thumb. She smells how she always smells: of whiskey and cocoa.

"It hasn't been easy, has it?" she says thickly.

I don't know whether she means the last few weeks or the last thirteen years, but either way the answer is the same.

"No," I admit. "I guess it hasn't."

Letting go of the embrace, but leaving one arm draped over

my shoulders, she picks up the Thermos again, offering me a sip. I gratefully accept.

"I feel like I've failed you, Izzy," she says, voice full of a regret I hate to hear.

"Absolutely not," I insist. "You've given up everything for me. I'll never be able to repay you. I'm so grateful to have you."

A tight smile. "But I've never given you an environment in which you could talk about your emotions. You've felt like you always had to put on a brave face, always had to be cracking jokes, because that's the way I dealt with my pain. And you had no choice but to do the same."

I let these words sink in for a while. I guess it's true. I've never thought Betty made me the way I am, but I suppose I learned a lot from watching her. Every single part of my personality contains elements of her, including her flaws.

Finally I say, "Well, every kid is screwed up somehow by whoever raises them. And if I had to be screwed up by anyone, I'm glad it was you."

We both laugh at this, but it's different to our usual defiant laughter. Softer. More real.

"We're going to do better, okay?" she says, gazing not at me but at my mom's grave. "We're going to talk to each other about how we're feeling. And we're going to cry when we need to. And we're going to admit that sometimes life just isn't fucking funny."

I take a deep breath, then let it out slowly. "Okay. Agreed."

We both watch as a cleaner leaves the back door of the church with a mop and bucket, emptying the dirty water over a wall and into the field behind.

"I miss them," Betty says quietly. "Your parents. They were wonderful people." Her voice is even thicker now, and this time not with mucus. A tear slides down her cheek. And then another. And then her shoulders are shaking and it's me with my arms around her. "I could use their advice sometimes, you know? Their reassurance that I'm doing right by them. With you. With everything."

A massive lump forms in my throat and before I can help it I'm sobbing too. But it actually feels good. We hug each other tight.

She sniffs. "You're a wonderful person, Izzy. And I'm just . . . proud. To call you my granddaughter. And I know your parents would be proud of you too."

More tears spill down my cheeks against my will. "But I messed up, Grandma."

She shakes her head fiercely. "No. You didn't. The fact that everyone is so damn interested in the sex life of an innocent teenage girl is more a reflection on them than you."

I snivel pathetically into her purple tunic. A pigeon watches with interest. "I know, but . . . I haven't told you the worst part. About Ajita."

"I already know, sweetheart," she says softly, which is not usually something she's capable of due to the eternal coughing.

I'm genuinely shocked. "You do?"

"Yes. Mrs Dutta rang me."

A coil of anxiety tightens in my belly. "Oh God. What did she say?"

"She was mad. Of course, she had to explain everything from beginning to end because as you know I do not understand the interweb, and hadn't seen the article in question." A pause. "Is it true? About Ajita?"

"I don't know," I whisper. "That's the problem."

Betty strokes my hair and takes a sip of coffee from the flask. "Mmmm. Mrs Dutta seemed to think it was impossible. Literally beyond the realms of possibility. I tried reasoning with her – saying she should be open to the idea that it might be true, and try to have an honest conversation with her daughter – but . . . well. I didn't get the impression that would happen somehow."

I rub my eyes, which have finally stopped leaking involuntarily. "I wish I could be there for her. Ajita. In case it is true."

Betty frowns. "You can be."

"How? Mrs Dutta won't let me see her."

A disappointed tsk noise. "You and Ajita have been best pals for so long. Are you really going to let her homophobic mother dictate your friendship?"

I pause. "I feel like you want me to say no here, but have you met the woman? She's terrifying."

She glares at me sternly, which she has literally never done before in my whole life. "Izzy."

"I know."

And I do.

Monday 11 October

7.32am

As part of the plan I made with Betty to intercept my *Lieblings-freundin* ["best friend" *auf Deutsch*, because even in my worst times I am an educator of the masses] on the way to school, I get to Ajita's house stupidly early. Seriously, early is stupid. Never trust morning people. They have deeply rooted psychological issues and, as a person with deeply rooted psychological issues, I consider myself something of an expert on the matter.

Parking my bike across the street [and slightly around a corner so Mrs Dutta cannot gun me down with an assault rifle], I pull out my flask of coffee, take a long, hard gulp like an alcoholic's first sip of the day, and I wait.

7.33 a.m.

After waiting for roughly forty-five seconds, I find it completely unreasonable that Ajita has not yet surfaced, and consider aborting the mission in lieu of a good old "hide in the bush and cry until you spew" session, but I tough it out.

[I know. My bravery is astounding.]

While I wait, I think about the screenplay competition. Yeah, it sucks that I got kicked out. It does. Mainly I feel bad for Mrs Crannon, and a little for myself over the lost opportunity. But something Carson once said soothes me like cooling gel on a migraine.

"You can love a thing without necessarily dedicating your life to it, you know?"

I love writing. I love performing. I love making people laugh.

The school system, and society in general, would have me believe I therefore have to make a career out of it – have to use my interests and talents to plow money back into the economy. That I have to be *productive*, above all else. A gerbil on a wheel, powering the machine with my success.

And yeah, it'd be cool to sell a screenplay to Hollywood; to hear actors speak my words on the big screen someday. But if that never happens, I think I'll be okay. My passions bring me enough joy to sustain me, even if they stay at hobby status forever.

Because what matters to me above all else? The people I love. And there's not a damn thing wrong with that. If people cared more about being kind than being successful, the world would be a much better place. That's why I need to mend things with Ajita. That's why I need to protect Betty, no matter what I have to give up to do so.

I don't think I would ever have had this epiphany if it weren't for Carson. A sharp pang needles in my chest when I think of him; of the night we spent playing at the basketball courts, meeting his mom and walking home together. Of the way he made me feel warm and fluttery and safe. Of his beautiful, painful art.

Could that boy really have betrayed me? As time goes on, I doubt it more and more.

8.19 a.m.

By the time I finally see Ajita rounding the corner toward school, I'm so jittery that I've splashed coffee all over my jeans. I'm just mopping the worst of it off with my roadkill scarf when I see her, all wrapped up in a duffel coat and carrying a stack of textbooks, which is incredibly alarming on account of the fact she's never voluntarily opened a textbook in her life. She looks like something out of *Gilmore Girls*.

It takes her a split second to see me, but when she does she stops in her tracks and stares at me vacantly. As if she has no idea who I am.

I edge toward her as though approaching a rabid wolf with morning breath.

"Ajita . . ."

Her massive brown eyes shine dangerously. She looks like she's about to burst into tears, and I hate myself so much for causing it. She bites her lip and stares at the ground, clutching those books so tightly her knuckles go white. It's so cold I can see her breath.

"I'm sorry. I'm so sorry." My voice wobbles as I talk. "They say you're not supposed to ruin an apology with an excuse, which is a relief, because I don't *have* an excuse. Not a single one. That text message was just . . . wrong."

A cold silence stretches out between us. Then: "That's the thing, though," she whispers. "You weren't wrong."

There it is.

I hug her. I can't help myself. She looks so cold and sad standing in the middle of the sidewalk, surrounded by dead leaves and empty chip packets and cigarette butts.

"I wasn't ready, Izzy," she mumbles into my shoulder. "I'm still not."

"I know," I say, unleashing her from my bear grip. She's crying a little. I am too.

"Everything's just so . . . uncertain. I don't know who I am; who I want to be. *What* I want to be. And this . . . it's just so confusing. It's like this gray cloud over my future. Everything my family want for me – to be a wealthy doctor, to marry a successful man from our community, to provide 2.4 grandchildren – I just don't know if I can give it to them. Or if I even want to." She scrunches up her face and shakes her head. "I hated you, you know. When I first saw it. I hated you so much."

"That's fair. I hated me too."

"I still do, a little."

"Again. Fair."

Pressing her lips together, she finally looks up at me. Her eyes are still glistening and red-rimmed. "I need you, though. You're my best friend. And I'm kind of going through a thing that I need a best friend for." A frown. "And you are too, right? So I'm guessing you feel the same. About needing me, and all."

"Yes. It's quite gross, isn't it? Admitting we need each other."

A smile, albeit smaller than her usual Cheshire Cat beamer. "So gross. Just like your face."

"I would retaliate with 'just like your mom', but I think she has several snipers pointed at me right at this very second. One wrong word and she'll give the command."

Ajita sniffs back a snot bubble. Neither of us are particularly attractive criers, but her nose takes on a life of its own when faced with a tear-inducing situation like this one. "I also have the authority to sanction your murder, so I'd tread carefully, Izzy O'Neill. Very carefully indeed."

"Noted. Do you have the authority over other killings? I have a hit list I'd like to start working through."

"Sure. Who's first? Carson?"

"Nah," I say, draining the dregs of my coffee. "Carlie, please."

Ajita smiles properly now. "I heard what you did. Thank

311

you for sticking up for me. I can't believe Schumer didn't suspend you."

I nod. "Yeah, I was kind of hoping he would, to be fair. I could do with a week off. But I think he knew that's what I wanted, and the bastard didn't give it to me. So rude."

"I never did like him." She sniffs against the cold wind. "Okay, Carlie first. Who next?"

"Danny. I found out he started the World Class Whore website."

Ajita's eyes flash wildly. "Wait, he did *what?*"

"Yep. Sucks, huh?"

All her sadness evaporates in lieu of world-ending rage. She splutters everywhere, stomping a Doc Marten angrily. "That little son of a . . . how dare he! And to think . . . to think! He's been playing the victim all this time, manipulating the crap out of me, out of both of us, and . . . he's the one who's to blame for all this! He ruined his best friend's life out of *jealousy*?! OH MY GOD, WHERE'S MY MOM'S ASSAULT RIFLE WHEN YOU NEED IT?"

10.02 a.m.

As Ajita and I leave math class we notice Carson lingering on the opposite side of the hall – the first time I've seen his face since he spoke to the press, although he's been texting me at regular intervals to promise me it wasn't him. I want to believe him. God, I want to believe him.

Before he spots me, Ajita grabs my arm and hauls me back into the classroom, nearly knocking out Sharon the deadpan queen with her backpack. Which wouldn't have been terrible on account of her horrid Twitter rant about my displeasing body shape.

We hunch behind the door and tactfully avoid Mr Cheung's glares by pretending to rummage in our purses for tampons, which we all know is a surefire way to get male faculty members off your case.

"Shit, Ajita, what am I going to do? Should I confront him?" I mutter as I slip quietly into cardiac arrest. "Carson, not Mr Cheung."

She considers this for a moment while dangling a paper-wrapped supersize emphatically in front of her face, like she's trying to hypnotize me on behalf of the period goddesses. "Look, Izzy, boys are like buses."

"They all come at once?"

"No, they're cheap, unreliable and smell like day-old dick cheese. Point is, you're awesome, and none of these pricks deserve you. Not Danny, not Vaughan, and not Carson." Something deep in my chest rebels at the idea Carson doesn't deserve me. If he's the man I think he is, he absolutely does. "Just go and give him a piece of your mind. You've got nothing to lose."

I frown. "What about my last remaining strand of dignity?"

"Don't be ridiculous. You lost that last summer when you touched your foofer after chopping chilies and had to squat in a bowl of Greek yoghurt."

"I have no idea what you're talking about."

"Don't you remember the moving funeral service I held for said dignity? Betty said a few words; Dumbledore peed on the casket?"

By now I am just so desperate for this conversation to be over that when she shoves me back out the door I'm beyond caring what happens in the next few minutes of my life.

Carson's eyes meet mine and sheer terror flits across his face. I attempt to fix some semblance of fury onto my own features and stride up to him, trying to forget Ajita's profoundly disturbing observations about dick cheese.

"Izzy, I —"

"What the fucking shit, Carson? Selling your story? Are you actually kidding me?"

Literally everyone on the planet is looking at us. Drivers on the highway have abandoned their vehicles to get a better look. Every drone in the world is pointed in our direction. Extraterrestrial life forms have finally breached the earth's atmosphere and nobody has noticed on account of the fact everyone is focusing on this pathetic sex scandal in small-town America.

"You don't under—"

Red-hot anger bubbles through me. "I don't understand? I don't understand needing some extra cash? Really? You're really saying those words to me right now? For fucking, shitting sake, why —"

He looks genuinely devastated that I'm cursing so fluidly at him. "I can explain. Please. Let me explain."

"Okay. Go."

Carson seems taken aback by my bluntness. "Right here?"

Small crowds have gathered around us now, and I don't know whether surviving several shaming rituals in the last month has toughened me up a bit, but I actually don't even care who witnesses this exchange.

"Why not? You'll probably sell your story again and all of these people will find out all the gritty little details anyway, so it might as well be public."

He shoots me a genuinely pained expression, wincing like I've punched him in the kidneys. "I didn't sell you out. I promise. You gotta believe me."

"No? So how'd the *Enquirer* get those screenshots?" I'm starting to yell now, and the corridor is quieter than it's ever been so my words echo around the lockers.

He almost whispers, "It wasn't me, okay? Like I say, someone must've hacked my phone and screwed me over for a quick buck. I'm not like that, Izzy. I wouldn't do that to you. Or Ajita. I would *never*."

Something in the way he's clenching his fists and staring at me so urgently tells me he's desperate for me to believe him. And as someone who has also recently had her phone hacked and its contents leaked, I'm aware it's a thing that can happen, even in a tiny, pointless high school.

I remember the way he acted in the days after the website was made. He didn't treat me any differently, didn't talk to me with any less respect. He was sweet and reassuring and gracious.

And the way he is with his mom and siblings. The guy I saw looking out for his family is not a guy who would willingly ruin my life.

And I really, really want to believe him. Because my list of people who aren't weapons-grade douchebags is getting hella short.

When I don't say anything for a moment, he adds, "And you know I would never, ever call you a whore. Not even if they paid me a million dollars."

I smirk despite the situation. "Well, that's just dumb, Carson. A million dollars would solve both of our financial problems forever. I'd let you brand the word 'whore' on my ass cheek for a million dollars."

"That could be arranged!" someone jeers from a few feet away.

Another snarks, "Let's crowd-fund that shit!"

Everyone laughs.

This next part I say more quietly. "You didn't stand up for me."

"What?" he says, matching my soft tone. He steps forward, closing the gap between us. He looks like he might take my hands, but decides against it, leaving his to curl at his sides. "When?"

"In the hallway. When Baxter and your other teammates were discussing the pictures. 'If you're giving it away for free, ain't nobody gonna pay for it.'"

His face falls. "You heard that?"

"It's all I've heard for weeks."

"Oh God." He closes his eyes. "I should've said something. I nearly did. I just hate confrontation, you know? Makes me sick. But it's not an excuse. I should've told them to shove it, and I'm so sorry I didn't." He opens his eyes again, running a hand over the buzz-cut hair on the back of his neck. "You gotta believe me, though. I had nothing to do with that article. I was as shocked and disgusted as you were, I promise."

A thought dawns on me. "Hey, the . . . *person* who made the World Class Whore website knew we were texting." I remember Danny flinging my phone across Ajita's basement and storming out. It all fits. "He would've known to hack your iCloud account and read your messages. Probably thought I'd sent you a nude too."

Carson raises an eyebrow hopefully. "So you believe me?"

Random people start shouting, "Believe him!" and, "How can you resist that face?" and "What the hell is going on here? Why are none of you in second period?" [I think this last one was Mr Cheung, which is one hundred percent justified.]

I pause for dramatic effect before replying, "I'm thinking about it."

Dimples form in his smooth brown cheeks, like they always seem to when he's smiling at me.

He mumbles, "Yeah? So, uh . . . what about that pizza sometime? Cos I'm kinda tired of us pretending we're not into each other."

The dumb part of my heart that inconveniently fell for his puppylike nature all those weeks ago flutters.

"Who says I'm pretending?" I smile. "But I never say no to pizza."

4.56 p.m.

Ajita orchestrates a meeting between Danny and me in the woods after school.

She bids me farewell at the gates saying, "Good luck, old buddy old pal. Meet you in the diner in a half-hour? There'll be a s'mores milkshake waiting for you." A coy smile. "Oh, and Meg's coming too."

For the second time today, my stone heart melts. I love my friends. The old ones and the new ones. The real ones, who

318

don't make websites condemning me to an eternity in hell just because I'm not attracted to them.

Danny doesn't know that I know, so he unsuspectingly shows up to our usual clearing with a look of casual indifference about him. That's about to change, because I'm going to come raining down on him harder than a monsoon in, well, monsoon season.

I step out from behind a tree like a Bond villain revealing themselves. [It's probably quite clear that I have not watched many Bond movies, but I assume this is the sort of thing that happens.]

Before he has a chance to even blink, I launch my attack. "It was you. You started that website. It was *you*."

I don't have to force the venom into my voice. I just remember how low I felt after that screenplay email, before Meg messaged me, before I finally asked for help . . . and the anger comes rushing back.

"Izzy, I —"

"No! You don't get to talk. You've done enough damage, and there's nothing you can say to make this better. *Nothing*. You know there's a term for what you've done to me, right? Revenge porn. It's illegal in the UK, and it's becoming more and more illegal here. State by state, they're cracking down. It might not be against the law here yet, but it will be. Soon. And personally? I hope to God you pay for this."

He says nothing, staring at me without emotion. Remorseless.

319

"Are you hearing me?" I'm almost crying. "You nearly ruined my life, Danny. Did you know that I've been kicked out of the screenplay competition? Did you know Betty is being attacked by journalists and politicians every day? Did you know that now, when I walk down the street, it's so excruciating knowing how many strangers have seen me naked that I just want to disappear? Did you know that on Saturday night, after it felt like I'd lost everything, I genuinely wanted to not be here anymore?"

He drops his backpack to the ground and leans back against a tree, finally letting a crack of emotion show on his face.

I keep going. "*You* broke into Carson's phone, and *you* leaked those messages. *You* pretended to be him, and *you* spoke to a journalist. *You* allowed Ajita's sexuality to be revealed to the world because, why? Bitterness? I don't get it. Why would you do this? Why would someone who claims to love me want to systematically ruin my life? Have you enjoyed it, seeing me in this much pain?"

He still doesn't say anything, just rubs his face with his hands, looking like he might throw up.

I scoff, throwing my hands up in the air, letting my voice rise above the trees. "Or was that your goal all along? To annihilate my sense of self-worth so that I'd collapse into your arms and beg you to fix me?" I raise my voice and scream so loudly a flock of birds fly away from a nearby tree. "You nearly killed me! Is that what you wanted?"

This gets a reaction. He pushes off the tree trunk and flies toward me so fast I actually recoil.

"No, Izzy! All I wanted was *you*!" His eyes are shining too, but he yells like he's made of pure anger. "How do you think I feel? I love you so damn much, Izzy, and just because I'm not Channing Tatum I've been relegated to the Friend Zone for the rest of eternity. I have to watch you chase the same good-looking *assholes* that every other girl wants to fuck, then pick up the pieces after they inevitably screw you over."

My eyes narrow and I fight the urge to spit at him. "Oh my God, I'm so sick of your entitled bullshit. You didn't get what you wanted, so you lashed out with the sole intention of hurting me. Hurting me for not wanting you back. How do you think *I* feel, Danny? My supposed best friend thinks I'm obliged to go out with him just because he *wants* me to?" I clench and unclench my fist. "Yeah, I messed up when I kissed you, and I'm sorry if that led you on. But stop with this poor little Nice Guy crap. You really think being 'friend-zoned' is worse than finding out someone you thought valued you as a whole person just wanted to fuck you? If my friendship is not enough, then fuck you. Just . . . fuck you."

Danny snarls in an ugly way. Then he says: "You know what? This isn't about me. This is about you and your complete inability to be emotionally available. Are you even capable of love, Izzy? Or are you just too damn scared to let yourself feel anything? You're . . . you're dead inside."

This is like a stab to the chest. I genuinely double over a little bit. "So the only reason I could possibly not be attracted to you is psychological damage? I can't believe you'd . . ." I trail off, speechless for probably the second time in my life. And then the floodgates open, because I'm exhausted and just all-round devastated that my former best friend is being so cruel.

"What do you want me to say, Danny? That I'm so completely broken and fucked up that I've come all the way back around to detached?" I gasp as I choke on a sob, but I keep going. "That there's a gaping parent-shaped hole in my life? That I use humor as a coping mechanism? That yeah, I *am* terrified to fall in love because of what happened to my parents?"

"Iz —"

"No, Danny. Stop. You're butthurt, and you're lashing out at me again, and you think it's justified because you believe you have a *right* to have sex with me, a *right* to my love, but just . . . stop. We're done. Our friendship is done. Which is totally fine, because it turns out it was never enough for you anyway."

And then I walk away. Because for the first time since this all started, I genuinely believe this is not my fault.

I do not deserve this. Not one bit.

Friday 15 October

9.05 a.m.

As soon as I get to school I go straight to Mrs Crannon's office. I checked her timetable, and first period on Friday morning is one of her only frees of the week.

She seems surprised to see me as she's tucking into a delicious-looking Danish pastry. I briefly wonder if Mr Rosenqvist is wooing her into friendship with Scandinavian delights. I would *so* be here for a Crannon-Rosenqvist buddy comedy.

"Hi, Mrs Crannon," I say, standing awkwardly in the doorway. "Do you have a sec?"

From behind her towers of books, she says, "I'll always have a sec for you, Izzy. Take a seat!"

I'm feeling bolshy, so I plonk myself down into the Iron Maiden chair without a second thought. I'll apologize to my buttocks at a later date.

I take a deep breath, forcing myself to look at her rather than twiddling with my zipper as I usually do during serious conversations. "Can I be honest with you, Mrs Crannon?"

One of her warm smiles lights up the room. "Always."

"Okay. Well, ever since everything blew up with, you know, the pictures and everything, I've been too ashamed to come and talk to you."

"Izzy! That's –"

"Please, let me finish." I feel bad for interrupting her, but if I don't say this now I never will. "I know this might sound crazy, because you're my teacher and not my mom or anything, but I've been fighting the feeling that I let you down." I pause. "I made the shortlist." Her face lights up, and she goes to celebrate, but I stop her. "No. They kicked me out a few days later. They found out about the . . . scandal." I swallow the wave of shame that rises like nausea.

Her face collapses in sympathy. There are pastry flakes all over her tunic. "I'm so sorry, Izzy. I can't believe they'd do that."

I shrug. "I've been surprised by a lot of things these past few weeks, but that wasn't one of them. I get it. They don't want the bad publicity."

"But still. You're a talented young woman, and you deserve a shot, no matter what's going on in your personal life. Which, by the way, you should never feel embarrassed about. We've all had sex. We've all sent risky pictures. It's nothing to be ashamed of."

She says this last part so sincerely, without even blushing or mumbling or showing any sign of discomfort, that it emboldens me to carry on.

"Thank you. Really. You've been so supportive since day one, and I'm so, so grateful. I'm sorry you wasted your dad's fifty bucks."

"Wasted? Izzy, did you get great feedback from the judges?" I nod. "Is your script better for it?" Nod again. "And has it cemented in your mind that this is how you want to spend your life – writing?" My face says it all. She smiles. "Well then, I'd hardly call that a waste, would you?"

2.46 p.m.
Ajita, Meg and I are in Martha's Diner, being poured fresh OJ by my wonderful grandmother. Yes, at quarter to three on a Friday afternoon.

Half an hour earlier we're all in English class together, listening to Castillo trying in vain to make Emily Brontë even half as interesting as Charlotte by talking about the feminist undertones of *Wuthering Heights*.

That's when Sharon pipes up with a pass-agg comment definitely aimed in my direction. "I think it's interesting how everyone seems to think feminism in the twenty-first century is better than it's ever been. I think it's just the opposite. Women had so much more class back when the Brontës were writing. They'd probably be horrified to see how some girls behave these days. You know, sleeping around, sending tacky nude pictures, and all that."

Everyone shoots me the same judgmental/pitying/snooty looks as usual, but honestly it barely even registers. I just roll my eyes. It's funny how fast you get used to being treated like a piece of crap.

But you know who's not willing to just stay quiet and let me suffer?

Ajita.

She stands up haughtily, gathering her belongings. "Izzy, we're leaving."

"I . . . what?" I look up at her in shock, just like every other member of the class.

"I'm not going to sit here and listen to ignorant assholes say crap like that about you. Especially if the person who's supposed to be in charge of the class just lets it happen without saying a word." She shoots Castillo a look so withering it makes Medusa look mild-mannered. "So, in conclusion, we're leaving."

I fucking love that girl. She just threw cold tomato soup all over Castillo. You know, metaphorically.

I gather up my stuff and shove it into my backpack as fast as I can, stray highlighters scattering everywhere, but I don't care. I just do not care anymore.

Castillo finally finds her voice. "Now, listen here, girls. Don't you dare walk out of that door, or I'll have you suspended."

Ajita shrugs as if she has literally never cared about anything less in her entire life. "So now's when you speak up? Not when one of your students is being bullied relentlessly by her peers, but when she finally decides to stand up for herself? Shame on you, Miss Castillo. Shame on you."

And with that, she strides confidently toward the door. I follow. Everyone just stares in utter amazement.

Meg's in the back row. As Ajita passes, she adds, "Meg, are you coming?"

Delighted to be involved in the protest, Meg grins ecstatically and wheels herself out after us, abandoning everything on her desk. Literally abandoning her pencil case, textbooks, everything. Amazing.

Castillo calls meekly after us, "But wait . . ."

We barely hear. We're too busy whooping down the corridor like we're the most badass bitches on the planet.

So now we're slurping milkshakes (I went strawberry cheesecake, Ajita and Meg both chose mint Oreo) and chatting and feeling all fired up. The diner is almost empty, since it's mainly a hangout for high-school kids and all the non-rebellious ones are still in class.

"You know what?" I say, raising my voice over the clatter of pans from the kitchen, and the crooning of Elvis Presley emanating from the nearby jukebox. "I'm tired of lying down and letting stuff happen to me without resisting."

"Damn straight," Ajita says. "It's time we stood up for ourselves, you know? It's time we threw cold tomato soup everywhere. Why should I let my own mother bully me into silence over a major part of my life? Why should we let people make us feel like crap?"

Meg jumps in. "What's that Eleanor Roosevelt quote? Nobody can make you feel inferior without your consent."

"YES!" Ajita and I both yell. She smacks the table so hard in agreement that the salt shaker nearly headbutts its peppery cousin.

"I'm sick of it," I continue. "I'm sick of feeling like I live in a lose/lose world, and that there's nothing I can do about it. As a woman, you're damned if you do and damned if you don't. A slut if you send the nudes and a prude if you don't. A whore if you have sex and frigid if you don't. A bitch if you fight back and submissive if you don't."

"We should reclaim the word 'bitch'," Ajita argues, her eyes alight with passion. I love it when she gets like this. Meg watches in awe of her fiery new pal. "It's been used to silence opinionated women for too long. Women who have beliefs and goals and things to say. Women who won't stand for injustice or mistreatment. They're labeled bitches by men – and other women – who feel intimidated."

I nod along like one of those bobbing dogs middle-class people inexplicably have in the back windows of their cars.

Meg speaks up. "Bitches bite back. And men hate that. Society hates that." A charming little milkshake mustache has settled on her upper lip, but we're both taking her as seriously as a president addressing the nation.

A spark of an idea forms in my head; dim at first, then brighter than an exploding sun. I gasp. "We should start a website. A community of teen girls who refuse to stay silent any longer. And it could be called . . ." I grin. "Bitches Bite Back."

Ajita laughs excitedly. "That. Is. Awesome."

"I really think it would resonate with so many young women," Meg agrees. "From all walks of life. What teenage girl can't relate to being called a bitch?"

We all look at each other, magic and milkshakes in the air.

"Let's make this happen."

11.34 p.m.

It's hard to believe that less than a month ago my life was entirely different to how it is now.

I hadn't had my screenwriting dream almost within reach – and then snatched away again. My crush on Carson was yet to manifest, and I hadn't yet slept with him or Vaughan. Danny was still my best friend. Ajita was still in the closet. Meg wasn't in my life. I wasn't the center of a national sex scandal. My naked body wasn't on display to the entire world, and journalists weren't gathered around the school gates. Betty hadn't told me she was proud of me. I hadn't had my life torn apart on a public website made with the sole intention of ruining my life. Nor had I stitched my life back together with the help of the people I love the most.

Shame. It's a peculiar beast, especially when it happens in public. It leaves you powerless. It strips you of everything you thought you knew about yourself, forces you to examine the very core of your being. Do I like who I am? Am I proud of my choices? How can I become better?

And then: how can I change the world – and myself?

I don't regret sending the nude picture. I don't regret having two one-night stands. I do regret hurting my best friend.

That's what truly matters to me: the people I love. And it took a fuckup of epic proportions to realize that.

A month ago, if you'd asked me what three things I wanted to be, I'd have said: funny, cool, well-liked.

What do I want to be now? Bold. Fierce. Honest.

A fighter. A revolutionary. A bitch.

Because the way the world treats teenage girls – as sluts, as objects, as bitches – is not okay.

It's the exact opposite of okay.

Old White Men Love It When You Slut-shame
posted by Izzy O'Neill in *Bitches Bite Back*

Slut-shaming In which a woman is labeled a "slut" or "whore" for enjoying sex (or even just looking like they might) and is subsequently punished socially.

Interestingly, only girls and women are called to task for their sexuality; boys and men are congratulated for the exact same behavior. This is the essence of the sexual double standard: boys will be boys, and girls will be sluts.

Unless, of course, you're not a slut, in which case you are some variation of the following: a frigid bitch, a cock-tease, a boring prude, or matronly purveyor of the Friend Zone.

Basically, if you're a woman, you're damned if you do and damned if you don't. If you refrain from any expression of sexiness, you may be written off as irrelevant and unfeminine, but if you follow the male-written guidelines, you run the risk of being judged, shamed and policed. It's super awesome.

You might think: *But Izzy, given this set of circumstances, isn't it preferable for a girl or woman to abstain from sexual expression?* To that I say nay. Putting aside the inherent sexism of this assertion, it shouldn't make any difference whether a girl or woman is sexually active, or even utters any expression of sexuality. The problem is in the way in which society interprets this perceived behavior. Because here's the thing: slut-shaming is not really about women's sexuality. It is grounded in the belief that men have the right to assert themselves, and women do not.

It's not a new phenomenon – just ask Monica Lewinsky – but in the social-media age, it's becoming more toxic than ever. One scroll through my Instagram feed on any given day proves this. Hordes of (usually male) users comment on young girls' selfies and bikini shots, dubbing them whores and sluts just for showing a little flesh or wearing red lipstick (this normally follows failed attempts to hit on these girls, may I add – it's amazing how much slut-shaming is derived from rejection-induced bitterness). Don't these girls know nobody will ever respect them now?

As an aside, I actually really admire people who slut-shame on the internet. Usually when someone has a low IQ they try to hide it, but these guys just throw it right out there in the public domain.

Never mind that these same dudes then go and spend five dollars a week on top-shelf glamor magazines with oiled-up naked models splashed on the front cover. You can *buy* tits, but you can't *have* tits. That would be absurd!!

In fact, I think in the manual they hand out to girls at birth, the chapter on sexuality should start with the disclaimer: "Unless an old white man can profit from your sexuality, you better hide it, because if it can't be exploited, it will be punished."

Our sexuality is a commodity, and thus the principles of supply and demand can be applied. If we're sexy but untouchable, we're in short supply. Demand goes up. And because demand goes up, the aforementioned old white man can charge more money for it. But if we give it away freely? If we actually have sex – and have the audacity to enjoy it? Supply is booming. Profit margins die. Old white men can't make as much money, so they get out their sticks and beat us into slut-shamed submission. And the rest of society buys into it.

When you're a young girl, your developing sexuality is a loaded weapon. You should polish it to a shine for the sake of the male gaze, but you shouldn't seek any enjoyment from it yourself. Play with power, as long as you never claim it. Enact desire, as long as you don't follow through.

I call bullshit.

The Friend Zone is as Real as Narnia
posted by Izzy O'Neill in *Bitches Bite Back*

The Friend Zone An imaginary area filled with self-professed Nice Guys who've been sexually rejected by women they've been Nice to. *See also*: A convenient social construct designed to comfort men who cannot cope with rejection. *See also*: A manipulative tool used by Nice Guys to make a woman feel guilty for not wanting to have sex with them.

The Nice Guy Phenomenon In which self-entitled men believe that if they spend enough time with a woman and aren't explicitly terrible to them, it's unfair when the woman doesn't then suck their penis and/or fall in love with them.

Poor Nice Guys. It must be so difficult, putting all of that effort into pretending to be a decent human being without being rewarded with sex or love afterward. They listen to our problems, buy us gifts, shower us with compliments, talk to us about all the other horrible guys we're dating, and yet! And yet we still don't tear our clothes off and fall into their arms. We keep going for those other dudes, the ones with charisma and personality. The ones we're attracted to, the ones who make us laugh, the ones who make us feel good. It is just so unreasonable and infuriating. They must really regret falling for such a Bitch.

To that I say: cry me a river. You should be nice because it's the right thing to do. If you're nice because you want something in return, you're probably not that nice at all.

I mean, maybe we can blame Hollywood. The invariable message of most romantic comedies is that men can be as lazy or slutty or awkward or obnoxious as they like, but as long as they're relatively nice and keep trying, they'll get the girl in the end. The below-average and perilously flawed man always ends up with the beautiful girl if he puts in a little effort and isn't an outright dickhead to her. The bar is so low that Nice Guys who watch it must see it and think, huh. I can do that. And if I do, I'll get any woman I want. Who is *she* to say no? Who is *she* to have a choice?

But I've got a news flash for you, Nice Guys: the world doesn't work that way. Sure, it'd be great if you could get anything you wanted – a job, a promotion, a mortgage – by being a semi-decent person and trying quite hard, but that's not reality. Just ask the millions of disadvantaged people around the world who face discrimination based on their gender, race, sexuality, class and disabilities every day.

That's probably why the Nice Guys are so angry. In a system that inherently favors them, it's the first time they aren't automatically getting what they want just because they want it. Their privilege is no longer doing the heavy lifting, and they're mad about it.

This entitlement has to stop. The world owes you nothing. Girls owe you nothing.

We *do* like good guys. You just aren't one of them.

Epilogue

Dear Izzy,

I'm a screenwriting agent based in West Hollywood, and was a judge during the shortlisting phase of this year's Script Factor. I championed your screenplay from the get-go. It's clever, topical and downright hilarious. You have a big talent, and should be very proud of your work.

However, I've recently learned about the disqualification of your entry. I strongly believe this is a terrible (and, frankly, cowardly) decision on the part of the organizers, and I can't even begin to imagine how disappointed you must be.

Next time you're in LA, give me a call. I'd love to meet with you in person to discuss the future of your screenwriting — and the possibility of representation at our agency.

You're going places, Izzy O'Neill, and I'd like to be on that journey with you.

All the very best,

Eliza Kennedy

Acknowledgements

Honesty hour: I've been putting off writing these acknowledgements for yonks. Not just because it's vaguely panic-inducing (someone will be forgotten and I will feel their wrath), but also because I almost burst into tears every time I even think about all the wonderful people I have around me. But alas, my deadline is tomorrow, so I best get on with it. Send tissues and an assortment of woman-up pills.

Since I signed with my literary agent at the ripe old age of twenty-two, I've been incredibly fortunate to work with some amazing publishing professionals. Sara and Suzie, you are the best agents I could ever ask for, and I'm deeply sorry for the ceaseless neurotic emails you have to deal with on a daily basis. And the rest of the New Leaf family – in particular Chris, Pouya, Kathleen, Mia and Joanna. I'm forever pinching myself that I get to be part of your team.

Next up, the Egmont rockstars. You have all been the biggest champions of Izzy O'Neill since day one. From my epic editorial team – Ali, Liz, Stella and Lydia – to the amazing publicity and marketing team (I'm looking at you, Rebecca, Alice, Emily, Rhiannon and Siobhan) and the cracking cover design courtesy of Laura and Goodwives & Warriors, I'm so fortunate to have found such an amazing home for *The Exact Opposite Of Okay*.

Also, you preempted this manuscript on the day of Trump's inauguration, which is the ultimate middle finger to misogyny, bigotry and hatred. Your style is flawless.

Then there's the unfortunate bunch who have to put up with me in real life, which I assure you is no mean feat. To Mum, Dad, Jack (even though you claim to despise me), Gran, Harry (who is a dog, and a much less friendly one than Dumbledore, but awesome nonetheless) and the rest of my huge, mad family. To the best pals a girl could ask for: Toria, Nic, Hannah, Lauren, Lucy, Gaby, Amy, Steve and Spike. To Hilary, even though you technically come under the Mad Family header – your sarcasm and prosecco-drinking skills deserve their very own shout-outs. To the Book Club: Sophie, Jess and Laura – you guys are new friends, but I'm kinda hoping you'll stick around for a while. To everyone I work with at *Mslexia* – you're the best people to drink tea and discuss *Game of Thrones* with. To my beautiful goddaughter, Millie – I hope this world is a better place for young women by the time you become one.

And to Louis, my fiancé (!!). Thank you for the nacho-fuelled life talks, hilarious cases of the zoomies, karaoke-filled road trips, endless back tickers, always doing the dishes, and for making me smile no matter what. There's nobody else I'd rather have by my side. Which is good, since we're getting married and all. (Omg.)

Over the last few years, I've met some incredible writing

friends, both online and in real life. Victoria Aveyard, my agent sister and drinking pal – our annual cocktail tours of Edinburgh are one of my favourite summer traditions. Emma Theriault, another agent sister and critique partner – there is nobody better to complain, commiserate and celebrate with, and I can't wait to visit you in Canada. Claribel Ortega, yet another agent sister (Suzie, your children are out of control) – you are an amazing champion for diversity in publishing, and I feel so lucky to be your friend. Bring on our London date this spring! Everyone in the Electric Eighteens – the most supportive debut group on this earth. Bindu Pisupati – the chocolate bear to my vanilla bear, and the only other person who likes *Scrubs* as much as I do. Scarlett Cole, one of my very first writing pals – you are the biggest inspiration to me, and the hardest-working woman I know. Rebecca McLaughlin, PitchWars mentee turned lifelong friend – your pep talks are as epic as your taste in confectionery. And a whopping great shout out to Louise O'Neill, Katherine Webber, Samantha Shannon and Katherine Woodfine for the ridiculously nice quotes about *The Exact Opposite Of Okay*. I am more grateful than you know.

And finally, to the entire YA community – authors, bloggers, readers, reviewers, agents, editors, event coordinators and all-round champions. Thank you for welcoming me with open arms.

LAURA STEVEN

Laura Steven is an author, journalist and screenwriter from the northernmost town in England. She has an MA in Creative Writing and works for *Mslexia*, a non-profit organisation supporting women in the creative arts. Her TV pilot, *Clickbait*, was a finalist in British Comedy's 2016 Sitcom Mission. *The Exact Opposite of Okay* is her first book for young adults.

It's not the end for
Bitches Bite Back . . .

Still reeling from the aftermath of her sex scandal, Izzy is left to navigate a sea of body image issues, relationship drama, and dachshund Dumbledore's inappropriate new habit of humping her teddy bears. Then a terrible work accident leaves Betty bed-bound, with a humongous hospital bill to boot, and everything else must take a back seat so that Izzy can sell her screenplay – and escape their impending eviction.

The sequel to THE EXACT OPPOSITE OF OKAY

Coming March 2019